# Love . . . Under
# Different Skies

Nick Spalding is an author who, try as he might, can't seem to write anything serious. He's worked in the communications industry his entire life, mainly in media and marketing. As talking rubbish for a living can get tiresome (for anyone other than a politician), he thought he'd have a crack at writing comedy fiction – with an agreeable level of success so far, it has to be said. Nick lives in the South of England with his fiancée. He is approaching his forties with the kind of dread usually associated with a trip to the gallows, suffers from the occasional bout of insomnia, and still thinks Batman is cool. Nick Spalding was one of the top ten bestselling authors in eBook format in 2012. You can find out more about Nick by following him on twitter https://twitter.com/spalding_author or by reading his blog http://spaldings-racket.blogspot.co.uk/

# Love . . . Under Different Skies

## Nick Spalding

CORONET

First published in Great Britain in 2013 by Coronet
An imprint of Hodder & Stoughton
An Hachette UK company

First published in paperback in 2013

1

A CIP catalogue record for this title is available from the British Library

ISBN 978 1 444 76707 0

Typeset in Plantin Light by Palimpsest Book Production Limited,
Falkirk, Stirlingshire

Printed and bound by CPI Group (UK) Ltd, Croydon, CR0 4YY

Hodder & Stoughton policy is to use papers that are natural, renewable and
recyclable products and made from wood grown in sustainable forests. The
logging and manufacturing processes are expected to conform to the
environmental regulations of the country of origin.

Hodder & Stoughton Ltd
338 Euston Road
London NW1 3BH

www.hodder.co.uk

# Contents

This novel is dedicated to the people of Australia and the beautiful country they call home.

# Jamie's Blog
# Tuesday 4 October

I have a question for you, one which I would appreciate an honest answer to, if you'd be so kind: If you suffer a gigantic emotional breakdown at work and mortally insult your boss, what do you think are the chances of keeping your job? Go on, be honest.

Yeah. That's pretty much the conclusion I'd reached too. I'm basically more screwed than a hooker with a six-figure overdraft.

It's not been an easy few months for the Newman clan. In fact, it's been dreadful, like a slow-motion car crash with none of the excitement. Since Pops was born the financial thing has become a real struggle for us. Don't get me wrong, I adore my weird little daughter with a love that borders on the psychotic, but she's a bigger drain on the bank account than a classic British sports car.

Laura's still on part-time hours at Morton and Slacks, and I've been going slowly insane at my desk at the paper. The work hours have been growing longer and longer, while my nerves have been getting shorter and shorter. I've even started smoking again. This is the single most coloss-ally stupid thing I could have done, given that fags now cost an arm, a leg and several yards of intestines.

The recession hasn't helped. My cost-of-living increase was frozen last April and my yearly raise went out of the window in July.

You can imagine how delighted I was to hear that David Keene – the CEO of the newspaper – and his lovely plastic third wife, Kayleigh, had jetted off to the Seychelles for three weeks on the same day I was told I wouldn't be getting a pay rise. The knuckles on my right hand have only just stopped throbbing and the stationery cupboard wall will need a jolly good re-plastering sometime very soon.

Poor old Pete from Reprographics lost his job last month. Clare, the girl who once held my flaccid penis while I blubbed like a little girl, has been inconsolable. The two were married in the spring at a lovely reception, where he wore a Wolverine costume and she looked dazzling as Catwoman. I tried to point out the inconsistencies in that particular fantasy pairing, but nobody seemed interested.

Seeing the poor cow moping around the office for the past few weeks has really topped off the deep sense of dread and loathing I've felt each and every day for the past eighteen months. This was never a job I was in love with, but it paid the bills and kept me off the streets. In recent times though I've come to see it as some kind of punishment for my wrongdoings of the past. I've tried to remember what I might have done to incur such a horrific fate and I've narrowed it down to the time I drop-kicked the little baby Jesus during rehearsals for the school nativity play when I was eight, and when my drunken antics as a twenty-something adult led to a glob of my semen destroying an oil painting of His face.

This sorry state of affairs came to a rather inevitable head yesterday.

The morning started as it usually does these days, with an argument. Laura and I used to share a lovely breakfast together, discussing our day ahead while sipping hot tea and munching on buttery slices of toast. These days, though, we've decided that a better way is to conduct a blazing row over something incredibly trivial while our daughter screams her head off on the couch.

Yesterday the source of our lively debate was my inability to load the dishwasher properly. You wouldn't think that putting the cheese grater on the wrong level more than once in a fortnight would be the catalyst for a potentially marriage-ending conflagration, but my wife and I managed to achieve it, to the charming accompaniment of Poppy rupturing her vocal chords while sat in the corner.

'Maybe I should just stick my fu—my *fudging* head in the dishwasher and drown my stupid bast—*blinking* face, eh?' I spit at Laura from the doorway as I pull on my coat.

'You could try, you enormous bag of horseshi—*horsepoo*!' Laura replies eloquently, picking up the screeching Poppy. 'But there's every chance you'd stick it in next to the fu—*fudging* cheese grater and break the spray arm completely.'

'Good! I hope the spray arm breaks. I hope it breaks off and cuts my throat so I don't have to listen to you moaning at me about that blood—*blooming* cheese grater ever again!'

'Don't you say things like that, Jamie Newman. We haven't got the money to fix that dishwasher and I am not spending my evenings up to my ar—*bum* in greasy pans any more.'

From the outside, this sounds like the dumbest argument in human history, especially with the self-censorship going on thanks to the presence of our firstborn. I'm sure poor Mrs Withering two doors down certainly thinks it's all very strange as she puts out her rubbish bin and tries to ignore the appliance-based nuclear war on our doorstep.

'I'm going to go to work now, Laura.' I say, pointing a trembling finger at her. 'Where I'll try to earn enough money to keep you in cheese graters and spray arms for another few weeks at least.'

'You do that, Jamie. I'll stay here, look after our daughter and try to extricate our existing cheese grater from where it's now jammed against the spray arm. Then I'll go to work too . . . because I have to do that as well, in case you'd forgotten.'

'No! No I hadn't.' I blast, and notice Mrs Withering giving me a very worried look from over her wheelie bin. This dampens my rage somewhat. I turn back to Laura. 'Have a good day, dear.'

'Don't you tell me to have a good day, you sack of sh—Oh, hello, Mrs Withering! How are your joints this morning?'

'Better, thank you,' the old bat says from her new

vantage point looking down our hallway. 'Is everything alright, my dears?'

*Apart from the fact my wife and I may be getting divorced thanks to a ballistic cheese grater, you mean?*

'We're fine, Mrs Withering,' Laura says in as calm a voice as she can manage. 'Why don't you get off to work now, Jamie?' she orders.

I don't need telling twice. I wave at Poppy, who completely ignores me and buries her head in her mother's shoulder.

With that final dismissal I bid Mrs Withering a good day and stride towards the Mondeo with a lump of hot coal still burning its way through my stomach.

I call at least fourteen other drivers twats on the twenty-minute drive to the office, such is my foul mood. A tension headache has formed over my right eye, and my left eye has started to twitch and water so much I look like someone's just sprayed chilli powder into it. The four cigarettes I smoke during the trip no doubt contribute heavily to this, as do the three cups of awful coffee I consume in less than an hour once I actually get to my desk.

By half past ten I'm twitching like an arsonist in a match factory and the tension headache has now broadened its horizons to encompass my entire head, both shoulders and inexplicably, my arsehole.

With stabbing pain coming from my rear end and a throbbing dull ache emanating from my skull, it's a miracle I get through the morning and into the lunch break in one piece. I consume a limp Co-op chicken-and-disappointment sandwich, smoke another four cigarettes and drink a can of Red Bull, before slouching back inside and shutting myself away in my office to try and get to grips with the promotional campaign I'm supposed to be creating for our new Sunday supplement. It's exclusively for women and goes under the brilliantly bland title of 'Living'. It was thought up by David Keene's lovely plastic third wife Kayleigh, so everyone with a good survival instinct has jumped on board the idea enthusiastically.

I put forward a counter proposal for a supplement called 'Dead' to appeal to our zombie demographic, but – as ever – my suggestion is completely ignored. So with caffeine pumping through my veins, a head that feels like it's gripped in a vice, and an arsehole that for some reason still feels like it's in the middle of a prostate exam, I hunch over my keyboard and try to think of a good way to sell a supplement that mainly features stories about handbags, periods and Kim fucking Kardashian.

As you can imagine, my mental state is now incredibly fragile. Antique Fabergé eggs are robust in comparison.

If I had just been left alone for the rest of the day the disaster that unfolded wouldn't have happened and I'd still be in gainful employment. As it was though, at twenty past four I hear a knock on my door. I ignore it, knee deep as I am in my attempts to build a cohesive advertising blurb for Kayleigh's asinine supplement.

The knock at the door is repeated, this time a little louder. 'James?' says a mewling voice and my heart sinks. It's my boss, Alex. I was sure the little shit was off today, but here he is, standing at my door like a Jehovah's Witness with a death wish.

'Come in,' I grind through clenched teeth.

The door swings open and in walks the single most annoying human being it's ever been my displeasure to meet. Alex is scrawny, has a high-pitched voice, is going bald but won't admit it, wears stupid round little glasses and has a handshake limper than a piece of lettuce.

'I need to talk to you, James,' he whines at me nasally.

'I thought you were off today.'

'I was.' He perches himself on my desk and moves my coffee cup. Do you know how *infuriating* that is? When somebody not only invades your personal space, but takes it upon themselves to start re-arranging your things without permission? My stress levels, already at DefCon 3 thanks to the caffeine, aching arse and cheesegrater-versus-dishwasher incident, ratchet up another notch closer to meltdown.

'I had to come in today just to speak to you,' he continues.

'Really? What about?'

Alex clasps his weedy little hands together in a sure sign what he's about to say isn't going to be good.

'Mr Keene has expressed a desire to save money and I'm afraid that means we're having to cut back on some of our staff working hours.'

My heart sinks into an abyss darker than the contents of my recently moved coffee cup. 'Are you about to tell me I'm out of a job?' I say in a shaking voice.

'No, of course not!' Alex cries with a little laugh and pats me on the shoulder. Then the hands come together again. 'You're just losing a few hours, that's all.'

'How many hours, Alex?' I reply, carefully putting down the ballpoint pen I've been squeezing in my left hand.

'A few, I'm afraid.'

'How many exactly is a *few*?' I'm trying my hardest not to imagine what the ballpoint pen would look like inserted into Alex's scrawny little neck.

'You'll be going from forty hours to twenty-five.' He puts a hand on my shoulder again in what I guess he believes is a conciliatory fashion. 'It's bad I know, but in the current economic climate these kinds of cuts are inevitable, I'm afraid. We're all having to make sacrifices.'

'Really? *Really*, Alex? And what sacrifice have you made as manager?'

He's ready for this one, I can tell.

'Well, James, I'm afraid I'm losing my car and my expenses budget has been significantly cut for this year.'

The little prick actually thinks that this would make me feel better. That he's proving that we're all in this together because he can't drive an A5 anymore and buy lunch in Pret A Manger every day.

*Hold it together*, I order myself, *we still need this poxy job. Just hold your temper, get out of this office and calm yourself down before you say anything you'll regret.*

Alex thumps the table. 'Oh damn it! I forgot. I'm afraid you'll have to move offices as well. We'll be putting you over with the reprographics department on the big table.'

*Seriously, Jamie, take a deep breath and put the pen down again. You have to keep your shit together right now. Think of Laura and Poppy.*

'Mr Keene has said he's willing to discuss the cutbacks with you if you'd like,' Alex says, standing up. 'He knows you have a young child to look after and wants to make sure you understand how hard it was for him to make these changes.'

'Alright, Alex. I think I'd like to do that.' Preferably carrying a ballpoint pen. 'Is he up in his office on the top floor?'

'Oh no, I'm sorry, James. Mr Keene is out of the office right now. He's in the Maldives with his wife.'

*Oh fuck this shit. Go to town on the little bastard and we'll worry about the fallout later. Just try not to do anything that'll land us in prison.*

I stand up.

Slowly.

A variety of foul swearwords, phrases and insults are queuing up at the front of my brain, ready to spew forth all over Alex's stupid face.

My arsehole puckers – partly due to the throbbing which still hasn't abated, and partly due to the fact it knows what is about to happen and is having a mini panic attack.

'Alex,' I say in a voice laced with winter.

'Yes, James, how can I help?' The smug self-satisfied tone is accompanied by a thin, wet smile.

The Dalai Lama would have trouble resisting the urge to stab this idiot. Ghandi would have broken a lifetime vow of nonviolence and gone at this fucker's head like a rabid gibbon.

'Alex,' I continue, in the same ice cool tone. 'You are

without doubt the slimiest and most officious little cock-sucker it has ever been my misfortune to come across.'

I will replay the change in expression on the slimy cocksucker's face for many months to come in my head. It is a thing of absolute beauty.

'What did you say to me?' He stands up straight now, two bony knuckles depositing themselves on equally bony hips in indignation.

'Oh, I'm sorry? Has all that bullshit you've got floating around in that excuse for a brain finally filled up your ear canals?'

He points a finger at me. Even that looks limp – in defiance of all the laws of body language. 'You'd better stop talking, James,' he hisses. 'This could go very badly for you.'

'Oh really? What are you going to do exactly? Cut my hours even more? Maybe have me work in the toilets? I could balance a laptop on my knees – how would that suit, you little prick?'

'One more word and you're on a disciplinary.'

'One more word, eh? How about "weasel"? Or maybe "ferret"? Possibly "rat"? All three are equally good at describing you, you ponce.'

'Right, that's it. I'm putting you on a disciplinary, James!'

'It's Jamie, you brown-nosing little git! JAMIE. J – A – M – I – E. Always has been. If you took even five seconds to try and get to know the people who work for you, you'd know what my fucking name is!'

He's gone red now. A delightful shade of crimson that

would look nice in the bathroom with the new mats we bought in Tesco last week.

Alex holds up two knobbly fingers in front of my eyes, holding them a scant inch apart. 'I'm this close to firing you, *Jamie*.'

This is it then. My last chance to back down and keep my job. In such moments are the courses of our lives decided for good and all. I could calm down, apologise, and soldier on with Kayleigh's Living supplement. Alex will put this outburst down to the stress of having my hours reduced and within a fortnight everything will be back to normal. The bills will continue to be paid (more or less) and I'll continue to let my soul die by small increments.

Or I can go all in. Penny and pound. Sacrifice the next few weeks and months of my life for one glorious five-minute explosion that will destroy my bank account (and possibly my marriage), but will do wonders for my sense of self-worth. Sometimes in life you just have to leap without looking . . .

My eyes narrow. My voice lowers to a whisper. 'Fire me, you little scrotum. Go ahead.'

I'm rewarded with Alex's face going a whiter shade of pale, a colour which would go well with the curtains in the spare bedroom.

He goes to speak, but I hold out one hand. 'No, no. Let's not keep this monumental occasion to ourselves.' I throw open my office door. Outside a plethora of heads are already turned towards me. 'Hello, everyone. Alex has an announcement to make.'

Alex follows me out. 'This is ridiculous, James . . . Jamie.'

'Is it? As ridiculous as a newspaper making massive cutbacks while its owner suntans his hairy arse on a beach and his trophy wife seduces the pool boy back in the hotel penthouse?'

There are gasps from the audience – sorry, my work colleagues – as they digest this.

'I think this is a private matter between us,' Alex says and tries to pull me back into my office.

'Oh, I don't think it is, Alex. You're one of those odious little shitbags—' more gasps, louder this time '—who likes to dish the dirt behind closed doors where no one can see you. This time though, you're going to spew your loathsome words in front of everyone.' I put out an arm. 'So please, tell the boys and girls what you're doing with me.' I fold both arms and lean against the door frame, watching what Alex does next.

'You give me no choice, Jamie. Really no choice at all. I don't like to do things like this.'

I roll my eyes. 'Jesus Christ, get on with it, you oily tick.'

The gasps are joined by not a small amount of laughter. I might be leaving with my belongings in a cardboard box, but at least the poor bastards who have to carry on working in this dive can go home with a smile on their face and a decent anecdote to tell their friends down the pub tonight.

'You're fired, Jamie! Collect your belongings immediately and leave!' For once Alex actually sounds commanding. Then he ruins it by whispering, 'The HR department will be in touch later today about your final pay slip.'

'Excellent!' I shout and clap my hands together. 'You finally managed to grow a set and do it. Well done, Alex! And may I just say that working for you has been slightly less pleasant than lying with my mouth wide open under the back legs of a camel with diarrhoea?'

'You tell him, Jamie!' a voice calls from the back of the room. I think it's Clare, but I can't be sure as the speaker is keeping herself well hidden behind some filing cabinets.

'And while we're at it, I'd very much like you to pass on a message to Mr Keene. Please tell him that he is a cunt of the highest, *highest* order. Also, his wife is nowhere near as attractive as she thinks she is. She is also a moron. I know nothing about women and am fairly sure I could come up with a better feature for a women's supplement than "What's the best chocolate to eat while you're on a treadmill".'

'I suggest you leave right now, Jamie,' Alex spits.

'Oh don't try and order me around you slimy prick, you lost the power to do that about a minute ago.' I turn to address the floor and see a series of gobs well and truly smacked. 'Goodbye, everyone. Some of you I got on with quite well. Some of you I barely knew. I received a handjob from only one of you.' A snort of laughter erupts from behind the filing cabinets. 'I hope that things get better here for all of you as soon as possible. Alex could certainly start that process by jumping out of the nearest high window.' I smile at the skinny weasel and give him the finger for good measure. 'I'm leaving now,' I say to my enrapt audience, 'and will head home to tell my wife what has happened here today. If you wish to visit me in hospital, I would imagine I'll be at St Mary's as that's the nearest one to my house.'

I turn back into my office and slam the door so hard it can probably be heard in the Maldives. Fifteen minutes later I'm chain smoking my way out of the car park. Forty minutes later I'm sat outside the house, sheer terror gripping every inch of me . . . except my arsehole, which has completely stopped throbbing, I'm pleased to report.

On shaky legs I open the front door, walk into the house and straight through to the living room. Laura looks up at me and sees the expression on my face.

'What have you done now?' she says. I can almost feel the needles in her voice.

Placing the dining-room table between me and my concerned wife, I begin to weave my ugly tale.

# Laura's Diary

## Thursday, October 29th

Dear Mum,

First of all, let me offer you a couple of much-needed apologies.

I haven't left a diary entry for over three weeks now and for that I am sorry. A combination of unholy rage and sheer exhaustion have put me in the kind of mood that's not conducive to creative writing. Which leads me on to my second apology – for the foul language you were subjected to in that last entry.

I used words and phrases no person should ever have to listen to, even if they aren't alive anymore. I'm frankly surprised you didn't come back as a ghost to smack my bottom until it was red raw as punishment for the use of such obscenities.

I re-read the entry just before writing this one and even I am amazed that I could spout such evil filth over the course of two whole pages. I can never let Jamie read it. He'd be taking out five restraining orders on me before the sun went down.

I do feel my reaction was understandable, given my idiot husband's nearly successful attempt to ruin our lives completely, by getting fired from his job. We've never had an argument that lasted eight days before. I'm thinking of ringing *The Guinness Book Of Records*.

Thankfully, something has transpired in the intervening fortnight that has made my disposition a lot sunnier. I'm also absolutely terrified, but in a good way.

Allow me to explain:

A week ago it felt like my life was more or less over. I had a husband with no work and a new propensity for walking round the entire day in his dressing gown, while I still went to a job that I can't stand at the best of times, but where I now find myself begging for more hours to make up for Jamie's little outburst at the paper.

I was trying very hard not to feel towering resentment towards my husband, but given that he'd forced me to work more and see even less of my rapidly developing daughter, I could have cheerfully extracted his eyeballs with an ice-cream scoop.

It was in this frame of mind that I started my working day at the Morton & Slacks pit of misery, vaguely hoping that at some point there'd be an earthquake and I'd be crushed to death by a pile of luxury selection boxes.

What made this particular day even worse was that one of my staff – a timid thing of sallow complexion called Amy – had taken the day off thanks to a twinge in her back. I hardly felt that a slight pain above the pelvis constituted an excuse not to come into work, but employment law unfortunately disagreed with me, so I was forced to run the shop with just Jonathan in tow. Jonathan, as you may remember, could spend three solid years studying human anatomy and still not tell an arse from an elbow at the end of it.

Still, it was a Wednesday – customarily a quiet day in the shopping centre – so I was looking forward to some idle staring out of the window while Jonathan tripped over things in the storeroom.

And for a majority of the day, this is exactly what happened.

We have a grand total of eight customers before lunch – two couples, one businessman who's obviously forgotten an important anniversary, two single men who probably haven't, and Larry the local homeless bloke, who I have to shoo out of the shop before he sucks the alcohol out of all the chocolate liqueurs.

I eat a Sainsbury's wrap for lunch that I barely taste and settle back in behind the counter for an afternoon of much the same thing.

A further seven customers come in and buy a variety of tasty treats before five-fifteen rolls around and I begin to think about closing up. Then Maisie enters my life. I didn't know that Maisie was her name initially, but I do know it's one I will never forget for as long as I live.

At approximately five-twenty in she shuffles wearing a crumpled red plastic mac three sizes too big for her and a black pork pie hat stuffed over the worst blue rinse this side of an episode of *Coronation Street*, she looks more harmless than a baby deer covered in bubble wrap.

'Good afternoon,' I tell her, hoping she won't launch

into a story about how she managed to get nylons during the war.

'Hello, my dear,' she replies and shuffles over to look at the fudges.

I breathe a sigh of relief. No war stories today it seems. I go back to staring out of the window. Larry is across the way outside Boots and I'm taking mental bets with myself as to how long it'll be before he tries to piss up against the window.

This occupies me for a good five minutes, until Jonathan stumbles over.

'Er, Laura?' he says in a low voice.

'Yep?'

'I think that old lady is shoplifting.'

'What?'

'She's nicking stuff.'

I look over at her. She's shuffled over to the novelty stand and is examining the six-inch Barney Bear in dark chocolate with some intensity.

Is there a slight bulge in her over-sized mac where there was none before?

I continue to study her for some time, but she doesn't appear to be making any moves to steal our stock, so I look back at Jonathan. 'I think you're mistaken, Jon. She's not doing anything suspicious.'

'But I swear I saw her lift a box of the Belgian specials just a second ago!'

'Maybe you just *thought* you saw her do it, but—'

Barney the frigging Bear has disappeared. Where once his big gormless chocolatey smile was on display for all to see, what remains is an empty shelf that could probably do with a good dusting.

The elderly woman is now edging her way back towards the entrance, feigning interest in the mini hampers. For all the world it looks like she's completely innocent.

Thanks to Jonathan's timely warning though, I know better. The bulge of Barney Bear is quite obvious. In fact, looking closer at her coat I can see there must be several lifted items under there, given how much larger she looks than when she came in.

'Stay here,' I tell him in a gruff voice. I must confront this miscreant and bring swift justice down on her before she is allowed to get away.

I wish I had a badge and a gun at this point – or a cape of some description. I stride over to where the old bint is now nearly out of the shop.

'Excuse me?' I say in a strident tone.

She looks back at me with the kind of wisened expression that grandchildren love the world over. 'Yes, my dear?'

'Could you open your coat for me please?' I demand.

The look of cheery good nature disappears faster than a Greek savings account. 'Why do you want me to do that?' she snaps.

'Could you just do it for me please, madam?' I repeat in my best police voice. All those episodes of *Motorway Cops* I've been watching are now paying dividends.

Given how commanding and authoritarian I sound, I fully expect her to capitulate and give up the pretence. I'm already considering letting her off with a warning. Colour me completely surprised then when she says

'Bollocks to you, love!' and runs away. Actually *runs away*.

I would have pegged this old lass as the type who could barely get above a zombie-like shuffle, but here she is speeding past BHS towards the shopping centre exit as fast as her crabby old legs will carry her.

The shock is so extreme I descend into cliché. 'Stop thief!' I wail and point one finger skywards. This has no appreciable effect as we live in the twenty-first century and not 1955. Nobody comes to my aid so I shout 'Mind the store!' at Jonathan and take off in hot pursuit.

I sprint towards my elderly nemesis, who turns to see me hunting her down and increases her pace even more. She's like a fat little red pinball bouncing her way through the crowd, both hands clasped over her belly to prevent Barney Bear and the rest of my merchandise from falling out.

Fast as she is, I am a good forty years younger and catch up with her outside the British Heart Foundation shop within a few seconds.

'Give me back my fucking chocolate!' I screech as I grab her arm. All pretence of politeness has gone out of the window now I know she's a dastardly criminal.

'Ooooooohhh!' the old duffer wails. 'Somebody help me!'

It occurs to me that from the outside this situation doesn't look good. As far as any bystanders are concerned a healthy woman in her thirties is bullying a sweet little old lady by one of the local charity shops.

'Let me go!' she moans again, really laying it on thick.

'Let that poor woman go!' a fat man in a suit demands.

'No!' I shout. 'She's a bloody shoplifter!'

Everyone in the British Heart Foundation has come out to see what all the fuss is about. I'm now surrounded by pensioners who think I'm assaulting one of their own. Things could go downhill very rapidly here. I've never been run over by a mobility cart before, but I fear that fate awaits me if I don't calm the situation down as soon as possible.

'This woman is a shoplifter, and I'm not letting her go until somebody calls the police!'

'I'm no shoplifter!' she moans.

'Oh no!?' I grab her coat and pull.

Fantastic, now it looks like I'm sexually assaulting an elderly woman in front of a crowd of like-minded pensioners. Any minute now I'm going to be battered to death by the most arthritic vigilantes in human history.

'Aaaaargggh!' the shoplifting granny wails.

'Let her go at once!' an old man who has ex-army written all over him commands from the back of the crowd.

Thankfully the coat falls open and Barney Bear, two bags of fudge, eight Belgian chocolate bars and a jar of pear drops fall onto the floor with a clatter. Silence descends as the crowd absorbs this new revelation.

Into the unfolding drama comes Terry, one of the shopping centre security guards. 'What's going on?' he asks, surveying the scene.

'She attacked me!' the shoplifter says and points a calloused finger my way.

'Oh yeah?' I reply. 'Did I also force a load of chocolate from my shop into your coat?'

To give her some credit, the old harridan doesn't respond. I think she knows the game is up.

'Oh good grief, Maisie,' Terry says. 'Not again.'

'You know this woman?' I ask him.

'Yeah. Last time I saw her she was trying to nick four frozen legs of lamb from Waitrose. We had to call an ambulance because she caught hypothermia.' He sighs and grabs his walkie-talkie from the belt round his waist. 'I'll call the local bobbies. They can take care of her.'

'You're a bad boy, Terry Pruett!' Maisie says to him. 'I'm victimised, I am.'

It seems I've caught up with a notorious local felon. I don't know whether to feel proud of myself or just completely incredulous. My mobile phone, still stuffed in my trouser pocket, starts to ring. It must be Jonathan in a panic. There must be something very wrong for him to go to the trouble of calling my personal phone. Maybe the rest of the Women's Institute have invaded the shop and are stripping every shelf of stock.

'Hello?' I say, answering it.

'Is this Laura Newman?' a voice says to me in a strange, nasal accent.

'Jonathan? Have you been at the chilli mints again?'

'I'm sorry?'

'Who is this?'

'My name's Brett. I'm calling from the Worongabba Chocolate Company in Brisbane.'

'Sorry, what?'

'You applied for a job with us?' the accent is so thickly Australian it's hard to understand, especially with all the background noise. I stand still for a second trying to process what the hell Brett is on about.

Then it hits me. 'That was four months ago!'

'Yeah, I know!' Brett says with a chuckle. 'Taken us a bit of time to get round to it. No worries though, eh?'

'You want to interview me for a job?'

'Yeah! Definitely. We liked your resumé. My boss Alan Brookes is a big fan of you Poms, so he wants to speak to you. We can do it over Skype if you've got it.'

Maisie, Terry, and the rapidly melting Barney Bear have left my head completely thanks to this new development. I barely notice the fact that Maisie has attempted a break for freedom and is currently trying to bite Terry's hand. The effectiveness of this is slightly ruined when her dentures fall out and smash on the shopping-centre floor.

'Er, can I take your number and ring you back, Brett?' I ask as Maisie gamely tries to gum her way out of trouble.

'No worries. Sounds like you're busy over there. What's going on if you don't mind me asking?'

'I've just made a citizen's arrest. Someone's grandmother was nicking my chocolate bear.'

Brett doesn't respond immediately. I can tell he's thinking *very hard* about what to say next. 'Heh! You Poms, eh? Always up to something weird!'

I end the call with Brett by giving him my email so he can send his details over. I promise to ring him later that night and turn my attention back to the crime scene. Maisie has thrown in the towel and stopped worrying at Terry's wrist with her gums. Two of the local constabulary have arrived and proceed to question me over what's happened. I can't help but feel bad as I dob Maisie in. My ire at her thievery has waned, and now I just feel like I'm consigning a pensioner to a night in the cells.

'Don't worry about it, dear,' she tells me as they gently cuff her. 'The tosser in Waitrose rugby-tackled me and threw my hip out. You were a lamb in comparison.'

Inexplicably, this *does* make me feel a bit better.

I get home that evening a good hour late thanks to Maisie. The first thing I do after kissing Poppy hello and berating Jamie for not clearing out the dishwasher is phone Brett back.

A brief call later I have a job interview arranged, to be conducted with Alan Brookes, the owner of the Worong-abba Chocolate Company, over Skype the following Thursday.

That's *today*. In about an hour . . .

I'm so nervous I'm afraid I'm going to throw up all over the keyboard, which I suppose would be a near repeat of my last important job interview with a chocolate company. I'm very sure I'm not pregnant this time though. You have to have sex to get pregnant and Jamie isn't getting anywhere near my lady garden for a good few weeks yet, thanks to getting himself fired.

This whole situation is very bizarre. I applied for that job via an industry website on a whim four months ago. I never thought anything would come of it. Here I am though, about to be interviewed for a job across the other side of the planet. It's exciting, terrifying and destabilising all in equal measure.

For the first time in weeks though, I feel something

other than miserable and tired. That's got to count for something, right?

I did a bit of internet research about Worongabba Chocolate. It's a smallish company that only runs out of a few locations in Queensland and New South Wales, but anything's got to be better than Morton & Slacks, and its clientele of homeless drunks and shoplifting pensioners. Besides . . . it's *Australia*! A place where I could actually hold on to a suntan for more than a week.

Wish me luck, Mum . . . and pray I don't make a fool of myself.

Love you and miss you as always.

Your very skittish daughter, Laura

xx

# Jamie's Blog
## Monday 2 January

For the first time in two months I find myself wishing Laura hadn't landed the job with the Woolengobb . . . Warrengubb . . . Wobblebottom Chocolate Company.

There have been many moments of high stress since she put the phone down on Brett Michaels, the deputy CEO of the company, and started jumping around the living room shouting, 'I got the job!' at the top of her voice.

Telling my family and our collective friends that we were leaving the country – perhaps permanently – was definitely an experience I don't want to repeat any time soon.

Neither was organising an inexpensive place to store our worldly possessions for the short term, and transport to the New World as soon as we were set up in Australia.

Sorting out all the necessary paperwork for visas was a ball ache of the highest order. Australia appears to be the kind of country that only lets foreigners in for longer than two weeks if they can prove an ability to fill in complicated forms in triplicate and exercise the patience of a saint when on the phone to the immigration department.

But in all of that I never once regretted Laura's decision to take the job. Neither of us has been to Australia before, so we're entering a new and strange existence that for all we know will chew us up and spit us out. What was the alternative, though? Another few months of Laura having to work at Morton & Slacks? Me slowly going insane as I sit in my dressing gown scouring the job ads, while Jeremy Kyle berates Tracey from Ealing for eating her baby?

The decision to uproot our family and move ten thousand miles away was a bit of a no-brainer. Besides, it was worth it just to see a happy, excited smile on Laura's face. I'd frankly have moved to the moon if it meant getting her out of the depressed state she'd been in – a good part of which was caused by my idiocy back in October.

So no regrets and no worries (I'm trying to get used to the lingo already). Right up until today . . .

And why the change of heart? Why would I now be having second thoughts about this entire venture, despite all the effort and work that's gone into it? Because I'm in the smallest, most uncomfortable seat it's ever been my misfortune to be sat in. Part of the reason for that level of discomfort is because the seat is forty thousand feet in the air.

I am on a plane, a long metal tube of evil design, wherein I am being punished for all my past sins by having to sit in the same place for hours on end, while people around me fart and belch into the air conditioning system, which happily recycles their emissions right into my pale, dry face.

An hour ago the demonic minions that live in the belly of the metal monster force-fed me a meal they claimed was 'chicken hotpot'. I know the truth, though. They can't fool me. After one mouthful I understood that what they were actually feeding me was the distilled agony of a million tortured souls, trapped for all eternity in a congealed pile of white goo that wobbles when you bounce a spoon off it.

Further punishment is handed down by the tiny screen in front of my face that pumps out images and sounds designed to turn my already scrambled brains into runny cheese. The only things I have not seen on the 'extensive in-flight entertainment' menu are six episodes of *The Only Way Is Essex*, a documentary about Kim Kardashian and all four *Twilight* movies.

I can't bring myself to rewatch any films that I actually enjoyed. Not when they've been 'edited for airline use' and shrunk to accommodate the confines of the postage stamp sized 4:3 ratio TV screen. I need to watch *The Avengers* in glorious widescreen, damn it! I had a go at watching *Twilight*, but Kristen Stewart has the same soporific effect on me as a plate of sleeping pills, and I keep thinking some alien life form is about to burst from that enormous slab of flesh R-Patz calls a forehead, so I switched it off after ten minutes.

But, gentle reader, all these horrors take a back seat to the true cause of my pain. The real reason I wish Brett fucking Michaels had never called Laura in October . . .

Her name is Manjula. Manjula is all of six months old, but is a personification of the devil so perfect in its malice that God himself would quail from her tiny, evil presence. When I checked-in online yesterday (or about ten thousand years ago, as it feels now) I was delighted to discover that I could choose bulkhead seats for all three of us. This would provide Laura and me with a bit more leg room, while allowing Poppy a bit more space as well.

Quite why three-year-old children need so much space is beyond me, but they do and it's just best to accommodate them wherever you can to cut down on the tantrums. Picture then, if you will, Laura sat on the aisle in the left-hand seat, Poppy next her and then me in the third seat . . . which leaves the right-hand aisle seat free. Into which a small, pleasant-looking woman of Indian extraction deposits herself while the plane was still sat at the terminal.

She has a baby with her, with causes an involuntary groan to escape my lips, for despite the fact I am a proud father myself, I maintain the intense dislike for children I've always had. It's one thing to love and care for your own baby, but I'll be buggered if I'm going to love everybody else's as well. They are loud, smelly, bizarre little creatures that I always choose to steer well clear of, if given the option to do so.

Sadly this option is decidedly *not* available on a plane journey, when somebody parks one of the little bastards right next to you. Still, I'm well used to babies by now, having helped bring Poppy into this world, so am at least prepared for anything it can—

*Bloody hell!* She's thrown the kid into my lap. I now have a baby's head in my crotch. It stares up at me with a glazed expression and a lop-sided smile. I look to my right in horror. The woman has flopped her child over the armrest right into my personal space and is now changing the little bleeder's nappy. We haven't even taken off yet. Can't she have waited and done this in the bog once the plane was airborne?

The woman smiles at me like nothing is out of the ordinary. I, being British and therefore incapable of voicing a complaint in such a confined space, merely smile back and wait while the nappy change is carried out. Once it is, the woman gestures at me to hold the baby while she gets rids of the used nappy. To the accompanying giggles of my wife and child I do so, with mild disbelief.

'Daddy's got a new brown baby!' Pops laughs from beside me.

'Poppy! Be polite,' Laura chides from beside her.

My daughter has made an accurate assessment of the situation though, I do now appear to be the proud owner of a new brown baby – which smiles at me and rolls its eyes.

Back comes mother and grabs the kid from my arms, swinging the poor bastard around like it's a life-size action figure. It doesn't seem to mind one bit though and settles down to sleep the second the woman buckles herself back into her seat. I turn away from both, hoping and praying that will be the end of my problems with this strange twosome. Yeah, like that was going to happen, eh?

Three hours go by. The kid is now sleeping peacefully in the basinet attached to the wall. It's a big one, stretching across in front of my seat as well as my Indian friend's.

I myself have settled down for a kip. Laura is watching *Twilight* and Poppy is spark out next to me, dreaming of kangaroos and koala bears I have no doubt. I start to drift off, the whine of the plane engines lulling me into a doze.

Sudden, brief and sharp pain on my forehead snaps me awake instantly. I look down to see a small, square cardboard picture book in my lap. Looking up, the baby is now sat upright in the basinet looking at me with a wide grin on its face.

'Manjula!' the mother cries and picks the book up from my lap, giving me a slight but discomforting whack in the testicles with one knuckle as she does so. She looks at me and bobs her head. 'So sorry,' she says.

'Not a problem,' I reply, and finger the small indentation left in my forehead by the corner of the book.

I shut my eyes again and try to sleep some more. Once again, blissful unconsciousness begins to take me in its warm embrace and I feel myself—

*Ow*! *Fuck*! This time the picture book hits me square on the nose. Manjula laughs in delight.

'Manjula!' the mother chides again.

Through watering eyes I see her pick the picture book (which features a badly-drawn monkey on the cover) up off the floor and put it back in the basinet. She then shifts Manjula to the other end of the cot in an attempt to keep me out of ballistic range.

This works for about ten minutes.

The third time the stupid book hits me it's on the crown of the head – sharp corner first again. Christ knows how this kid can be so accurate and so strong to have thrown the bloody thing so high. If nothing else the Indian shot put team will have no trouble scoring the gold at the Olympics in twenty years. This time I hand the book back to the mother, a dark look on my face. 'Sorry, sorry,' she says with a smile that indicates her deep regret may not be as sincere as I'd like.

'Maybe you shouldn't give her the book again?' I ask. She shakes her head with incomprehension. I drop into typical English behaviour and speak slowly and loudly to her. 'Don't give her the book again!' I enunciate clearly into her confused face.

She seems to get the message and puts the monkey book by her side. Manjula isn't fucking happy about this turn of events and starts to wail. Mother then starts to tickle her, which stops the crying, thankfully.

There's no way I'm going to sleep now. I daren't drop my guard in case Manjula decides to launch an all-out aerial assault on me. I do however shut my eyes again in the universal signal for *I'm now ignoring you and your child for the rest of the flight, madam.*

With the picture book removed, there are no more incidents for the next few hours. In that time I end up watching the Kim Kardashian documentary for the simple reason she has nice tits, while munching my way through the evil chicken hotpot concoction with grim determination.

The final battle with Manjula commences two hours out from Singapore, our stop-off on the way to Australia. A majority of the people on the flight are now either fast asleep or watching to see if R-Patz is about to give birth to a forehead alien. Laura is catching flies, Poppy is dribbling over the armrest and even Manjula's mum is sound asleep and snoring gently.

I am not sleeping. I am watching Manjula like a fucking hawk. The reason? The little cow has stepped up her game. I'd eventually succumbed and decided to watch *The Avengers* again on the tiny TV screen. It was just at the good bit when the Hulk starts smashing everything in sight when my viewing pleasure was ruined by the monkey picture book thrown at my face with the power, style and deadly accuracy of a ninja. I narrowly avoid losing my right eye.

I pick the book out of my lap and waggle it at Manjula. 'If you think you're getting this back now,' I hiss at her, 'you've got another thing coming!' I stuff the book down by my side and flick Manjula a V-sign.

I'm a man in his mid-thirties making obscene gestures at a small baby. This is not my proudest moment. Manjula accepts the insult with good grace and looks down into the basinet. I take this as a sign of defeat and return to watch Robert Downey Jnr flying around Manhattan with a hoard of screaming aliens chasing him.

The next thing I know a plastic baby bottle is bouncing off my forehead. To add insult to injury, the rubber teat on the end falls off as it lands in my lap, splashing the remnants of the milk left in it all over me. Manjula laughs with delight.

'You little sod!' I gasp in suppressed fury.

Manjula's mother stirs next to me but does not awaken. In the dim light of the plane cabin I can see my enemy rock back on her pudgy little legs in devilish glee. A baby barely out of the womb is making me her bitch.

I am rendered utterly impotent. There is simply no way I can respond to this in any conceivable way that won't make me look like a complete maniac. I've been targeted by a demon who knows I can do nothing to stop her tormenting me. As if to exemplify this point a rattle hits me on the right ear before clattering onto the floor. Even with the noise it makes nobody wakes up to come to my aid. I am trapped and at Manjula's mercy.

Thankfully she's running out of ordinance and is reduced to chucking a sad-looking stuffed elephant my way. This bounces harmlessly off my cheek.

'Ha!' I exclaim in furious delight. 'That one didn't hurt one little b—'

Another cardboard picture book, this time featuring a hippo on the cover, hits me square on the chin. *She was hiding it!* The vicious little cow was deliberately lulling me into a false sense of security before unleashing her final victorious salvo. I am *incensed*.

Without thinking about what I am doing I lean forward and very smartly flick Manjula on the end of the nose. She immediately starts to cry.

*Ha! Ha! Not so clever now are you, you bloody monster?!*

I shake my fist at her. Yes . . . I actually shake my fist in triumph at a baby not yet a year out of her mother's womb, having just physically assaulted her. I should be ashamed of myself, but I'm not. Not by a long shot.

*That's what you get for fucking with Jamie Newman!* I

scream in the vaults of my mind, while continuing to waggle a vengeful knuckle sandwich.

Manjula's mother snaps awake to see her adorable baby girl screaming her head off while the mental white man in the seat next to her threatens her child with his balled-up fist.

'Manjula!' she cries, waking Poppy, Laura and the surrounding passengers.

I stop the fist waving and immediately concentrate my complete and undivided attention on the end credits of *The Avengers.*

'Oh, Manjula!'

Who'd have thought Robert Downey Jnr needed three hairdressers?

'Ēkachōtāsārōnābandakarō!'

My my, they do use a lot of people for the special effects in these movies don't they?

'Kyābātahai?'

Filmed on location in New Mexico, Pittsburgh and Stuttgart. How very interesting.

'Apanēnākaujjvallālakyōṁhai?'

'What's going on, Jamie?' Laura asks in a hazy voice.

'Daddy hit the baby!' Poppy cries and collapses into hilarity.

Majula's mother nails me to my chair with a look of deep suspicion. It seems the woman knows more English that she's let on.

'What? No, no!' I lie, feigning complete innocence. 'Pay no attention to my daughter. She's a moron.'

'Jamie!'

Pops doesn't seem too bothered by the insult. She's still laughing like a loon and bouncing one hand off her nose. Manjula is quieting down now, so the Indian woman puts her back in the basinet and returns to her half doze. I can't help noticing her left eye remains slightly open though.

For my part I offer Manjula a final, smug grin of victory and then try to give *Twilight 2: The Search For Kristen Stewart's Personality* a go. I last twelve minutes before turning it off and doing something more constructive by picking my nose.

Yes indeed. There's nothing like several hours of airline travel to reduce you to the level of casual child molestation, I always say. As I sit here writing this now we're on the second leg of the journey from Singapore to Brisbane. Manjula and her mother did not get back on the flight I'm pleased to say.

I am now next to an elderly Chinese gentleman who could be anything from sixty-five to four hundred and fifty. I think he's getting a bit annoyed with my constant tip tap on the laptop keyboard, so I'm going to shut it down and try to entertain myself with something on the TV. I say try – the Kardashian documentary has been replaced by one about Paris Hilton, *Twilight* has given way to all three *Transformers* movies, and I've already seen every episode of *Fawlty Towers* about seven times.

I'm starting to wish Manjula had taken my eyes out with her ninja throwing books.

# Laura's Diary
# Monday, January 9th

G'day Mum!

Sorry, I won't write that again, I promise.

We've been here a week now and I've never been so hot in my bloody life. Australia, it seems, is a mere ten-minute walk from the surface of the sun. My *eyelids* are sweating. I have never experienced sweaty eyelids in my life. It is a new and strange phenomenon I'm not entirely sure I approve of.

Two words have become of paramount importance to me in the last week: air conditioning. Without it I would have wilted into a small heap in the corner within five hours of getting off the plane. As it is, the dull drone of the air conditioning unit is the most pleasurable sound in my life these days.

And what a few days it's been! A real rollercoaster ride. We've well and truly been dropped into the deep end of Australian culture without a life jacket.

The first two days of the trip were spent getting over the horrific jet lag. My new employers had arranged three days in a fairly bland hotel in Brisbane to start us off, giving me forty-eight hours to stop yawning every five minutes and prepare myself for my first meeting with the boss. Said meeting took place in a rather elegant office building overlooking the botanical gardens.

Alan Brookes is possibly the most Australian Australian to ever walk the face of the planet. In his fifties, he speaks with a nasal twang it's impossible not to find endearing and has a tanned, lined, and ruggedly handsome face that speaks of many an hour tramping manfully through the outback. Well over six feet tall, he wears a hat that mercifully doesn't have corks on it, but is exactly the kind of bushman's hat you'd expect a working class Australian millionaire to have perched on this slightly thinning head of blond and white hair.

I have to confess to a slight crush on Paul Hogan when I was a very young girl, so I can't prevent myself from blushing slightly when we're first introduced, as he shakes my hand in a gentle but firm manner. Having said that, Alan looks like the kind of man who knows as much about chocolate as I do about crocodile wrestling.

'The wife's idea,' he tells me when I voice this rather impertinent opinion. I feel relaxed enough to ask this after only ten minutes around the man. He's one of those open, funny, down-to-earth types that make you feel instantly at ease.

Alan Brookes probably makes friends easier than most people shake hands, firm or otherwise. 'She loves the bloody stuff,' he continues. 'Always wanted to own a chocolate company, she has. Hasn't got a head for business though, so I'm running the show for her.'

You know you're rich when you can buy your wife an entire chocolate company for Christmas. I wonder what he bought her for her birthday? New Zealand, possibly? Still, I'd love it if Jamie had enough cash to buy me my own chocolate manufacturer. It'd make a nice change from all the electrical kitchen appliances he keeps purchasing in an unconscious display of Yuletide misogyny.

Alan Brookes made his fortune in the opal mines out west, then semi-retired with more money than God. It appears he now buys up small businesses as a hobby to keep himself busy when not strangling crocodiles in the outback. This chocolate venture is the latest of these little experiments. One that I'm going to be an intrinsic part of.

'Yeah, we'll get you going down on the Goldie in a few weeks,' Alan tells me. This sounds like he wants me to do unspeakable things to a dog.

'The Gold Coast, Laura!' he explains when I tell him I don't understand. 'We'll send you down to the store in Surfer's Paradise to use as your base of operations.'

He goes on to explain that he wants me to get a feel for how the three stores in Southern Queensland are faring and provide him with a detailed report within the month.

'This month though we'll keep you here in Brizzie,' he says, 'just so you can get your feet on the ground. Okay there, Laura?'

'Yes. That's fine. Thank you,' I say in stilted fashion. I'm used to a typical level of polite British prevarication, so this Australian get-to-the-point bluntness is somewhat disconcerting.

'Great! What hotel did Brett stick you in?'

'The Brisbane Metro.'

'What? That's a shit-hole! Brett's a good bloke to have as your right-hand man, but his taste in hotels leaves a lot to be desired.' He pulls out a mobile phone. 'Got a much better idea. You can go stay with my cousin Grant and his wife Ellie while you're here.'

*What?*

'They live in a beaut of a Queenslander over in Wynnum. Gorgeous bit of countryside they've got, you'll love it!'

*But I want to stay in a hotel like a typical foreigner!*

I'd been told back in England that the Australians do stuff like this all the time. They can be accommodating and welcoming to an aggressive degree. As two bog-standard socially repressed British people, Jamie and I were mildly terrified this kind of thing might happen – I just wasn't expecting it to happen *this quickly*.

Alan's on the phone for five minutes arranging our bed and board for the next week.

'Right!' he says, shoving the phone back in his pocket. 'You're all set. Grant's expecting you this evening. You got a car yet?'

I blink several times. This sudden shift in conversation topic nearly gives me whiplash. 'No.'

'Ah, you'll need a motor, Laura! We'll get Brett to drive you over to Grant's today and I'll set something up with my mate Bushy who runs one of the local car dealerships for tomorrow.'

'Okay.'

I certainly can't complain that my new employer isn't helpful.

'Great. Good to have you on board then, Laura.' Alan thrusts out a rugged, tanned hand and I once again feel a blush coming on as it envelops mine.

Within the space of half an hour I have a new place to temporarily live, my first work task and a viewing on some cars.

My head is spinning as Brett drives me back to the Brisbane Metro.

'I'll pick you all up in an hour, Laura,' he says as he drops me off. I nod and make my way back to our hotel room, still in something of a daze.

'You bloody what?' Jamie says in horror when I tell him of our change in accommodation.

'It's a very nice gesture by Mr Brookes,' I tell him, trying to convince myself of that fact as much as anyone.

'But I like it here!' Jamie whines. 'The air con is fairly quiet and the swimming pool downstairs is like a sauna.' The corners of his mouth drop. 'We've even got cable.'

'I'm sure Grant and Ellie will have cable as well, Jamie.' I say and start to gather our things.

Jamie then pulls the child card. 'Poppy likes this hotel. Don't you Pops?'

Poppy looks up from the intense game of plastic horsey versus plastic cow she's been playing on her bed all this time and giggles.

'See?' Jamie says, as if a chuckle from a three year old is a solid and well-presented argument.

'My new boss has made a generous offer and I'm not

about to get off to a bad start with him by refusing. Pack, Jamie!'

Poppy, realising her mother won't be swayed on this one, climbs off the bed and puts the cow and horse in her pink plastic rucksack. Jamie produces the time-honoured expression used on occasions such as this – the one that makes him look like he's chewing a lemon – before sighing heavily and joining me in the grand clean up.

Brett arrives right after we've checked out, and it's not long before we're motoring our way east towards Grant and Ellie's Queensland abode.

'You'll love it!' Brett exclaims. 'We went there for a barbie a couple of weeks back. Lovely garden they've got.'

'Hmnm,' Jamie huffs from the passenger seat. He's really not happy about all of this. Not in the slightest.

The first inclination I get that my decision to agree to a change of accommodation was a grievous error is when we pull off the main road and hit a long tarmac strip surrounded by thick foliage. The further we venture down this street the worse the condition of the road becomes. A couple of rights and a left later we arrive at a street replete with the kind of greenery you'd usually see Tarzan swinging through of an evening. It's completely unbeliev-able how this kind of environment can be only a couple of kilometres from the built-up twenty-first century Brisbane suburbs. Brett pulls up in front of one of the houses along the street and my heart starts to hammer.

What Alan Brookes referred to as a 'beaut of a

Queenslander' is an enormous rambling wooden house that looks as ancient as the gnarled, gigantic trees surrounding it. Set in a garden over-flowing with the local flora, the house is a wide, squat bungalow finished in a fading dark blue.

Next to it is a massive lean-to, under which an antique boat sits. Captain Pugwash would have looked right at home standing at the prow. All in all it's more rustic than an episode of *Escape to the Country*.

Brett leaps out of the car. Jamie gets out very slowly, like someone on their first parachute jump leaving the safety of the plane fuselage. I manhandle my wriggling daughter out as well, and walk to the rear of the vehicle, where Brett has already removed our suitcases from the boot. 'Here comes Grant!' he says and I turn to see a skeleton walking towards us.

No, scratch that, this guy's a bit thinner than that.

Grant is about six four, has long grey wispy hair, an equally wispy beard and big bug eyes that wouldn't look out of place perched on the front of an owl. He's wearing a grey paint-splattered vest that hangs off his bony frame, along with a pair of bright orange board shorts and flip-flops that look like they're hand-me-downs from Moses. Around his neck is a stone pendant with that peace sign from the sixties painted on it in what looks like Tippex.

'G'day!' he exclaims brightly. I'm amazed he has the strength to even talk, let alone sound so cheery.

'How you going?' Brett replies.

'Hello,' I say.

'Hmnmn,' Jamie grunts. No matter what else happens today, I know I'm getting a right earful later before we go to bed.

'I'm gonna leave you in Grant's capable hands,' Brett tells us. 'I'll come back tomorrow to take you to look at cars.'

'Thanks Brett,' I say, trying as hard as I can to sound happy about all this.

'Hmnmn,' says Jamie, who couldn't hide his displeasure right now if you put several guns to his head.

'Great!' Grant says and ruffles Poppy's hair. 'She's a cute one, ain't she? Have to make sure the pythons don't get her!'

*Oh good God.*

'Pythons?' Jamie stares at the nearest patch of undergrowth.

'Only messing about!' Grant tells him. The look of relief on Jamie's face is palpable. 'They don't come in the house much anymore, so I'm sure she'll be fine!'

*Yeah. I'll be getting a divorce pretty soon, I just know it.*

Grant picks up my suitcase, further proof that his emaciated frame doesn't necessarily square with his levels of strength. 'Let's get you inside, eh?'

'Yes please,' I reply with genuine gratitude. The lure of air conditioning in this baking thirty degree heat overrides all other concerns.

We say goodbye to Brett and follow Grant through the dense foliage up a garden path that weaves its way between a variety of odd garden ornaments – including a rusty tin bath sunk into the ground as a pond, a plastic statue of a fat naked aborigine man squatting in front of an enormous didgeridoo, a small sculpture of a snake made from old beer cans – and Steve Redgrave.

Not the real one, needless to say. I'm sure getting a multi gold medal-winning Olympian to come and stand in your garden all day would probably prove quite expensive. This is a framed picture of Sir Steve nailed to one of the wooden banisters that runs around the sides of the house.

There is nothing to indicate a reason why Steve Redgrave is positioned thusly. You could almost understand it if there were pictures of other Olympians decorating the banisters at regular intervals – a moving shrine and testament to the soaring endurance of the human spirit. But Sir Steve is all on his own, staring out over the rambling Australian garden like a watchful guardian. Whatever else happens I must question Grant about this later. I have to know the reason behind this oddity.

'I'll take you through to your room,' Grant says as we walk across the wide veranda towards the front door.

Every door and window in the place is thrown open. This is not a good sign that cooling air conditioning is to be had inside.

'Do you have air con?' I ask as we enter the confines of the house proper.

'Nah! Don't need it,' he replies, pointing up at one of four fans in the ceiling that are doing a good job of pushing the baking air around the broad expanse of the living room we've just walked into.

I say living room but 'flea market' would be more appropriate.

Every surface is covered with crap.

Plastic crap, metal crap, wooden crap, ceramic crap, glass crap.

A lot of it has a nautical theme. There are at least three of those lifesaving rings that always hang off the side of the boat. One is for the HMS *Purbright*, another is for the HMAS *Sandcroft* and the last came from the HMS *Chucklebottom* – which I assume is a joke, unless the navy got really drunk once while naming the new fleet.

I could list every item included in the room, but this diary only has two hundred pages available to write on and I still have something of a life to lead. Suffice it to say that an episode of *Antiques Roadshow* has raped eBay and this room this is the unholy product of that union.

'Fuck me,' I hear Jamie whisper under his breath. Poppy giggles from his arms and points at a plastic flamingo sitting on a small black and white portable TV, which probably last saw action when Jimmy Tarbuck was still popular.

'Through here,' Grant says, oblivious to the fact he has a serious hoarding disorder, and shuffles through a broad open doorway. I enter the room and my heart sinks so far even the ring off the HMS *Chucklebottom* couldn't save it.

We've walked into 1957.

I'm sure that's when the gigantic wooden bed squatting in the centre of the room was built, anyway. Another smaller, but equally ancient single bed sits along the wall opposite.

'Here you go, guys,' Grant says, depositing my suitcase on the mattress. The ancient bed emits a protesting creak loud enough to echo round the room.

I'm struck dumb. The walls are painted with what I assume was once canary yellow, but is now roughly the same shade as the stuff that comes out of a large spot when squeezed. The floorboards are bare and look like they'd insert several nasty splinters into your feet should you walk across them without shoes on. A monstrosity of a ceiling fan squeaks its way round slowly above, and the large oak wardrobe in the corner looks like it's been sat there for so long it's now fused to the walls and floor like a giant wooden limpet. A wide set of double doors lead back out onto the veranda, which then gives way to the chaos of the back garden.

The fan and the open doors do nothing for the temperature. It's like an oven in here.

'Quaint,' says Jamie, doing his best maintain an air of polite Britishness – and keep the shrill tones of insanity out of his voice.

'Glad you like it!' Grant says happily.

I turn round and notice something. 'Er . . . is there a door?'

'Nah! We don't like doors, me and Ellie. Too restrictive in the heat, you know? You got this blind though.' Grant grabs a thin bit of rope next to the doorway and proceeds to lower a set of blinds that wouldn't look out of place on the set of the next *Saw* movie.

Fantastic. Not only are we now expected to spend the next few nights in a house Stig of the Dump would run screaming from, we won't even have enough privacy to argue about how stupid I am for agreeing to it.

'Right. A few things to tell you about,' Grant says. 'There's a few things you need to know about the area.'

'Go on,' I say, trepidation writ large across my face.

'First off, ignore the koalas at night. The little bastards like to use the back garden as a shortcut to the gum trees across the road. You can hear them snorting like pigs at all hours.'

*Oh dear.*

'Also, if you see a big brown spider with long legs you're fine, it's just a Huntsman and they're harmless.'

'Good to know.' There's a squeaky quality to Jamie's voice that worries me deeply.

'If you see a little black bastard with red on its back though, you might want to avoid it. They can kill you faster than a croc with a toothache.'

'And what do you suggest we do if we can't avoid it?' Jamie asks, the squeak now so bad he's starting to sound like Sooty.

'Ah, stick a glass over it and come get me. She'll be right.'

'Okay.' Jamie is holding Poppy much more tightly in his arms and is slowly backing into one corner.

'Lastly, Monty might make an appearance at some point. He normally does when it's really dry like this.'

'Monty?'

*Please let Monty be a neighbour, or the postman.*

'Yeah, Monty. He's the ten-foot scrub python we've

got hereabouts. Likes to sleep in the eaves on the roof, so if you hear something moving around up there, don't panic.'

*Don't panic?* This lunatic has just told me there's every chance a snake large enough to swallow my daughter whole is going to be our room-mate and he tells me not to fucking panic?

Jamie has started to make a high-pitched keening noise and is holding Poppy so tight she's starting to turn blue.

'Thanks, Grant,' I say on autopilot.

'No worries! Ellie will be home soon and she'll get on with tea. We're having tofu burgers and lentil salad.'

'Sounds lovely.'

It does not sound lovely. It sounds like the kind of thing they'd serve up in a Japanese internment camp.

'I'll leave you folks alone for a while then. You've got your own dunny when you need it. Just head out of the double door and straight down the garden path. Make sure you don't trip on a koala in the night. I did that once and the little bastard bit my ankles.'

*This is hell on earth.*

Grant ducks under the blind, leaving me with my red-faced husband.

'Why, Laura?' he intones. 'Why would you do this to us?' he holds Poppy up. 'Why would you do this to our daughter?'

'It's not that bad,' I say, not believing a word of it.

'Not that bad? We're all going to die in our sleep, Laura. That skinny maniac will come in tomorrow to find my rigid corpse covered in redbacks, you torn to pieces by the local koala gang, and Monty the giant fucking python sunning himself in the garden with a Poppy-shaped lump in his belly!'

'Don't be so silly.'

'Oh no, you're absolutely right. I am being silly. That won't happen to us at all. We're just going to get murdered by the living skeleton of a hippy sailor and his tofu-cooking wife.'

'Keep your voice down.'

'Why should I? I want to make the most out of my voice box before it gets torn out by the nearest marsupial.' Jamie's voice then lowers to a hiss. 'And why the fuck is there a picture of Steve Redgrave in the garden?'

'I have no idea!'

'Hellooo!' From the living room we hear a new female voice. This must be the lady of the house.

'Shut up, Jamie! We have to go and meet Ellie.'

'Yes, we'd better say hello fast, before she gets attacked by something.'

Giving Jamie a look laced with venom, I raise the hideous blind and storm out of the bedroom, husband and child in reluctant tow. We're greeted with what looks like the ghost of Joseph and his Amazing Technicolor Dreamcoat.

A small ball of brightly coloured material is floating its way across the hardwood floor. The ball has an enormous smile perched on top of it. 'Hi! You must be Laura and Jamie. It's just delicious to meet you.'

*Oh great*. A podgy colour-blind Australian cannibal.

Ellie hovers up to me, her feet completely obscured by

the diaphanous rainbow dress she's wearing. I go in for a polite British handshake. She goes in for a hearty Australian hug.

This results in me punching her in the boob, which she ignores and throws her arms around my waist. 'So lovely to see you both!'

My nostrils are assailed by what I can only assume is the outflow from a nearby perfume factory. Either that or Ellie must bathe in the stuff.

'It's so fantastic to have you stay with us!' she says and noisily kisses me on both cheeks.

Grant has reappeared from another room with a big smile on his bony face. I turn to look at Jamie. We've been married long enough for something of a telepathic link to have been established between us. I know without a doubt that what's currently going through his mind is, *She's going to hug me next. I'm going to be suffocated by a walking haystack of technicolour vomit. I must find a way to avoid it at all costs.* He looks down at Poppy who is still wriggling in his arms. I see an idea forming in that over-cooked brain of his. The bastard is about to sacrifice our daughter to save his own hide.

'Hey, Poppy! Go say hello to the nice lady!' Jamie squeaks, planting Poppy on the floor and giving her bottom a swift pat. He then backs away in the manner of a bomb disposal expert.

Poppy is of course oblivious to the treachery and with arms outstretched she runs towards the delighted Ellie, who gathers her up.

'Hello, little Poppy! I've heard so much about you too!'

From the sound of things Alan Brookes has been bloody thorough.

Poppy giggles. Then her nose crinkles. The perfume has found its way to her delicate three-year-old olfactory membrane.

Small children don't have the social niceties us adults are forced to obey. They therefore think nothing of sneezing right in someone's face.

Ellie emits a high pitched squawk and lets my daughter go. Thankfully Grant has what appear to be catlike reflexes and grabs Poppy before she can make friends with the floorboards. 'Easy there, sweetheart!' he says, putting Poppy back on the ground, who proceeds to sneeze two more times and run back to her daddy.

I can see the smile trying to work its way onto his cowardly little face so I turn quickly back to Ellie. 'Sorry about that, Ellie. Must be the strange pollen in the air.'

'No worries,' she replies, wiping Poppy snot off her forehead.

'Well, now that we've all met,' says Grant, 'I suggest we get some dinner on the go. What do you say?'

Ellie suggests that this is a marvellous idea. I smile half-heartedly. Jamie tries not to grimace at the thought of eating tofu burgers and Poppy sneezes three more times, wetting herself. This breaks up the meeting and we retire to our room to take care of our damp and angry three year old.

So that was how we came to be staying in nineteen-fifties Australia, Mum. Grant and Ellie are extremely nice people, but I don't know how long they're likely to stay like that with us living under the same roof.

Love and miss you, as ever.

Your awkward British daughter, Laura.

xx

# Jamie's Blog
# Tuesday 10 January

The night.

It clings to me. The stifling heat. The cloying darkness. I lie in a pool of sweat, watching the broken ceiling fan rotate above my head, its low hum starting to lull me into an uneasy sleep. I'm responsible for the fact it's broken, for reasons I shall come to shortly. My eyes close, the drowse of sleep overcomes me. Then it happens again . . .

*SNORG!*

My eyes snap open. A small wail escapes my parched lips.

*SNORG!*

I would cry but I've sweated out every millilitre of water from my body since climbing into bed.

*SNORG! SNORG!*

They're fucking koala bears, for crying out loud!

Koala bears are supposed to sit in eucalyptus trees, eating leaves and moving their heads around slowly while Japanese people take photographs. Every TV show I've ever watched about them has taught me that. And you know what else? They're always bloody *quiet*. Silent little balls of fluff that wouldn't say boo to an entire flock of fucking geese. Not the koala bears in my current neck of the woods though. These bastards would give a pack of hooting gibbons a run for their money in the decibel championships.

*SNORG! SNORG! SNORG!*

I'm going to kill myself. But first I will kill Laura. It's been a fairly decent marriage up to now, but I'm afraid it must end with homicide. There's nothing else for it. Poppy can be adopted by Grant and Ellie, if she isn't eaten by snakes in the interim.

Speaking of snakes, when there's a brief surcease from the koalas shagging one another outside I can hear the occasional bump and creak coming from above my head.

With sleep impossible, I've brought the laptop out onto the veranda to chronicle this most bizarre of days. Grant and Ellie are indeed very nice people, but they're also hippies. What's more, they are hippies living in a world they are ill-equipped to deal with. It's all very well preaching love and tolerance from a quiet rural Queensland suburb, but you try applying those philosophies to an average Monday morning on the M25 and see how far it gets you.

Laura and I are very much products of our own environment and therefore have little in common with our new hippy friends. Dinner was a prime example of this disconnect. I'm sure in their world a limp green salad, a couple of grey tofu burgers and a round of goat's milk is a hearty meal. Grant looked positively stuffed after eating a single spinach leaf. I, on the other hand, hoovered up the meagre fare in thirty seconds and immediately started wondering what roasted koala tastes like.

After dinner I was looking forward to an early night. Poppy had already buggered off to bed and I was feeling intensely jealous of her good fortune. Grant and Ellie had other plans for Laura and me, sadly.

'So then!' Grant says over a goat's milk moustache. 'Who's up for a game of Rummikub?'

'What?' I reply, around my last morsel of tofu.

'Rummikub! Me and Ellie love a game, and whenever we have guests we always insist they play!'

This day has now descended into levels of surrealism Salvador Dali would have been baffled by.

'Rummikub? What's that?' Laura asks.

'You've never played Rummikub?' Ellie's tone suggests that Laura has missed out on one of the greatest pleasures in the known universe.

'I have,' I offer up in a bland voice.

Rummikub is awful. A confusing mish-mash of gin rummy and dominoes, it's harder to pick up than molten lead, goes on for hours, and demands a level of mathematical ability most of us lose five seconds after we leave our final GCSE exam.

'Fantastic!' Ellie shrieks and magically produces the oldest looking Rummikub box I've ever seen. With combined looks of obsessive glee, Grant and Ellie start to hand out the game tiles and the wooden racks you put them in. They then proceed to fill Laura in on the rules of the game.

My wife is a very intelligent woman, who can grasp

complicated theories and equations with relative ease. Therefore, it only takes what feels like eight weeks for her to grasp the infernal rules of Rummikub. This is excellent. It takes most people the better part of a year. And thus the game begins.

Two point eight nano-seconds later I want to choke myself to death with my own fist.

We spend the next ninety-three years of our lives playing the first game, which Ellie wins by a country mile.

'Never mind!' Grant tells Laura and me. 'You'll pick it up better in the next game.'

And indeed, seven centuries later I'm surprised to find myself beating Grant. Ellie is still way ahead, but at least I've got one up on the bony head of the house.

Another forty six millennia go by (including two ice ages) before Laura finally plucks up the courage to put an end to the evening. She gives a yawn of such overblown theatricality I can hear Laurence Olivier turning in his grave. 'It really is time for bed I think. Got a long day tomorrow car hunting!'

Ellie couldn't look more disappointed if you told her tofu had bacon in it. 'Oh, okay. That's a shame. The game was really getting exciting.'

'Never mind,' offers Grant. 'We'll leave it here and pick it up tomorrow.'

If I could insert the dining table up Grant's narrow arse right now I would.

'Well done,' I whisper to Laura as we head to our room having said our goodnights.

'I couldn't take it anymore. My soul feels like it's been repeatedly hit with a hammer.'

'Yep, that's Rummikub for you.'

'What the hell does that word mean anyway?'

'It's translated from the original Hebrew. It means to suffer a slow and agonising death.'

I'm joking of course, but in that instant Laura is more than prepared to believe me. I lower the blind across our door and lie on the bed. This is a jolly painful thing to do. I've slept in uncomfortable beds before, but this one actually causes me physical harm. It's quite incredible.

I watch Laura check on Poppy, who is sound asleep. I watch my wife's face change from one of sleepy discontent to abject horror.

'What's the matter?' I hiss, trying hard not to raise my voice too loud given that Grant and Ellie can probably hear everything we're saying, thanks to the lack of a fucking door on our room.

Laura points at Poppy's head. 'Mosquito!'

I jump up and peer down at my daughter. Perched on her forehead is a mosquito roughly the size of my fist. It's looking back up at me and squinting – as if daring me to take a swipe at it.

'Get rid of it, Jamie!' Laura whispers as vociferously as possible. Quite why I've been automatically designated mosquito killer is beyond me, but I start flapping my hand around just above Poppy's forehead in the hope of dislodging the bugger without waking my daughter up.

This succeeds, but instead of having a calm mosquito sucking Poppy's blood in fairly contented fashion, I now have an enraged mosquito flying directly at my face, intent on sucking my eyeballs out of my head.

I flap ineffectually at it. Mosquitoes are not the most acrobatic of insects, but this one doesn't have to put much effort into avoiding my hands as they're both suffering repetitive strain injury from the twelve years of Rummikub I've just played. The fat insect flies up towards the ceiling.

'Hit it with something!' Laura suggests helpfully.

I desperately look around for a suitable weapon. If I don't deprive the sodding creature of its life right now it will go off and hide until we're fast asleep. Then it will spend the rest of the night snacking on our extremities.

Laura is bent over Poppy, no doubt checking for signs of a bite, so she can't help with my search. I can't see anything that looks like it has swatting potential, so I whip off my T-shirt and start chasing the mosquito around the room. Of course the T-shirt is just slightly too short to reach the bastard as it bobs around the ceiling, so I have to climb up onto the bed. This puts me precariously close to the ceiling fan, which is still turning slowly and wafting the soupy air around the room.

The mosquito has settled briefly on the coving a scant few feet in front of me. I lunge at it and smack the bastard square on.

Woo-hoo! That's one dead mosquito that won't be munching on my face tonight.

In my moment of celebration I forget that I'm standing on the bed and lose my balance. One arm goes out reflexively and my hand latches onto the first thing it can gain purchase on: one of the lazily swinging blades of the ceiling fan. This helps to regain my balance for the briefest of moments, before the blade continues its sedate pace around on its arc and carries me off the bed.

At this point I should have let go. Unfortunately in situations like this my brain often likes to take a quick holiday from proceedings. It's been in similar circumstances enough times to know things aren't going to end well and wants to get as far away from the blast zone as possible. I don't think to release my grip on the blade of the ceiling fan and therefore start to drop to the floor still holding it. With a horrendous shriek of ancient metal the blade snaps clean off the fan.

I hit the floor, spraining my ankle in the process and sit back on the bed with a look of pained befuddlement on my face.

'Jamie!' Laura cries. 'What the fuck have you done?'

'I didn't mean to. I was trying to kill the mosquito.'

She looks down at the long piece of bent metal I'm still holding in my hand. 'Well you certainly did a good job of killing the fan, you silly sod.'

I start to object, but am interrupted by Grant, who has appeared at the open double doors, clad in a brown terry dressing gown that barely reaches his skinny little knees. 'What's all the racket there, Newmans?' he asks and yawns.

'There was a mosquito, Grant,' I reply. 'I had to kill it.'

Grant looks up at the broken fan still turning lazily above our heads, only now with a pronounced lean to one side. He then regards the broken fan blade I'm still clutching like a sword. 'Must have been a big bastard. I usually just hit 'em with a pillow.'

'I . . . I'm so sorry Grant.' I stammer. 'I'll pay for a new one.'

Grant waves one skinny hand. 'Ah, no worries. The bugger hardly worked anyway. You've given me an excuse to get a new one myself. Just do me a favour though, will you?'

'What's that?'

'If you see any more mozzies, just hit 'em with the pillow. That bed's been in my family for generations and I don't really want the headboard ripped off.'

'No problem,' I reply sheepishly and delicately put the fan blade on the dresser next to the bed.

'Well, night again then, Newmans,' Grant smiles and shuffles his way back from whence he came.

I breathe a sigh of relief. 'That could have been worse.'

'Yeah? You haven't seen the size of the bite on Poppy's forehead yet.'

I trot over to the small single bed where my daughter has apparently grown a third eye. An angry red welt juts out from the middle of her forehead.

'Oh, Christ,' I say.

'He's not going to help us, pal,' Laura replies. 'Pops is a deep sleeper, but that thing is going to itch like crazy. It's only a matter of time before it wakes her up.'

And wake up she does about twenty minutes later as Laura and I are negotiating our way into semi-comfortable positions on the rock hard ancient bed. I hear a plaintive moan from the other side of the room.

'Mummy? Itchy.' She's asking for Mummy, but Laura gives me a look from where her head is buried in the pillow that suggests that if I wish to keep breathing the baked air hanging around us I should probably get up and attend to Poppy's new bite.

I go over to where Poppy is lying, scratching at her face like a dog with fleas. 'Don't scratch, honey. It'll make it worse.'

'It itches, Daddy. Don't like it!'

'Perfectly understandable, poppet. That mosquito was the size of a camper van.'

I open my suitcase and take out the medical kit we've brought with us. Thankfully, Laura and her Teutonic levels of organisation were responsible for packing it, so it's stuffed to the rafters with every conceivable medicine. If I had been left in charge, I'd be looking down at four Elastoplasts and half a bottle of Beechams' All In One. I pick out the sting relief cream, squeeze a healthy blob of it on my hand and lazily slap it on Poppy's forehead.

'Just leave it alone now, Pops. Let the cream do its stuff.'

'Stinky,' she growls at me and frowns in an exact carbon copy of her mother's best annoyed expression.

'I know, sweetie, but better stinky than itchy, right?'

'Don' wanna sleep here,' she continues.

'It's not for long, poppet.'

'Too hot, Daddy. Want the airy con.'

I want the airy con too. More than anything else in the world right now. 'They don't have it here, Pops. Just the fan.'

'Why's it broken?' she asks, looking up.

'Er . . . Daddy had to kill the mosquito honey. The fan broke while I was doing it.'

'Daddy broke it,' Poppy says in her most accusatory tone.

My daughter is developing so fast these days it amazes me. It seems like it isn't five minutes since I was spoon feeding her brown mulch and here she is at two in the morning halfway across the other side of the world berating me for removing the only form of air cooling available in this wooden monstrosity of a house.

'Just try and go back to sleep, Pops. And don't touch your forehead.'

'Daddy . . . stinks.'

I don't know if she's insulting me or just reiterating her displeasure with the sting cream's aroma, but I'm frankly way too tired to care and blow her a half-hearted kiss before shuffling back to bed.

'That's some wicked parenting there, Newman,' Laura says, her words muffled by the pillow.

'I'm up for this year's award,' I snark, before I close my eyes, and try not to think about the temperature of the air, or the solidness of the bed.

The night. It clings to me . . .

*SNORG!*

So that's been our first day and night at Grant and Ellie's. There will not be a second one. We're supposed to be here for *weeks*, but I don't think I can handle even one more day. That's an awful thing to say I know, but I can't help myself. Uprooting your entire life to travel thousands of miles is bad enough, but when you get to the other end and find it's unbearably uncomfortable, you have to do something about it.

I haven't as yet thought of a good enough reason for us to leave tomorrow that will not mortally offend our guests, but I'm hoping that one will spring to mind as I sit here, enjoying the slightly less stifling heat afforded to me by being outside. This does mean I can hear the koala bears snorging their way across the garden even more loudly, but it's a small price to pay for not having sweaty teeth.

Mind you, as I look out across the ramshackle expanse of ground to the rear of the house, I can see a disconcerting lump sat square in the middle of the grass. In the dim light of a moonless sky the lump could be any one of a number of things. Most of them with teeth.

The chances are it's just one of a number of thick tree branches dotted around the place – I can see three of them just off to my left near the veranda as I type – but it could equally be a ravenous crocodile or ten-metre snake just waiting for me to make the wrong move.

Intellectually I know that neither is that likely. I've been staring at the lump for a good few minutes now and it hasn't budged. If it were alive it would have surely shown some signs of life by now, wouldn't it?

This is one of the less attractive aspects of trading the British Isles for the sunny climes of Australia. If the disconcerting lump was sat in the middle of an English garden I could be fairly sure it was either A) a large sleeping badger, B) a bin-liner dragged out of the wheelie bin by one of the local foxes, C) somebody very drunk and lost on their way home from the pub, or D) a large dead badger. None of these would present much of a danger to me. Here in Australia though, I can be damn well sure that if the lump is not a thick tree branch then it probably has the capacity to deny me my continued existence on this planet in a heartbeat.

There's part of me that wants to retire – slowly – to the relative safety of our bedroom. The thing is, we're going to be in this country for a long time, so I have to get used to the local flora and fauna, no matter how scary it may or may not be. I can't run away in terror at the first sign of anything that may look even remotely reptilian. Living with dangerous creatures is just one part of living in this beautiful country, so I'd better get used to—

*Oh fuck me it moved.*

It's twenty minutes later. My arsehole has stopped twitching. It's now hotter than the surface of the sun in the bedroom thanks to the fact I've closed the double doors, but better that than being eaten to bits by whatever that thing is out there. I'll take a sleepless night over having no intestines any day of the week, thank you so very much.

# Laura's Diary

# Thursday, January 12th

While I have to confess that I'm glad Jamie got us out of Grant and Ellie's and back into the Brisbane Metro hotel, I do wish he'd gone about it in a way that hadn't made me out to be clinically insane. The problem with my husband is that he has no appreciation of the term 'over-kill'. He'll have what amounts to a pretty good plan of action and then he'll ruin it by over-egging the pudding when things don't go according to plan.

But I'm getting ahead of myself, Mum.

First came the car.

'Did you sleep well?' Ellie asks brightly from the kitchen as the three of us shuffle in for breakfast. I've had less than three hours sleep, Jamie only got two thanks to the run-in with his crocodile (which turned out to be a tree branch once the sun had come up) and Poppy now sports a bite the size of a golf ball in the middle of her head.

'Yes,' I lie through my teeth in a manner so British it's quite pathetic.

'Lovely bed,' Jamie adds.

'Itchy!' is all Poppy can contribute.

'That looks like a nasty bite you got there, Poppy,' Grant says from where he's making porridge at the kitchen counter. He goes over to a cupboard in the back wall and produces what looks like a jam jar full of liquidised frogs.

'Er, what's that?' Laura asks.

'Mozzie remedy, Laura,' Grant replies. 'My dad came up with it back when he was a ranger in the bush.'

Grant puts two fingers in the concoction, making a splooging noise as he does so. He bends down to address Poppy, who is now staring at his sludgy fingers like they've just transformed into lit sticks of dynamite. 'Hold still there, Poppy,' Grant tells her and wipes the strange solution across her forehead.

Poppy's face crumples briefly, before she hesitantly opens both eyes again and looks up at me. 'Tingles,' she says.

'Is it making the bite better, honey?' I ask.

Poppy thinks about this for a second before giving one emphatic nod of the head. 'Yes, Mummy.'

'There you go!' Grant hollers. 'Home remedies are always better than the rubbish you get at the pharmo.'

That may be so, but pharmacy medicine doesn't tend to leave you looking like the Incredible Hulk has just sneezed on you. Poppy seems quite happy though. The sludge is above her nose after all, so she can't detect the aroma of decaying vegetable matter.

'Thanks,' I say to Grant, but not sure I mean it.

'No worries. You Newmans want some brekko?'

I trust he means breakfast. 'Yes please.'

Just don't offer me anything from an old jam jar and we should be fine.

Breakfast turns out to be very pleasant. Grant rustles

up some very tasty omelettes, and by the time I've sunk my second cup of coffee I'm feeling almost human. Even Jamie is looking quite perky, though he has had four cups of coffee by the time he finishes his omelette. This will no doubt leave him needing the toilet every fifteen minutes, but at least he's got a smile on his face.

Poppy's frog poultice has gone yellow around the edges and now smells like the centre of London, but she's not scratching at the bite so we'll take that as a win.

'What are you guys up to today?' Ellie asks from over her cup of ginseng.

'We're buying a car!' Jamie says with unconcealed joy. Men, for some reason, always find car hunting an enjoyable pursuit. They may sulk and moan their way around the shopping mall on a Saturday afternoon before Christmas, but you stick a copy of *Auto Trader* in their hands and tell them to find something with less than sixty on the clock for under four grand and they're in hog heaven.

'Ah right,' Ellie says. 'Good luck with that.'

'Don't buy a Mitsubishi,' Grant warns. 'I've had two of them and neither even got as far as three hundred thousand kilometres.'

*Three hundred thousand kilometres?*

That's how far it is to the moon isn't it? Back home we're lucky if the car gets to its first service without rusting into a heap by the side of the road.

'What would you suggest?' Jamie enquires.

'Get a Holden,' Grant tells him. 'They'll do you half a mil' no problem.'

Half a million kilometres? Does this man think I'm commuting to Paris every day?

'I was kind of thinking of getting a Ute,' Jamie adds. This is a new word he has picked up since we arrived here. 'Ute' is short for utility vehicle – or in simple terms, a flat-bed truck. Only not like the big, rusty Bedford sort we're used to. Out here they turn their Utes into day-glo green monstrosities with lowered sports wheels and blacked-out windows. It's the Australian equivalent of the council estate F-reg Vauxhall Nova decked out with a neon kit and an exhaust you could drive a moped into.

'We're not getting one of those,' I intone from over the last of my omelette. 'I have to drive the bloody thing a lot more than you, Jamie, and there's no way I'm buying one of those clown cars.'

This makes Grant laugh like a drain. Jamie sneers and gets up to make more coffee.

I knew this would be an issue. Until Jamie finds work I will be the one using the car ninety per cent of the time, so it really should be something I'm happy with. Jamie knows this on an intellectual level, but on the more visceral, emotional side of things he's just a typical little boy and wants to buy something very fast, stupidly powerful and epically noisy that will prove to the world he has a large penis. I'm all for bolstering his self esteem, but not if it means potentially crashing the car if I sneeze, hit the accelerator involuntarily and slam into the nearest gum tree.

The doorbell goes. It's a rendition of 'Waltzing Matilda'

in a bingly high-pitched chime. If there's one thing Australians don't appear to be worried about it's coming across as too Australian.

'Morning all!' Brett says enthusiastically when Grant lets him in.

'Good on ya, Brett. How you going?' Grant asks, in an equally robust voice.

'Good lookin' day out there, Brett,' Ellie adds.

'Sure is!' Brett replies.

Have I pointed out its only just gone seven-thirty in the morning on a Sunday?

How are these people so fucking *jovial*? My eyes are still crusted with sleep dust, Jamie's complexion can best be described as thousand-wash grey and even Poppy – who should be young and sprightly enough to be up there with her Australian hosts – is frowning and poking at her sludgy head while taking a long draught of warm milk from her sippy cup.

'Morning, Newmans!' Brett shouts at us from across the lounge diner. 'Ready to go car hunting then?'

'Will anywhere be open?' Jamie asks incredulously.

'Oh yeah, for sure. No point in hanging around on a day like today, eh?'

And right there's the reason for all the early morning jocularity. These people live in a country where you actually *want* to get up early in the morning, just because it's so flaming beautiful outside. Sunday morning weather in the UK usually consists of drizzle and an over-riding sense of disappointment – and can only be dealt with by the swift movement of duvet over head.

It takes the Newman family another half an hour to assemble themselves into a presentable state.

Brett whiles away the time with Grant and Ellie talking about the vitally important matters of the day, the issues that Australia as a nation holds close to its heart and the things that define its people's lives above all else. The cricket team are three wickets up as they go into the third day of the test against the West Indies and the bastard cane toads have been sighted just outside Broome for the first time.

Brett almost seems disappointed when I say we're ready to leave. Once an Aussie gets stuck into a conversation about something they're passionate about, pulling them out of it makes yanking barnacles off the bottom of a boat seem like child's play.

Grant and Ellie bid us farewell from the porch. I have to confess to a small shudder of pleasure as we get into Brett's air-conditioned car and drive away from the decidedly non air-conditioned house we've just endured a sticky night in. The air con is set at maximum, thanks to the fact it's positively *baking* outside, even at eight o'clock.

'Is it always this hot?' I ask Brett.

'Nah. This is way up there, Laura. They're saying we'll hit thirty-eight today.'

*Thirty-eight?* You can boil an egg in that can't you?

'What are they saying it'll drop to tonight?' Jamie asks quickly. I know what he's thinking.

'Not much lower than thirty-two, mate,' Brett tells him.

Another night with the mosquitoes and grunting koalas in the kind of temperature that can kill off pensioners? I sink down into the car seat, close my eyes and try to concentrate on the glorious cold air pumping from the dashboard vent in front of me.

We arrive at the car showroom. I say showroom, it's actually a car park the size of a football pitch with one small building at the back. The Australians definitely take their cue from their American cousins when it comes to selling used cars. A honking great sign held up with thick scaffolding towers over the whole enterprise. 'BUSHY'S MOTORS: The cheapest high quality cars in Wynnum!' it screams at the world in bright pink letters on a black background. I have to look away before it sets off a tension headache.

Row upon row of cars in varying states of repair are lined up in front of us as Brett pulls up to the kerb.

'Loads to choose from here, Newmans,' he says and grins.

I look out across the hundreds of cars, and then up at the scorching sun. This is likely to take all day.

'Woo-hoo!' Jamie exclaims and pumps his fist. The sight of so many potential automotive purchases has called to the small boy deep within him and he's jiggling on his seat with excitement.

Did I say all day? I possibly meant all month.

'I'll just go and get some petrol while you guys have a look about,' Brett says.

'Okay,' I say in resignation and take in the look of barely contained glee on my husband's face. There's no getting around it, I'm just going to have to walk around a baking hot car park with two small children by my side for the next hour or so. At least I can shut Poppy up with sweets.

Brett roars away, leaving us by the side of the road. My eyelids have already started to sweat.

'Come on!' Jamie cries and beetles his way off between two large grey sedans like a man possessed.

Poppy gives me a look from under her broad floppy hat. 'Daddy's silly,' she says.

'You're not wrong, Pops,' I reply, watching him poke his head into the cabin of the nearest day-glo green Ute. 'Daddy's very silly.'

The following thirty minutes can be summed up simply by my responses to Jamie's suggested purchases:

'No, Jamie, it's too large.'

'No, Jamie, it's got two seats. Where's Poppy going to sit?'

'No, Jamie, the wheels look like they should be on a tractor.'

'No, Jamie, it has flames down the side. I'm not driving anything with flames down the side.'

'No, Jamie, it has flames and skulls down the side . . . didn't you hear what I said about the other one?'

'Yes, Jamie, it does look very sporty, but it's also done over five hundred thousand kilometres and will probably fall apart the minute I apply the brakes.'

'No, Jamie, that's a monster truck.'

'No, Jamie, that's still the same monster truck.'

'Jamie, if you don't shut up about the monster truck I'm going to shove your head up the exhaust pipe.'

Then a miracle happens.

'What about this one?' he suggests.

I turn with the words *'No, Jamie'* ready to tumble forth from my lips – and bring myself up short.

The car is called a 'Magna' and is a large, standard looking white saloon. It shines cheerfully in the hot Queensland sun. It has no flames down the side, does not feature tyres bigger than Poppy, looks roomy inside, and – according to the notice on the windscreen – has only done a hundred thousand kilometres. It's also inside the relatively modest budget the Worongabba Chocolate Company has allowed for the car's purchase. It's still a monstrously large contraption, but it's by far and away the most sensible car Jamie has found thus far.

My husband suddenly looks crestfallen. 'It's a Mitsubishi,' he says dejectedly. 'Grant said not to buy a Mitsubishi.'

'Grant also wears hemp clothes and enjoys Rummikub, Jamie. Let's get the manager over here and have a chat.'

'Ah, the Mitso? That's a nice motor. Only came in yesterday,' says Bushy the manager. Used car salesman in the UK usually dress to impress. About the only people Bushy is likely to impress are surfers, students and the homeless. 'I'll grab the keys and you can fire her up.'

Jamie leaps into the cabin. 'Look, Laura, it's got an MP3 connection in the stereo!'

*Oh fantastic.*

That's that then. It won't matter if the car belches out black smoke and drives like a shopping trolley, Jamie has spotted a piece of technology that makes him squeal like a little girl. If we don't buy this car now I'll never hear the end of it.

For her part, Poppy has flopped onto the back seat,

glad to be off her feet and out of the sun. The satisfied way in which she's crashed out on the soft, springy seat suggests she's happy with the choice her father has made as well. I sigh and await the return of Bushy with my new car keys.

'Here you go,' he says and hands them to Jamie through the window.

With an expectant smile on his face Jamie inserts the key and turns it. What sounds like an entire pride of lions humping a grizzly bear breaks the relative peace and quiet of the parking lot. Jamie laughs. It's such an honest and heartfelt show of genuine happiness I find myself joining in despite myself.

'Why the hell is it so loud?' I holler at Bushy as Jamie guns the accelerator again.

'Sports exhaust!' he replies at the top of his voice.

'On a car like this?'

'Welcome to Australia!' Bushy says and waggles his eyebrows with a chuckle.

'Can we—'

BRRUUUMMMM.

'Sorry, can we—'

BBBRRRRRUUUUUMMMMMM.

'Can we—'

BBBBBRRRRRUUUUUUUUUMMMMMMMMMMMM.

'Jamie! Stop doing that!'

'Ow! Don't pinch me like that, Laura!'

'Can we please take the car for a test drive?' I eventually get to ask Bushy.

'No worries. Take her for a spin.' He gives Jamie a look.

'I wouldn't put your foot down that much, mate. The cops will be all over your arse if you're not careful.'

The test drive goes well. Jamie even relinquishes control of the steering wheel long enough for me to have a go. This is nice, as it'll be me who will actually be driving the bloody thing most of the time. This is the first time I've driven in Australia and I'm a little nervous. It becomes quickly apparent that their road layouts are strikingly similar to the ones back home though, and I'm happily pootling round the streets of Wynnum in no time, trying hard not to rev the engine too loudly. Mind you, it's not like I'm going to wake anybody up. Everyone around here has been awake since the crack of dawn and is on their third choc ice of the day.

By the time I pull back into parking lot Brett has returned and is standing with Bushy near the office building. By the animated way he's waving his hands around I can only assume the third test isn't going all that well.

'Found one you like there, Laura?' he asks as I climb out.

'I think so yes.' I look to Jamie for confirmation, who bobs his head like a nodding dog in an earth tremor.

'Great stuff! Let's go do the paperwork with Bushy.'

The process of buying a car in Australia is not as straightforward as it could be. In the UK you just put your details on the registration document, take your new owner's slip and other documents, and hand over your cash.

In Australia you first buy the car from the vendor, and

then you have to drive it across town to a garage where they complete something called a roadworthiness certificate, which is much like an MOT without the hand wringing and casual over-charging. Finally, you drive across the *other* side of town to pick up your registration (or, rather inevitably considering we're in Australia, your 'rego') from the Department of Transport.

All this takes the best part of a day.

Yep . . . a *day*.

The Mitsubishi Magna isn't officially ours until gone three in the afternoon.

'Right then, that didn't take too long,' Brett says unbelievably as we walk back out into the glaring afternoon sun from the cool confines of the department of transport building.

'Really?'

'Oh yeah, the queues were pretty short. It took me four days to get my Commodore. Still, no worries eh?'

'No. Absolutely not.'

Do these people ever get irritated by *anything*?

'Right then, I've gotta shoot off. Got a footie match at five. You guys okay to find your way home?'

Unfortunately we are. 'Yes thank you, Brett. Jamie's phone has sat nav.'

'Great! I'll see you Monday morning.'

And with that, we are left alone once more, this time in charge of a three-litre automobile that's so large it makes me look like a little girl while I'm driving it.

It's on the drive back to Grant and Ellie's that Jamie comes up with his plan to get us out of there.

'Look, they're lovely people and very hospitable, but I don't think my nerves, lower back or survival instinct can stand another night,' he says as I follow the digitised female voice back along the Wynnum Road.

'What do you suggest?'

Jamie looks back at Poppy, who is fast asleep on the back seat. 'I think Poppy should develop a hideous fear of koala bears.'

'What?'

'We'll tell them she's frightened of koala bears and we can't stay another night because it might traumatise her for life. All the grunting is keeping her up at night and causing night terrors.'

'That's ridiculous.'

'Not it's not. They *are* keeping *me* up at night.'

'Why don't we just say it's your problem then?'

'Don't be ridiculous, I'm a grown man.'

'Sometimes I wonder.'

All in all though, it's not the worst idea in the world. We can leave Poppy in the car while we broach the subject with our hosts when we get back.

I hate lying to people, especially good, kind folks like Grant and Ellie, but I also hate mosquitoes big enough to play the harmonica, a bed harder than the Orloff diamond and the kind of heat usually reserved for browning the tops of cupcakes.

By the time we pull up outside the ramshackle Queenslander, we have our story straight.

'She's scared of the koalas?' Ellie says doubtfully from where she sits in her rocking chair out on the veranda. Jamie and I are standing sheepishly in front of both her and Grant as they relax the afternoon away.

'Yes, deathly afraid of them unfortunately. It's the grunting,' Jamie explains.

'I've always found it quite soothing,' Grant offers and takes a sip of what looks like the frog sauce he smeared over Poppy's head watered down to drinkable levels.

'We're really very sorry,' I add. 'It's been lovely staying here, but we do think we should probably go back to the hotel in Brisbane for her sake.'

I can see your face, Mum. Please stop scowling like that.

I don't like this any more than you do, but did I explain the mosquitoes, noisy wildlife and oven-like temperatures?

Grant and Ellie both look disappointed, but there's a definite note of sympathy in their expressions as well, suggesting that our ruse is working.

'Well, I guess you've got no choice then,' Ellie says. 'We don't want the poor little thing suffering do we?'

'Nope!' Jamie says, with unnecessary levels of happiness.

Grant snaps his fingers. 'I've got it!'

'Got what?' Jamie asks.

'You guys can have our room!'

'What?'

'What?'

'Yeah . . . our room looks out onto the side garden. The bears never go past us there, no trees to get to. Little Pops will be fine. The room's a little warmer than yours, but she'll be right.'

A little *warmer*?

Seriously, are these people lizards?

We're trapped.

No way out.

Out excuse hasn't worked – and if anything we're now even worse off as we have to sleep in a bed that Grant and Ellie have probably had hippy sex in, and in a room that will be even hotter at night.

'That's very kind of you!' I say too loudly. 'Isn't that right, Jamie?' I add through newly gritted teeth.

'Yes,' he says, his head dropping to his chest. 'Yes it is.'

'Great! That's all settled then!' Grant moves to get up.

'Laura can't poo,' Jamie blurts out.

'What?'

'What?'

'What?!'

'She can't poo. Didn't want to say anything . . . obviously very embarrassing for her. That's the other reason why we need to leave.'

'I can't *poo*?' I spit at him.

I can't believe he's doing this.

I can't believe he's *humiliating* me like this.

I can't believe I didn't think of it first and say it was *him*.

'Yes honey. I'm sorry to bring it up, but we should be honest with these guys, don't you think?'

My nails dig into the back of the chair I'm standing next to. 'Not really, Jamie, no. That's not what I'm thinking *right now*.'

Jamie does his best to ignore the danger signs and

swiftly looks back at Grant and Ellie. 'It's a nervous thing. She can't go to the toilet in other people's houses. The poor thing is more backed up than the M25 at rush hour.' He gives me a pleading look. 'Isn't that right, baby?'

I'm now bright red in a combination of gut wrenching embarrassment and a rage so unholy it should be confined to the pages of the Old Testament. 'Yes, that's right,' I say in a strangled voice. 'I don't seem to be able to go properly. Not at all.'

Grant and Ellie both look like I've just pulled down my shorts and bent over to prove my point.

'Well . . . that must be quite uncomfortable for you,' Ellie says slowly.

'It is!' Jamie jumps in. 'That's why we'd like to move back to Brisbane, so Laura can have a proper shit.'

*Oh my God.*

There will be nowhere for him to hide. He could have a week's head start, ten thousand dollars and access to a plastic surgeon in Kiev and I will *still* track the bastard down and make him pay for this.

'Okay,' Grant says. 'I guess we'd better help you pack your things up then.' He fixes me with a sympathetic gaze. 'Would you like me to make up some of my home remedy, Laura? It might help you get things moving again.'

I shake my head vociferously. The last thing I need right now is Grant trying to shove liquidised frog up my bum.

And so, some twenty minutes later I am sat in the driver's seat of the Mitsubishi Magna, wringing the life out of the steering wheel with whitened knuckles. Jamie is collecting the last of things and saying a final farewell to Grant and Ellie.

One swift phone call has booked us back into the Brisbane Metro and a short drive west is now the only thing between us and the joys of a comfortable king-size bed and climate control. But first there will be suffering, the most suffering a man can endure while sitting in the passenger seat of a car, without it being on fire and covered in scorpions.

I'd already said my goodbyes to our hosts, before running to the car as fast as my legs would carry me. I just couldn't bear to look at their faces ever again. These perfectly nice people, who brought us into their home and let us play Rummikub with them, now think I have a daughter who's scared of her own shadow and that I have antisocial bowels.

Only Jamie has come out of this unscathed. This is an unacceptable state of affairs.

As my husband loads up the last of the suitcases, slams the boot lid down and lowers himself into the passenger seat, I wind down my window.

'Grant! Ellie!' I shout up the tangled driveway.

'What are you doing?' Jamie asks as he slams the car door.

The two Australian hippies re-emerge onto the veranda. 'What's up, Laura?' Ellie asks as I start the car engine.

'I just thought you both should know . . . Jamie has an extremely small penis. He wanted to leave before either of you accidentally caught sight of it and called the *Guinness Book Of World Records.*'

Yes, it was childish, but by crikey it made me feel a lot better as I drove away at speed, my husband's shrieking protests ringing in my ears.

Jamie did get the ear-bashing he so richly deserved for blaming our hasty move on my bowels, but as I sit here in the Metro with the gentle breeze of the air con playing across my shoulders, I have to confess that the embarrassment was almost worth it.

I start a brand new job on Monday and really could do with the next few days being as stress-free as possible. This is more likely here in our modern hotel than it would have been back in nineteen-fifties Australia.

Love you and miss you Mum. And I can assure you that my bowels are functioning with clockwork regularity.

Your relaxed daughter, Laura.

xx

# Jamie's Blog
# Wednesday 22 February

Stop raining.

*Please* stop raining. This is Australia for crying out loud. It's supposed to be warm, sunny and potentially carcinogenic for the skin three hundred and sixty five days a year. Here I am though, sitting on the balcony of our apartment on the *eighth* consecutive day of incessant rain.

And you thought the August bank holiday weekend in the UK was bad. I'm glad we're not camping anywhere, as by now I would have probably been swept out to sea on my inflatable mattress, never to be seen again.

Apparently this kind of weather is not actually that surprising in this part of the world at this time of year. The Gold Coast is in Southern Queensland on the east coast of the country about a hundred kilometres south of Brisbane, and it has a sub-tropical climate. Essentially, this means it is either hot and sunny or hot and wet. And in January and February the chances of it being the latter are quite high.

They fail to mention this in the brochures and travel shows. Not once have I seen a family from Cleethorpes standing outside a Melbourne detached bungalow in the pouring rain while a bedraggled Phil Spencer tries to convince them that open-plan living rooms are a good idea.

The constant downpour is lovely for the rainforests and gardens I'm sure, but it's not so great for an out-of-work writer with a short attention span and borderline ADHD.

It wouldn't be so bad if I had Poppy to look after, but Laura's annoyingly efficient new employers have access to an excellent daycare centre a scant few minutes' walk from the their Surfer's Paradise store, so Poppy is currently having the time of her life playing in a state of the art ball-pit with her new Australian toddler friends.

Actually, this is probably just as well. I can only imagine the psychological damage I'd do to her if we were left alone for days on end. It would be virtually guaranteed that I'd lose her in a department store again before the week was up. Either that or I'd poison her the first time I tried to whip us up a cooked lunch on the tiny two-ring electric hob in the kitchen. She's far better off picking up an Australian accent with her peers and trying not to feel bad about not having much of a suntan.

Similarly, my wife is no doubt extremely busy right now with her new job. Worongabba Chocolate didn't hang around, that's for sure, and put her to work as soon as was humanely possible. We were only back at the Brisbane Metro for a few days before Alan Brookes decided to send us down here to The Gold Coast early, because as he so eloquently put it: 'You're a bloody miracle worker, Laura. I want you down there and up to your elbows in it as soon as possible!'

This came after only a few days of Laura getting up to speed with the company's operation. Within forty-eight hours she'd already identified several key areas that would increase turnover and lower expenditure. Brookes knew a valuable asset when he saw one and didn't want to waste any time getting her up and running.

So I barely have time to work out the electronic programme guide on the hotel room TV before we're upping sticks again and driving the Magna (which for some reason Laura has started to call 'The Randy Lion') to the apartment Worongabba has rented for us in the strangely monikered but delightful town of Coolangatta. This beautiful place sits at the very edge of the state of Queensland and is bordered by equally picturesque places such as Tugun, Tweed Heads and Currumbin.

I don't think I'm ever going to get used to the names in this place. Every time I try to use the sat nav it has a mild panic attack and refuses to cooperate until I agree to use abbreviations. I was highly amused to discover a place less than an hour's drive away called Wonglepong. I'm going to suggest a day trip there to Laura just to take pictures of me standing beside the road sign with an idiotic grin on my face.

Coolangatta is half an hour's drive south from Laura's place of work – but according to Brett, 'It's a lovely place. My gran lives there. Much prettier than Surfer's if you ask me. That place is all shiny skyscrapers and Jap tourists.' Jap tourists who enjoy luxury Australian chocolate I trust, given the decision to locate the company's shop there.

Laura hit the ground running and I barely saw her for the rest of the week. Her job is partly to oversee the three chocolate stores across the southern Queensland area, and partly to deal with the production and distribution of the chocolates themselves. It's like running her own shop again, only times by four and with a shitload more suntan lotion.

'It's a fantastic company,' she told me one evening as I was giving her a foot rub. I still wasn't entirely out of the doghouse after using her bowel movements as an excuse to leave Grant's and Ellie's. 'Everyone seems delighted to be working for it and they're actually happy to come into the store every day. It's quite disorientating.'

'That'll be the sun,' I reply sagely. 'Well, that and the fact the economy here isn't flatter than a deep-sea pancake.'

'A what?'

'A deep-sea pancake. You know, because the sea pressures are high, which would make the pancake even flatter than it would be if—'

'Right, I understand. I think all this sun is boiling your head, Newman.'

'Possibly so.'

'Anything come up for you?'

'Nope,' I reply downcast.

We'd come out here thinking I would have absolutely no problem finding work of some description. In a country with a strong economy and low population you'd think they were handing out employment opportunities on every street corner. I had every intention of landing myself a nice part-time job doing a bit of copywriting or marketing to supplement the already healthy wage Laura was bringing in, thus leaving myself enough time to write a couple of dreadful novels.

This had been the plan we'd agreed on when we flew out last month, but within a few weeks it had become apparent that finding me some gainful employment wouldn't be the breeze I thought it would be.

First of all, there are no writing jobs of any kind in this area. Any rare positions that do open up are snapped up at near light speed before I get so much as a chance to fill out an application form. Which brings me to the other reason I can't find work: I was unlucky enough not to be born Australian. If you weren't educated in the Australian system you can forget about any of your qualifications meaning a damn thing here. I have degrees and post graduate certificates coming out of my arse, but as they were all earned in the UK I might as well have a PhD in advanced chicken molestation.

'Something will come up,' Laura tells me and gives me one of those sympathetic smiles you never want to have aimed at you.

She then launches into a lengthy diatribe on how chocolate manufacturing out here is ten times more efficient than it is back home. I continue to rub her feet while drifting off into a morose fantasy where I have to offer sexual favours to passing Japanese tourists to earn enough money to buy myself a degree in creative writing from an online Australian university.

When this chance for a new life came along I spent all

my time fantasising about long golden beaches, thirty-degree temperatures and barbecues. I really didn't think about what I was going to do for a long-term career until we actually got here. I was so happy that Laura had been offered a well-paid job – and would therefore dig us out of the mire I'd resolutely put us in thanks to getting fired from the paper – that I didn't stop to think about the ramifications on my own future employment, and my sense of self-worth should I not find something remunerative to do with my time.

Right now I'm a kept man, and it frankly makes me feel a bit sick. I'm very proud of Laura for what she's accomplishing with Worongabba, but I hate the idea of her having to support us both. Oh, I can clean the house from top to bottom every day and rub her feet until they're worn down to nubs, but I still don't feel like I'm providing much to the family unit. It's a very caveman-like attitude to take I know, but I just can't help myself.

The lack of work and acres of free time wouldn't be so bad if it would just stop fucking raining for five minutes. In previous weeks I've been able to take constitutional walks along the breathtaking beaches we're lucky enough to be living right beside. Our apartment is less than a hundred yards' walk to the kind of sandy slice of heaven you only usually see glaring at you from the pages of the nearest travel brochure. I've grown quite used to ambling my way along the boardwalk, dropping into the town centre to pick up the local paper, and spending the next twenty minutes in a fruitless search for employment before throwing my hands up and buying an ice cream. It's the kind of lifestyle I'd be insanely jealous about if I wasn't the one living it.

But then it started to rain and my life became a living hell.

The two-bedroom apartment we live in isn't all that big. It's part of a three-storey complex built around a small swimming pool, and is obviously designed with the transient holidaymaker in mind. Not a day goes by without seeing a new collection of tourists wheeling their suitcases in through the main gate, happy expectant looks on their faces.

The lack of floor space is fine when you can get out and about, but when you're confined thanks to the inclement weather it's akin to being in a prison – admittedly, the minimum security kind with cable TV and attractive views from the window, but a prison nonetheless.

Thus I am bored out of my tiny mind.

Which is frankly ridiculous considering I'm in one of the most beautiful countries in the world, with access to a plethora of entertainment venues designed to keep the locals happy when the weather is a bit crappy, as now. The fine public transport system of Queensland could carry me to any number of cinemas, theatres, bowling alleys, amusement arcades and shopping malls.

I'd also like to think I have a pretty creative intellect. I could be spending all this free time writing a novel of such great import and significance that it will change the face of modern literature.

So what have I accomplished in the past few days, you

may ask? What constructive and pro-active tasks has Jamie Newman completed in his days on The Gold Coast so far?

I have finished *Plants Vs Zombies*, learned how to say 'my elephant has a purple bum' in German, and wanked off a grand total of six times in one afternoon. By the end all I could produce was a fine dust. My life is truly blessed . . . or *'mein elefant hat einen lila unten'* as they say in Bavaria.

Thanks to the fact this is an apartment block largely full of tourists I haven't had much chance to get to know anyone. No sooner have I broken through my British sense of reserve and introduced myself to a neighbour, it's then time for them to leave. There was a particularly nice couple from Munich I was trying to get to know last week. I'd just got to the point where I was attempting to work elephants into the conversation when Jurgen announced they were both leaving the next morning for Perth.

In fact the only people I've seen on a regular basis so far have been Sandra the housekeeper, her husband Bob who tends the grounds, and Mindy the pretty twenty-year-old letting agency trainee, who sits in her small office at the rear of the apartment complex texting on her iPhone. Sandra is an ex-pat so we have some common ground on which to base a conversation; Bob is quite happy to baffle me with the rules of Aussie football, and while Mindy isn't the source of great conversation, I can at least stare idly at her fabulous breasts.

I can't talk to the girl for more than five minutes at a time though, as she makes me feel older than shit. Mindy speaks in a language I can barely understand, using words like 'stoked' and 'wrapped' in contexts I am completely unfamiliar with. Apparently they are both indicators of excitement and happiness judging from the way she says them in a high-pitched squeal while bouncing around on the spot.

I have tried to put pen to paper (or fingertip to keyboard) and write something in the empty rain-soaked hours of the past week. It did not go altogether well.

I initially started to write a thriller about a British journalist living in Australia who has to fellate Orientals to survive and gets embroiled in a human trafficking operation, but decided after three thousand words that this was probably hitting a bit close to home and left it there.

Then I had a pop at writing erotica. I just can't do it. Every time I start to describe how his throbbing manhood sailed majestically towards her heaving sex I feel a combination of horny and nauseous – and start to giggle like a ten year old looking through a porno mag for the first time.

Then I wrote a poem about the rain. I'd only got three stanzas into the bugger when I realised that all I'd been writing was a weather report in rhyming couplets: *Heavy downpours all this morn, leaves me feeling all forlorn. Precipitation from the west, creates a weight inside my chest.*

Complete crap, I'm sure you'll agree.

I've come to the decision that I'm not cut out to write anything of great import and significance, so I should probably just knock out a derivative action pot-boiler, featuring large explosions and women with chests that defy gravity. I am therefore now halfway through chapter one of *Max Danger And The Boobatrons* and am heartily looking forward to our muscular hero's first confrontation with the evil Doctor Smegma.

We've been here in Australia for six weeks now and that's been long enough to get a pretty good idea of what it's like as a country. So, for your delight and edification, here's the six-week report card:

The Good:

Free Parking. I know I should probably start with the beautiful beaches and all that blather, but FREE PARKING, PEOPLE – EVERYWHERE! We haven't once had to pay for parking at any one of the various beauty spots and tourist attractions we've been to. The petrol's cheap as well, even though the price is more up and down than an overworked prostitute some days.

The weather. Yep, here's the inevitable one. It's hot, and for the most part sunny. It hasn't dropped below 25 degrees yet, and we're all permanently living in shorts and flip-flops (sorry, thongs). This makes people happy and friendly, which makes you happy and friendly – those of us with jobs that is. Yes, it's summer here, but as their winter is generally the same temperature as *our* summer anyway, we'll go ahead and give this one resoundingly to the Aussies, eh?

Safety. This place, or the Gold Coast at least, seems a lot bloody safer than a majority of UK cities. There's little to no vandalism other than a smear of graffiti, the teenagers are all too busy rolling around on skateboards

93

looking happy and suntanned to attack any pensioners in the street, and folk are happy to leave their possessions lying around on the beaches with little fear of them being stolen. Some of the police cars here are partially coloured pink. Yes, pink. Can you imagine how that'd go down in the UK? What little respect the local scabs have for the old bill would evaporate the second a unit drove by in a car that looked like a marshmallow. Here, on Friday and Saturday nights, you're just as likely to see a family out and about with little kids as you are drunken people. I've seen no anti-social behaviour whatsoever – unless you count middle-aged men flying past you on a skateboard as anti-social.

Scenery. The other inevitable one. Beach after beach of bright sand and roaring surf, mountains covered in lush rainforest, clean sun-dappled parks where people can congregate and look tanned together. Frankly, it's sickening. These people don't know they're born. Even the town centres look lovely.

The food is excellent. Walk into your average British shopping mall and the meal choices you have will consist of a variety of brown fried shit from the fast-food outlets, or a limp bit of lettuce parked on a burned slice of bruschetta in one of those Italian café chains – a meal which is about as authentically Italian as a bowl of Asda spaghetti hoops. In Australia the food courts are enormous and the variety is great. Laura and I must have spent at least a month trying to decide what to choose from the wide selection of cuisines from around the world (we generally go for Thai). The portions are big too. Other than the mall food, the coffee, even the cheap stuff, is far better than the sludgy crap we are used to, and the meat is fabulous, especially the beef – none of that slightly grey stuff that generally lurks at the back of the Tesco meat counter. I've also found the best peanut butter I've ever had here, and you can buy a ton of delicious watermelon for about tuppence.

The people are friendly and open. This is largely because of all the things I've mentioned above, of course. Okay, you get one or two chav-like individuals who shout a bit and dress like they really want to be extras in the next *Mad Max* movie, but for the most part the Aussies are a happy, friendly bunch. It's quite a culture shock to have somebody genuinely interested in helping you out, rather than getting the usual look of contempt and that wall-eyed vacant stare when talking to an official person in Blighty. The Australian people live in a beautiful country and that's reflected in their demeanor, although I do wish they wouldn't go around being so chuffing smug about the place all the time. It's just not British.

The Bad:

Communications. Let's start with the internet. The internet in Australia is laughably bad. African bushmen in the middle of the Kalahari can't believe how backward Aussie broadband is. Slow, hideously expensive and unreliable, it boggles the mind how it can be this awful. We're currently paying over £30 a month for a mobile broadband service that'd cost me less than half that at home. And it drops out all the time (twice since I started typing this). If somebody so much as sneezes anywhere near the wi-fi router it refuses to work for twenty minutes.

TV: Woeful. We have Freeview here but it's not like the Freeview back home, where there are fifty channels to choose from, plus radio. Australian Freeview consists of sixteen stations, which are all the major mainstream broadcasters and no music channels at all. *On the Buses* is still broadcast here, believe it or not. If you missed any UK dramas or comedies from about three years ago, no worries – just come to Australia, because they're all still on in primetime slots. When you do find something half decent to watch the thirty-four advert breaks an hour ruin it somewhat (Australia has the most unrestricted and worst advertising controls in the world it seems). Australia has followed the USA in terms of its TV, rather than the UK. That's the clinching indictment you need on the dubious standards here. I miss the BBC.

Prices. Everything here is bloody expensive. This is partly due to the pound being weaker than an asthmatic vegetarian mountain climber against the Aussie dollar – but even so, things here are a lot pricier than back home. A takeout is double what it would be in the UK, cars are astronomically priced, groceries vary from mildly expensive to frickin' ridiculous, and you have to carefully pick and choose what entertainment you want to indulge in if you don't want to bankrupt yourself. As far as I can see this is all due to some of the dumbest competition and commercial rules I've ever seen in Western civilisation. There are just two supermarket chains here (as opposed to our eight or more): Coles and Woolworths. Nobody else seems allowed to get into the game. There's no real competition so prices stay high. The banks (there are actually four or five of these) operate like UK banking institutions did fifteen years ago. You can't draw cash out of a competitor ATM without being charged, for instance.

Australia is a lovely place, but if they think I'm paying five quid for a small bag of jelly babies, they've got another thing coming.

Bugger. I forgot one last thing that's bad about this place: mosquitoes.

Utter bastards of the highest order. Like small, multi-limbed insect ninjas they sneak up on you unawares and bite you where you least expect it. To prevent the little sods having a go at you, you need to spray yourself with so much insect repellent you end up smelling like a malfunctioning chemical plant. And even then a few of the hardier ones slip through the net and find the one place on your body you didn't smother in the cancerous gas. I know Australia is supposed to be full of murderous creatures poised to rip your face off as soon as you debark from the plane, but I've not seen any of them yet and most of the wildlife has actually seemed pretty friendly. The mosquitoes though . . . they're evil buggers with no remorse and I want them all dead. My back looks like the surface of Mars right now and Poppy's forehead still shows evidence of the golf ball sized bite she was subjected to back at Grant's and Ellie's.

Anyway, that's quite enough of all that. It's been at least

half an hour since I last stared forlornly at the clouds trying their best to squeeze out every drop of rain they can. If I'm not there to watch it they may start to think all their hard work is being underappreciated.

I'll just make myself a peanut butter sandwich and get back to it.

# Laura's Diary

## Friday, March 3rd

Dear Mum,

I could get used to being an Australian.

I'll never like watching cricket and will never idol-worship Ned Kelly, take up surfing or end every sentence with a question-mark, but by gum I could get used to everything else this country has to offer.

The past few weeks have been amazing, not least because my legs are beginning to take on a very healthy golden tan and my hair has achieved a natural bounce I couldn't reproduce back home with three hundred pounds' worth of John Frieda.

The job is everything I wanted it to be.

Hell, it's everything I *needed* it to be.

Since I was forced to close the shop back home my career in the wonderful world of chocolate consumables had been royally in the toilet. Morton & Slacks sucked the life out of me every day, and it got to the point where I never wanted to look at another chocolate fondue set ever again. That was the worst thing about the job – it made me start to hate one of the major passions in my life.

I really feel like I've won the lottery now, though.

Working for Worongabba is the best job I could possibly have without owning my own business again. The money is great, the working conditions are fantastic, Poppy is in the best daycare I've ever come across, and I get to go to work every day in a series of light summer dresses that make me look and feel about ten years younger.

I always wake up with a smile on my face and Jamie gets the biggest kiss possible at the door before I leave. This, if nothing else, should give ample evidence that I am enjoying life again.

Kissing my husband goodbye of a morning is something I haven't been all that keen on doing in recent months. Jamie and I have lived what can only be described as a strained existence this past year. The mere fact that I am happy to give him a big smacker as I leave for work now marks a very healthy and much-needed change in our relationship. Things still aren't *quite* how they used to be when we were first married, but this move to Australia has improved matters no end, and I'm confident that any damage that might have been done back home thanks to all the stresses and tensions we were under will be mended out here in the sun in no time at all.

After Poppy and I have said goodbye to Jamie, I drive us up the highway in the monstrous white car we own, with its exhaust that's several decibels above the safe limit for most people's eardrums. I try to ignore the looks from the passing pedestrians as much as I can and just turn up the radio.

Australian radio is very strange. There's no real analogue for Radio One over here. They don't seem to have any stations dedicated to new songs. I was listening to the area's most popular station yesterday and they played a Kaiser Chiefs song back-to-back with Eddie Grant's 'Electric Avenue' with no trace of irony whatsoever.

Usually by the time Poppy and I reach Surfer's Paradise we've been treated to hits from the last three decades. And Crowded House. There always must be Crowded House. It's written into the Australian constitution.

Surfer's Paradise is the crown jewel in the Gold Coast's expansive tiara. It's the nearest you get to a proper city anywhere in these parts. By Australian standards it's huge, but all New Yorkers would laugh at the notion that this collection of skyscrapers perched right on the edge of the ocean could in anyway be classed as a *city*. You can cheerfully walk the entire length of the place in an afternoon if you had a mind to.

What buildings it does have though are impressive. The collection of soaring monstrosities loom over the golden sandy beaches, casting their long shadows out over the water at dusk. From the heights they reach, you'd be forgiven for thinking they were running out of space around here.

I once visited Miami for a few days back in my youth while on holiday, so I can appreciate the rampant plagiarism going on here. It's like somebody picked up everything from Fort Lauderdale to the Everglades, put it on a hot wash until it shrunk four sizes and plonked it down on the east coast of Australia.

I love it though, partly because I haven't seen a cloud in the sky for a week, and partly because this is where I work. I love living in the quieter, smaller town of Coolangatta further south, but give me somewhere bustling and lively to go to every day to earn my daily crust. Surfer's has more energy than a litter of puppies drunk on Red Bull. Hordes of tourists mingle with the local surfers and party people among the forest of glass and metal. The sun beats down relentlessly on thousands of people who know they are lucky enough to be in paradise and are damn well going to enjoy it every second they can.

Worongabba Chocolate is situated in the shopping mall underneath one of the skyscrapers right next to the beach. It's a prime bit of real estate with very high foot traffic all day long. I saw how much the rent was for the floor space the first week I was here and nearly had a heart attack.

Today promised to be a particularly important day in Laura Newman's new antipodean life. Alan Brookes, owner of Worongabba Chocolate and my boss, was visiting for the first time since he sent me down here to run the place and was expecting a report on what I'd accomplished so far. Therefore I dropped Poppy off a good hour earlier than usual at Surf Tots Day Care and was upstairs in my office by eight a.m., finishing off the Excel spreadsheet I'd been compiling for the past week.

It's a masterpiece of financial brilliance, even if I do say so myself. Not only have I collated an accurate overview of turnover from the past six months, I have also identified a forty thousand dollar tax overspend that can be claimed back. I have no doubt Brookes will promote me instantly once he realises I've saved him that much money in barely six weeks of work. It may have taken all of my free time over the past seven days to complete, but the results will be totally worth it. Yes, I was one of those insufferable kids at school who always handed their work in early and made you look bad – how did you guess?

Alan is due in at ten thirty and I have everything ready for him a good half an hour beforehand. The spreadsheet is projected on my white office wall in all its Powerpointy glory; a stack of neatly folded financial reports sit on my desk, awaiting his eager gaze should he wish to view them; and I even have a selection of new chocolate flavours I intend to bring into our collections sat on a plate next to the reports, awaiting his equally eager taste buds.

Everything is set. Everything is ready. This will be my finest hour.

My finest hour will have to wait it seems, as ten thirty comes and goes with no sign of Brookes. By ten fifty I'm boosting the air con in my office to make sure the chocolates don't melt. By eleven I'm pacing down on the shop floor, worrying shop staff and customers alike.

By eleven fifteen I'm back in the office checking my diary to see if I've got the day right.

By eleven forty I'm back downstairs telling the shop floor manager Jake that he needs to rearrange the mint fondues in the front window so they don't spell 'MINTY!'. I appreciate his efforts at creativity, but I don't think it's really giving the right impression of the store, seeing as we're supposed to be upmarket.

Being upmarket is obviously not something Alan

Brookes is all that concerned about either, as he eventually rolls in at eleven fifty, wearing an ancient bushman's hat, a pair of board shorts, a bright orange vest and a pair of leather thongs that look like they're about to fall apart. He's accompanied by a stern-looking oriental woman in a power suit and the number-two man in the business, Brett Michaels, who is as shabbily dressed as his boss, given that he's wearing a Captain America T-shirt over a pair of board shorts that look like they've been savaged by a shark.

'You alright, Laura?' Brookes says to me as he walks up.

'Yes, Mr Brookes,' I reply in accepted subordinate fashion.

'Ah, drop the formal crap there, Laura. Call me Brooky. Every other bastard does!'

'Okay . . . *Brooky.*'

'Sorry I'm late. Stopped to chat to a mate of mine down the surf club. Great bloke he is. Got his left arm bit off by a salty up in Mackay last year. I wanted to see if it had grown back!' Brookes collapses into gales of laughter, as does Brett. The oriental woman doesn't so much as crack a smile. I have no idea what Brookes is on about, so elect to maintain a neutral expression.

'Right!' he says, having got over his laughing fit. 'Let's get a look at what you've been up to, Laura. I brought Sangwen along to look at this spreadsheet you emailed me about.'

Sangwen gives me a short but courteous nod. 'Pleased to meet you,' she says in a soft Aussie accent tinged with a subtle Thai flavour.

'And you.' I turn back to Brookes. 'Shall we go up?'

I lead the trio up the stairs and through to the expansive office at the rear of the shop.

'Hey, chocs!' Alan Brookes exclaims happily and proceeds to polish off two of my carefully selected tasters before he's so much as sat down. I'd planned on a good fifteen minute build-up to those. Never mind, I'll just have to give him the speech without them.

I stand behind my desk and clear my throat. 'Thank you for coming today. I'm going to take you through my findings so far in a presentation that should last no more than half an hour.'

'Half an hour?' Brookes protests. 'Bugger that for a game of soldiers.'

'Er . . . but I thought you wanted a report on how I'm doing?'

'I do. So, how are you doing?'

'What? You mean the shop?'

'Yeah! Things going alright, are they?'

'Yes.'

'No big problems on the horizon?'

'No.'

'We're in profit?'

'Yes.'

'And you lot have settled in okay?'

'Yes.'

'Great stuff!' He turns to address Sangwen. 'Give Laura your email and she can bung you the spreadsheet to have a look over.' He then looks back at me. 'Right, you got anything else?'

'Er. The chocolates on the desk . . .'

'New flavours?'

'Yes.'

'You like 'em?'

'Yes.'

'Great! Chuck 'em in then. I trust your judgement.'

'Er . . . thank you.'

'No worries.' He leans forward. 'Now then, how about we all go for a swim before lunch?'

Brett nods his head enthusiastically. Even Sangwen cracks a smile.

I do neither. This meeting has slipped out my grasp faster than a greasy halibut. I was prepared for some awkward questions and a concerted grilling of my facts and figures. I was not prepared for an invite to go paddle around in the surf.

I don't want to go for a swim. I want to dazzle my new employer with my prowess. Besides, I don't have my swimming costume. I say as much to Alan and company.

'Oh yeah, good point,' Brookes says. 'Should've told you ahead of time really. Bit of a silly suggestion all round, I guess! Going for a swim before lunch. I should get my head tested!'

*Thank God for that.*

'We'll go after lunch!'

*What?*

'Yeah, we'll have a bite to eat next door at Hong's, then you can go grab yourself a cozzie with some petty cash. Sangwen can go with you to help you choose if you like.'

The Thai woman can't help but look me up and down

in a disconcerting way that makes me feel extremely self-conscious.

This is horrible. This is absolutely *awful*. I'm being ordered by my employer to take the afternoon off and go have some fun.

'Do you think it's . . . it's appropriate, Mr Brookes?'

'Brooky!'

'Sorry . . . do you think it's appropriate, Brooky? I really should be working.'

'It's my flaming company, Laura, and if I say we're gonna cool off in this heat, then that's what we're doing!'

*Oh God.*

This is the worst boss I've ever had.

We pop to the Chinese restaurant next door for lunch, and end up sitting outside in the sun, al fresco style. In the hideous knowledge that I'm shortly going to be in a bathing suit in the company of my employer, I elect to eat a small salad and drink a bottle of sparkling water.

I try to join in on the conversation my colleagues are having, but my mind keeps going back to the potential embarrassment factory that the next couple of hours of my life are likely to be.

'Right then,' Brookes says, downing the last of his beer in one swift gulp. 'That's us fed and watered. Let's go see what the waves are like.' He looks at me. 'You surf, Laura?'

Oh no. It just gets worse.

I know how this conversation will go. I'm going to tell him I don't know how to surf, and then he's going to suggest he gives me some lessons. An excruciating hour of me repeatedly falling off a floating plank of wood will then ensue. At some point the swimming costume that I have yet to buy will probably fall off. Some things are just written in the stars.

I have to head off any suggestion of me surfing to avoid all of this.

'No, sorry. I have an inner-ear problem that stops me doing it. Shame really, but the doctor warned me not to.'

*Well done girl.*

An excuse of fiendish brilliance.

'Ah pity,' Brookes says. 'Sangwen doesn't surf either, so you two can just have a swim about. The surf looks a bit low anyway so Brett and I probably won't do much ourselves.'

*Phew.*

Brookes takes a look at his watch. 'You go find a costume, we'll go get our boards and see you back here at the shop in twenty minutes.'

*Twenty minutes?*

Does this man have no comprehension of how long it takes a woman to clothes-shop, especially when it's an item that *revealing*? It takes me an hour just to pick out the right chunky-knit sweater in December, for crying out loud. Purchasing a swimming costume is enough to take up an entire morning – and that's mostly just dealing with the self-loathing.

If Jamie had suggested such a short timescale I would have probably punched him. As it is, this is the man who writes my pay cheques. 'Okay,' I say in a strangled voice.

'Great.' Brookes gets to his feet. 'See you in a bit then,'

he tells me before marching off with Brett and Sangwen dutifully in tow.

If you like, feel free to hum the *Mission Impossible* theme to yourself as you read the next few paragraphs.

I look at my watch, take a deep breath and I'm up out of my chair like a shot.

My first port of call is Billabong, three units along. I scuttle through the crowd of tourists, arriving at the surf shop only slightly out of breath. Inside, I start riffling through the bikinis and swimsuits. All of them are very pretty and would no doubt flatter any very thin, bouncing nineteen-year-old girls that happen to be passing.

I am neither nineteen nor very thin these days, and the last time I bounced anywhere I was still in pigtails. Therefore I can't buy any of these tiny pieces of material. The idea of squeezing my carcass into something constructed out of half a small flannel and two strips of elastic is enough to make me lightheaded and nauseous. I scuttle back out of Billabong and scan the rest of the shops in the mall.

As there isn't store nearby called The Post-Birth Cellulite Swimsuit Company, I decide to leave the immediate area and head to Caville Avenue. That takes me a good five minutes, so I now have about seven to find a swimsuit and five to hurry back to the shop and my expectant boss. I duck into a place called Le Sande, then duck straight back out again when the price tag on the first swimsuit I see gives me a nosebleed.

What I need right now is a Kmart. But this is Surfer's Paradise, a place far too cool for Australian's answer to

Primark. I come to the end of the block and reach a crossroads. Roads lined with shops disappear off in three directions, offering me far too much choice in the three remaining minutes I have allotted to this desperate mission. Panic sets in.

*Which way do I go?*

My brain may be frozen, but my feet know what's best for them and take a left. This is a bad choice. There's not one clothes shop down this road that I can see.

I'm just about throw myself under the next party bus that goes by when I spot an extremely tacky looking souvenir store. It's called Surfers Paradis Attractive Gifts. Normally, the lack of the 'e' at the end of 'paradise' and the fact that the shop smells vaguely of cannabis would be enough to put me off, but I now have two minutes left and can see a rack of one piece swimsuits just inside the main door. They come in a variety of bright colours, and are made of the kind of material you don't want to touch for too long for fear of getting an electric shock.

But they do seem to be cut quite modestly and there are plenty in my size. I won't have time to try one on, so I need to go with something that looks like it will cover as much of my body as possible. I spy a likely prospect in a halfway decent powdery blue colour and pull it from the rack. There's a rather tacky illustration across the front unfortunately. It features a cartoon surfboard with a slogan above it in big stupid letters that reads *Surf Lovin'*. This is bad, but the costume will have to do as my time is officially up.

I throw twenty dollars at the guy behind the counter

and sprint back towards The Worongabba Chocolate Company as fast as my legs will carry me.

'You found one then?' Brookes says as I arrive at the shop's entrance.

'Yes,' I reply, still a bit out of breath.

'Good. There's changing rooms down on the esplanade and I've got you a towel already.' He hands me a fluffy roll of material that probably cost ten times as much as the stupid costume I've just bought.

So off we go to the beach – two enthusiastic Australian men, one stoic Thai woman and one terrified British berk.

In the changing rooms I'm relieved when the costume goes on okay and fits relatively well. It's a bit tight around the boobs and a touch loose at the bum, but it could be far, *far* worse.

The *Surf Lovin'* epithet and badly rendered surfboard are frankly ludicrous, but I'll just have to put up with it. Other than that though, I think I've done rather well, considering. My legs look healthy and tanned, and even my arms and face have a warm, summery glow about them that contrasts quite nicely with the powder blue of the swimming costume. I won't be giving any of the bikini-wearing Australian sex goddesses a run for their money, but I can at least hold my head up high.

I apply a liberal amount of suncream from the bottle Sangwen has given me. She obviously has to do this kind of thing with Alan Brookes quite a lot and always comes prepared.

Stepping out into the Gold Coast sun, I see Brett and

Alan Brookes standing with their surfboards at the steps leading to the beach.

'Ready?' a soft voice says from my side. I turn to see Sangwen in a beautiful black two-piece swimsuit, and instantly start chewing my own liver.

'I think so,' I reply.

She offers me a warm smile. 'I know this seems a bit strange, but Mr Brookes means well. He only does this kind of thing with people he likes. You're doing a very good job for the company, you know.'

'Am I?' I say disbelievingly, given how all my hard work had been dismissed earlier.

'Oh yes. Alan trusts you, that's why we're doing this and not sat poring over figures in the shop. If you're out for a swim it means he's more than happy with the work you're doing.'

'But he didn't look at anything.'

'Don't let the relaxed attitude fool you, he knows exactly what's going on with every aspect of Worongabba at all times.'

'Right.'

'I don't think I've ever seen him take so well to a new employee, actually. He talks about you a lot.'

'Really?'

'Absolutely. I'd say you have nothing to worry about.'

'Thanks very much. That's a real relief.'

She smiles again. 'Let's go join them, shall we?'

'Okay,' I agree and walk off in front of her.

She catches up with me. 'Was that the only swimsuit you could find?' she says.

'Yes, in the time I had.'

'Pity about the slogan.'

I look down at *Surf Lovin'*. 'I know, but I had no choice.'

We reach Brett and Alan, who both look like excited little boys.

'Okay then! Let's go see what the water's like!' Alan exclaims happily and takes off towards the rolling waves.

'We'll have a bit of swim for a few minutes and then sit on the beach,' Sangwen says as she watches Brett follow our boss down to the sea.

'Sounds good,' I reply, with a sigh of relief. The Thai woman has set my mind at rest somewhat. I'd rather not be spending my afternoon frolicking in the surf with people I hardly know, but at least she's reassured me that I'm doing a good job right now.

I spend ten minutes in the water before getting out and sitting on the hot sand.

Sangwen and I spend the next hour chatting idly about living in Australia, working for Alan, and the pitfalls of buying swimming costumes. We're just discussing the horrors of cellulite when Brett and Alan return, having given up on the surfing thanks to the inferior waves on offer this afternoon.

'That'll about do it for today I think,' Alan says, spearing his board into the ground. I have to say that for a man in his fifties he has a startlingly good physique. If that's what skiving the afternoon off to go surfing can do for you, I can begin to see the merits of doing so on a regular basis.

Brett looks like he's carved out of granite, but he's in

his twenties and Australian, so that's more or less par for the course and not worth mentioning, to be honest. 'You guys have a nice swim?' he asks us.

'Yes thank you,' Sangwen answers in her calm, level manner as she rises from her towel.

'Think I've managed to top up my tan a bit,' I say to him as I get up too.

'Yeah, you're not bad for a Pom,' Brett replies and smiles cheekily.

'Nice, er, nice cozzie you've got there, Laura,' Alan says. There's a doubtful tone to his voice that gives me the distinct impression he doesn't really mean it.

'Thanks,' I say anyway. I figure if he's trying to be polite, the least I can do is accept the comment at face value.

'Interesting slogan,' he points out.

I don't think *Surf Lovin'* is all that interesting myself, but these Australians do seem to have a fairly blunt sense of humour.

We make our way back to the changing rooms on the esplanade and it's actually with some regret that I retrieve my clothes from the locker and enter the nearest free cubicle. I've enjoyed the hour or so we've spent in the sun this afternoon, safe in the knowledge that my enigmatic employer is satisfied with the work I'm doing.

I take off the twenty-dollar swimming costume and hold it up, giving it a more thorough once over now it's off my body. I don't ever intend to wear it again, but it's seen me through the impromptu dip in the ocean, so I can't complain too much.

Quite why Sangwen and Alan thought the slogan on the front was worth mentioning I can't fathom. After all, it only says—

I turn the costume in my hands to look at the back and my blood runs cold.

*Surf Lovin'* was only the first part of the catchphrase. There is more on the back. Oh sweet Jesus Christ on a kangaroo, there is *more on the back*. Above a crude cartoon of a voluptuous beach bunny lying on a surfboard with her two enormous breasts exposed for the world to see are the words *BEACHWHORE* written in big, bold block capitals.

Yes, for the last hour I have been proudly proclaiming to everyone in Surfer's Paradise that I not only enjoy the foaming waters of The Gold Coast, but that I also like to indulge in giving oral pleasure to strangers behind the beach huts for money.

Still, this is quite a nice changing-room cubicle. As a place to hide in for the rest of my life thanks to cringe-worthy levels of embarrassment, it certainly beats the men's bathroom at the offices of Hotel Chocolat. Jamie will have to bring Poppy for regular visits, and they'll of course have to pass food over the top of the door, but at least I have a bench to sit on and can while away the years reading the graffiti on the walls.

So today I well and truly managed to snatch defeat from the jaws of victory, Mum.

I've also once again highlighted the absolute importance of taking your damn sweet time when out shopping for clothes. Being in a rush will only cause you to purchase the wrong item, and inform everyone in the general vicinity that you like to earn your living lying on your back with your legs in the air.

I didn't mention my new found status of beach whore to my colleagues as we made our way back to the shop. Thankfully, neither did they. I'm going to hope that my good work with our financial figures will mitigate the fact that I like to advertise the fact I'm a dirty street walker. Alan and Co. certainly didn't seem too bothered about it as they happily bid me goodbye at the store entrance.

The walk over to pick Poppy up at the end of the day was a bit disconcerting though. I'm sure I got a few funny looks from people who passed me in the street, and there was one guy who looked suspiciously like he was trying to fish his wallet out and offer me something before I ran around the nearest corner and out of his line of sight.

When I got home that evening I told Jamie what had happened. This was a colossal mistake, of course. I don't know which was worse, the abrupt gales of laughter on conclusion of my story, or the request later that I wear the costume the next time we had sex.

Love you and miss you, Mum.

Your shameful daughter, Laura.

xx

# Jamie's Blog
## Sunday 16 April

Here are the top things I miss about the UK, having been resident in Australia for over four months (time really does fly when you're looking for a job, while applying insect repellant and suncream in equal measure):

Marmite. Oh dear Vegemite, you try so very hard, but you're just not *quite* there, are you? It's a brave act you put on, but we all know you're still Marmite's bitch whether you like it or not. You're like the plain girl who goes to the prom, only to find out that the hot cheerleader is in the same dress as you. You're like a Rolling Stones cover band who play all the hits, but just aren't the same thing at all. Yes, I miss Marmite a great deal. I miss Bovril too. You can eat kangaroo in Australia, but can you find a decent meat flavoured drink anywhere? Hell no!

Sleeping under duvets. Out here . . . forget it. You'd die of heat exhaustion in three minutes. The sheets are a pain in the arse, as they have a knack of entwining themselves in your limbs to such an extent that you become virtually pinned to the bed. I miss my duvet.

Wearing long trousers like a proper adult. I've been walking around in shorts so much I'm starting to feel like a naughty schoolboy from the nineteen-fifties. I actually pulled on a pair of full-length jeans the other day. It felt like coming home. I then took them off again as nobody likes a sweaty knee cap.

The English countryside. Now don't get me wrong, the Australian flora and fauna is gorgeous. All those golden beaches, fragrant rainforests and striking mountains are fantastic. But damn it all, there's something about the rolling English countryside that just can't be beaten.

The British sense of humour. Yup, nothing like it. While the Australians can be quite amusing, it's a very blunt kind of humour. I've watched both the UK and Aussie versions of *Top Gear* and the difference is obvious. They don't really do sarcasm or irony here much.

Accurate weather reports. We'd love to be able to trust the Australian weather, but it's about as accurate as Michael Bay's *Pearl Harbour*. Yesterday for instance it was supposed to be showers, cloud and occasional sunshine – and it was blue skies all day. Two days before that it was supposed to be showers, cloud and occasional sunshine – and it drizzled all day. I think they just say it's going to be 'showers, cloud and occasional sunshine' to cover all bases for every day of the year.

Thankfully, the weather report said it would be windy and grey on Friday, so it was a lovely sunny day to get out and about. Miraculously, Laura also had the day off work.

This was her first day off since she started in the job, and I decided it would be a good idea for us to do something 'touristy' together. She's been pretty knackered after work and at the weekends, so we haven't thus far ventured further afield than the local beaches of the Gold Coast. As soon as she said that she was taking Friday off, I jumped on the laptop to see what interesting places we could take Poppy to see that were within a drivable distance. I figured if nothing else, it would give Laura and I quality time together, as well as get me out of this apartment for a while and stop thinking about job applications. I miss spending time with my wife and this trip would be a great way of rectifying that.

The rainforest is a fascinating place that I'd been keen on paying a visit to since we touched down at Brisbane airport, so I planned us a lovely drive inland to Springbrook National Park, the vast green forest that lies to the rear of the Gold Coast in slumbering vegetative glory.

I have learned lessons from this day trip that I will now impart in full, so that others may learn from my experience and avoid the discomfort and mind-numbing terror I've just been through. I'll start with a tip for you: should you ever decide to visit this fair country and take in some of its wondrous natural landscapes and beautiful national parks, do bear in mind that visiting an Australian forest is not like visiting one in Britain.

This may seem obvious, but I really want to hammer the point home as heavily as possible, because the differences are far greater than you can appreciate. Or rather, *you* might be able to appreciate them, but I sure as hell didn't until it was way too late to do anything about it.

In England, it's very easy to pop out for the day to feed the New Forest ponies and grab a pub lunch. A nice time is generally had by all, providing the rain holds off and there are no road works between you and the wildlife. It is resolutely *not* easy to conduct a similar day trip to your nearest Australian national park.

First of all, you won't be *popping out* anywhere. One simply does not 'pop out' to a place like Springbrook National Park. It may look relatively close on Google Maps – no more than sixty kilometres and less than an hour's drive away – but contained within that short distance are obstacles and horrors that generally require several changes of underpants before you so much as reach the sodding park.

'I'll drive us there and back,' I confidently say as I plug Springbrook's post code into the sat nav.

'Will you?' Laura replies with apparent relief.

'Yeah, sure. You're doing that drive to work every day, the least I can do is take over for something like this.'

'Thank you. I don't think I could stand another minute behind that wheel this week.'

'My pleasure,' I smile back, completely unaware of the terror about to unfold.

We pile into the Magna and set off from Coolangatta on the kind of beautiful warm sunny day you dream about when you're stuck in traffic on the M4 at seven in the morning in the middle of January.

The first section of the drive is fine, right up the Pacific Highway and off at the Mudgeeraba exit. Even the second stage is more or less a breeze, as you wend your way through the low lying fields and forests of the hinterland. Then you come to the road that leads up to Springbrook

National Park. The most important word in that previous sentence is 'up'.

The further you travel towards the park, the more you come to appreciate just *how* important the word 'up' really is. You see, unlike the New Forest, Lake Windermere, Dartmoor (or any one of a thousand other forests in Britain) Springbrook sits on a mountainous plateau just slightly higher than the tip of Mount Everest.

I find it incredible that no one has noticed this before me. All the encyclopaedias would have you believe that the highest point on planet Earth is Everest, but I am here to tell you from personal experience that it isn't. Springbrook National Park is. I know – I've driven up the bastard in a second-hand Mitsubishi Magna.

Everything is fine until we leave the last remote homesteads behind and really started to push uphill. The road goes from a straight ribbon cutting through the countryside, to a snaking series of U-bends and hairpin turns that hug the side of the rapidly ascending geography.

'Woah, this is getting tricky,' I say in a half amused, half anxious voice to Laura.

'Yeah,' she replies in a vague sort of way and tightens her hand on the seat-belt strap ever so slightly.

Up and up we go, my whitened hands working at the steering wheel, while my brain wonders just how long this ascent is likely to take. I'm also starting to get a bit worried about how much petrol we've got. All this low gear stuff is not conducive to high miles per gallon when you're in a three-litre car.

Then the first real bottom-trembling moment occurs.

The height we are at has until now largely been hidden by the thick, dense foliage all around us, but as we reach yet another switchback we arrive at a point where the trees haven't grown and you can see right down the side of the mountain.

'Jesus fucking Christ!' hollers Laura.

Poppy lets out a high-pitched squeal. 'Mummy said a swear!'

'Mummy is sorry,' I tell her and slow the car even more to look down at where an ashen faced Laura is indicating. 'She promises she won't do it agai—*Jesus fucking Christ!*'

It isn't a mountain slope I'm looking down, it's a sheer cliff face that drops into infinity.

Unbridled terror vies for supremacy with sheer incongruity. Here I am in a second-hand saloon car with a noisy exhaust and odd smell coming from the boot, and I'm driving it at a height only birds and a few hardy mountain goats usually get to experience. Anywhere else in the world I could confidently expect to pass a team of Sherpa on their way to the summit.

This is Australia though, where they take a more relaxed attitude to aggressive geography and never let it get in the way of a nice day out. Cars and trucks are still thundering down the mountain from the direction we're going towards. I get a few odd looks from the locals as they pass the Magna by, no doubt wondering why it's going so slowly.

Mercifully, the trees once again close in as I nurse the car at three miles an hour round the top of this particular hairpin.

'How . . . how high up are we?' Laura asks in a shaky voice.

'I don't know, but I'm beginning to wish we'd packed a few oxygen tanks.'

My heart rate slows down a bit and I put more revs into the protesting engine.

Still the upward climb goes on.

And on.

*And on.*

At least the forest hides the mortifying view for the most part, so I'm able to concentrate on the blissfully solid two-lane tarmac road in front of me. Then things get worse. Much, *much* worse.

On yet another hairpin where the forest has neglected to grow, the two-lane road becomes a single lane. Not only that, it narrows by a good three feet and streams of water flow over it from cracks in the rock face above.

I let out a noise that sounds like a kettle coming off the boil. Laura sketches a cross on her chest – which is truly indicative of our precarious situation as she's an atheist.

Poppy is sitting up at the rear window, her nose pressed against the glass. 'Mummy, Daddy, look at the big sky!' She points a happy little finger out at the magnificent view beyond the Magna. I don't have the wherewithal to respond as I begin to negotiate the car along the slick narrow road. Did I mention there was no barrier at the edge of the road? No, I didn't think I had.

THERE'S NO BARRIER AT THE EDGE OF THE ROAD.

Nothing between us and certain plunging death other than my dubious driving skills. If you recall, I once crashed my car trying to park it at work.

We're all going to die.

The next thirty seconds last eighteen months. Slowly – *ever so slowly* – I drive us around the turn, my eyes fixed ahead with grim determination. My arsehole is trying to eat the seat below it. My hands shake like a palsied pensioner with frostbite. Laura's nails dig in to the dashboard. Poppy starts to sing 'The Circle Of Life' from *The Lion King*. The epic scenery around us has obviously inspired her into song.

I knew we shouldn't have bought her the flaming Blu-ray. She's watched it so many times she even knows the African bit at the start, so as I try my hardest not to slip off the road into oblivion, from the back seat I hear, '*Nasss ingoymaaaa! Ba boo be baba!*'

'Poppy, be quiet honey. Daddy's trying to concentrate,' Laura says. Unfortunately it's in a tiny scared tone that my happy singing daughter doesn't hear a word of.

'*It's the Circle of Life!*' Poppy continues at the top of her piping voice.

There are times when I am profoundly glad that Poppy is extremely advanced for her age. This is not one of them. She also has a singing voice akin to her mother's, which rather resembles a cat having an air-raid siren inserted into it.

'*It's a big shiny circle!*' Poppy keeps going. '*I've gotta circle of life! And it's got big bells on!*'

I'm pretty sure those aren't the right lyrics, but there's

no way I'm breaking my unholy levels of concentration right now to tell her so.

Finally I get the car around the turn and back to where the road once again splits into two. By now my arse has digested the seat cushion and is full, so it relaxes somewhat. Laura removes her fingers from the dash, leaving small dents in its plastic surface. Poppy has now moved on to 'I Just Can't Wait To Be King'. Personally, I just can't wait to get down off this fucking mountain. But we've come this far, so there's no turning back now . . .

The road unbelievably continues upwards for another ten minutes before we reach the plateau and it straightens out again. Very soon we see the first sign for Springbrook and the end of this harrowing journey.

I've never been so glad to apply a hand brake in my life. 'Maybe we'll just have a few minutes rest here in the car,' I suggest in a light voice.

'That's a very good idea,' Laura agrees.

'I wanna see all the big trees, Daddy!' Poppy demands.

'Very soon, sweetheart. Just let Mummy and Daddy have a couple of minutes to gather their thoughts.'

Being three years old must be wonderful – you have absolutely no idea what the word 'mortal' means.

We eventually alight from our vehicle and go for a look at the map. If today's trip has thus far highlighted how much the Australian topography likes to do height, a quick study of the map shows that it loves to do width even more.

Springbrook is bloody enormous.

Stretching across the impressive Macpherson Range at

the rear of the Gold Coast, you could drop the Lake District inside it and have a bloody hard time finding it again.

We've arrived at the Springbrook Plateau section, which is replete with all manner of majestic waterfalls that drop over the side of the plateau in curtains of foaming white water. There are several walks you can go on around the park, taking in the incredible views and natural beauty around you.

It all sounds lovely, but all I can think about right now is the fact I have to negotiate that terrifying hairpin turn again at some point today to get us back down into the world again.

Unbelievably, there are a lot of vehicles up here with us in the car park, suggesting that I'm not the only lunatic who's braved the journey. There's even a minibus. I haven't seen the driver as yet, but he must have testicles the size of my head.

Further to the multitude of cars parked around me, there are toilet facilities, refuse bins and seating areas available to those who choose to visit this area of Springbrook. Does nobody realise we're at the end of a treacherous uphill climb and are currently seventeen miles above sea level, at the very top of the world? There's a fucking *barbecue* set up next to several of the seats just in front of me. I can just imagine the conversation:

'D'ya fancy a barbecue today then, Sheila?'

'Yeah, Bruce, that sounds bonza. Just let me go pack the crampons, oxygen masks and altitude sickness tablets.'

Laura takes Poppy off to the toilet and I fish out the

rucksack from the boot containing our packed lunches. If I'd have known about the barbecue I would have picked up a few steaks, but as it is, we'll be munching our way around the walking paths of Springbrook on cheese and vegemite buns.

'Which way do you want to go?' Laura asks, pointing up at the map which shows us three separate tracks.

'The one with the least altitude,' I reply.

'You do remember the drive up here don't you, Newman? It's all altitude in these parts.'

'The waterfall circuit then, that's sounds nice.'

'Okay, come on, Pops. Let's go see the waterfalls.'

My daughter lets out a happy little cry of pleasure and toddles off in front of her mother and father, straight past an enormous red sign that reads DO NOT LEAVE PATH. STEEP DROPS AHEAD. DANGER OF DEATH without so much as a glance up at its straightforward message of doom. I would put it down to her lack of advanced reading and writing skills, but it's more likely to be the daredevil side of her nature – the one that's likely to leave me grey-haired and deeply neurotic before I'm forty.

'Hang on, Poppy!' I shout and we take off after her as she starts to clamber up a rather steep set of steps cut into the hill in front of us.

It has to be said that provided you do stick to the path and keep your wits about you, Springbrook's waterfall circuit is a rather delightful place to spend an afternoon.

The path snakes through the dense rainforest around

and through enormous boulders and rock formations that you can cheerfully imagine a dinosaur rubbing itself against. The waterfalls themselves are also impressive. Some you walk over the top of, others you wend your way past the bottom. There's even a couple you can walk behind, which is a unique experience to say the least. There's something very odd about staring out at the world from behind a curtain of water as it cascades past your eyes. *'I wonder if this is what having a cataract is like?'* my treacherous brain pipes up, rather ruining the mild feeling of awe I've got going on.

What it can't ruin is the happy feeling I have inside as Laura and I amble our way through the forest holding each other's hand, with Poppy bouncing around in front of us. This is exactly what I wanted from this trip, a chance to just spend time with my wife and daughter away from everything. I even begin to think that the horrific journey here was worth it just to feel the warmth of Laura's hand in mine as we make our way through Springbrook's wonderful forest.

The path does snake its way past some pretty bowel-loosening heights as well, though. I was royally put off my cheese and Vegemite bun as we walked out onto a man-made gantry that seemed relatively innocuous until I looked down through the wooden planks to see a two hundred foot drop straight down into the tree canopy below.

'Meep,' is about the only sound I'm able to make as I start to back slowly up towards the safety of the forest.

My heart rate soars again when three Australian teenagers come bouncing past me like they're on steroids.

'Wow!' one of them exclaims as she leans right out over the barrier that separates her from becoming jungle pancake.

'Get your camera out, Milo!' another girl squeals at the only boy in the group. He whips out his mobile phone and proceeds to lean out with his friend and snap happily at the sheer drop below him.

I always knew Australians were a healthy bunch, with a refreshingly down-to-earth way of dealing with life, but I never knew they were also completely fucking crazy. It's like vertigo was banned by the government in 1986 when they became independent from the Brits. Mind you, the way Poppy is sat dangling her legs over the drop from between the railings suggests this place is really starting to rub off on her.

'Pops,' I say in a strangled voice from my perch ten feet behind. 'Maybe you should come back here with Daddy.'

'Looking at the sky, Daddy!' she pouts from between mouthfuls of bun.

'Leave her be, Jamie. She's perfectly safe,' Laura chides.

'When you're standing on a precipice with only a couple of inches of wood between you and certain death, "safe" is a relative term, wife of mine,' I respond and shuffle back to make room for the hyperactive teens as they bound back past me.

I breathe a sigh of relief as the path changes to a comfortably downhill direction. My happy feelings return as we reach an apparent low point on the course, and I retrieve what's left of my bun from my pocket, secure in the knowledge that no great heights are about to leap out at me and force it back up my oesophagus.

I have to say that these tasty cheese and Vegemite treats are something I've fallen deeply in love with since we arrived in Australia. I must be helping to keep the profit margins of the local Coles supermarket very definitely in the black, given the amount of them I've bought from the bakery section in recent weeks. I'm just licking the last few crumbs off my fingers when Laura says something that part of me must have been expecting, as I don't feel that much surprise when she comes out with it.

'I think we're lost,' she says, coming to a halt next to a particularly large fig tree.

*Hello, Jamie. This is your brain.*

Hello, brain, what's up?

*Well now, you remember what happened a couple of years ago in Wookey Hole don't you?*

Ah yes, the day I got us lost on the way back to the campsite?

*That's the banana.*

What of it, oh soft and squishy originator of all my worldly thoughts?

*If you recall, we had a conversation with one another in bed that night and you promised me something. Do you remember what that something was, Jamie?*

I do brain, I do indeed.

*And what was that very thing?*

That in future, if we ever got into a similar situation, I would immediately and wholeheartedly defer to Laura, thus saving us from potential embarrassment and physical injury at her hands.

*That's right, Jamie. Well done. So, to that end, what do we say to Laura right now?*

'Which way do you think we should go, baby?'

*Well done, Jamie. I'm very proud of you. Have another bun.*

Laura looks back the way we came. 'Not sure, it looks like we strayed off the path without realising it. We should probably back track.'

'Okay, whatever you say, sweetheart.'

Laura takes the lead and I pick Poppy up, putting her on my shoulders. This is a pre-emptive strike. She hasn't said anything about being tired yet, but I know the signs. For the past two hundred yards she's been doing that funny stamping walk kids do when they're getting sick of putting one foot down in front of the other. I dutifully follow my wife in what feels like the right direction.

Ten minutes later we're back at the fig tree.

'That's the fig tree,' I helpfully point out.

'Shut up, Jamie.'

'Just thought I'd point it out.'

'I said shut up, Jamie.'

'Yes, dear.'

And off we go again, this time in a more lefterly direction from the one we went previously.

Now, I should be somewhat concerned when we arrive back at the fig tree about quarter of an hour later. After all, this is fairly dense rainforest we're talking about here.

Being lost in it is not a trifling matter. However, I don't feel that concerned for two very important reasons.

One, the feeling of smugness that I'm not the one who got us lost is quite overwhelming. It's quite unprecedented for Laura to be the one with a poorer sense of direction than me, and by golly I'm going to wallow in it for as long as possible.

Two, I'm pretty sure the way back to the path is to go right at the big boulder that looks like an upturned boob. Its breast-like qualities caught my eye the first time we passed it, and that was only ten or fifteen yards on from the well marked pathway.

In a few minutes I will suggest we make a move towards boob rock, but for now I am content to let my wife huff and puff her way past the same fig tree for the third time. I love Laura with all my heart, but she did once let me nearly drown in a tent, so fair's fair and all that.

Eventually though, the vein on her forehead looks ready to pop, so I pipe up. 'Why don't we go back to the boulder with the bit on top that looks like a nipple? It could be that way.'

'I doubt it. That was nowhere near where we came off the path.'

'Well, let's try it anyway. It's getting a bit hot and Pops is wilting. We could do with getting back to the car.'

'Oh, alright, clever-clogs. Let's see if you can do any better than me.'

I give my wife a shit-eating grin Ed Milliband would be proud of and march off in the direction of the stone tit with purpose and aplomb.

Aplomb gives way to barely concealed smugness when I march us back onto the pathway headed back up the hill.

Laura eyes me suspiciously. 'I don't know how, Jamie Newman, but I know you know something I don't. Rest assured I will find out what it is.'

'I don't know what you mean,' I say in a voice dripping with honey and turn to follow the path back to the car park.

We arrive back at the Magna tired, but otherwise fit and healthy, which when you think about it is some kind of miracle for this family . . . a miracle that lasts for another three or so miles until we arrive back at everyone's favourite single lane hairpin turn.

This time the harrowing passage is made even more fun by the fact it's started to rain. Great big drops of Australian rainwater hammer off the car windscreen as I slow the Magna to a crawl and drive past the point where the road narrows into one lane. Everything is going fine – or as 'fine' as anything can be when you're less than two feet away from falling off a cliff – when the Magna decides it really doesn't like all this heavy wet stuff and conks out.

'Meep,' I utter in a very small voice.

'That's not good,' Laura remarks, the understatement fairy having paid a swift and invisible visit to her cerebral cortex.

I turn the key and the engine sputters.

I try again with much the same result.

'Meep,' I repeat.

'What does meep mean, Daddy?' Poppy asks.

'It means Daddy is having a little moment to himself, Poppy. Just sit back and everything will be fine in a few minutes.'

I look out of the window at the cliff face beside me and wonder just how Laura expects this situation to resolve itself happily in the next few minutes – unless Superman is passing on his way home to Metropolis and offers to carry us down to the motorway.

It's not Superman that turns up to offer aid, but the three hyperactive teenagers I mentioned earlier. They're in a bright orange Ute that has alloy wheels slightly shinier than the surface of the sun. It pulls up behind us, and scarcely ten seconds have passed before the boy is out of the driver's seat and bounding over in muscular Australian fashion. He rocks up to my window and leans in. I steal myself for the inevitable barrage of swear words about how we're blocking the road.

'You need some help there, mate?' he says and smiles.

The little shit. Teenagers are supposed to be aggressive and threatening, not helpful and cheery. I hate Australia.

'The engine won't start,' I tell him and fiddle with the key fob.

'No worries. My gran's got one of these. They don't like the water much. My name's Miles, though everyone calls me Milo. Jump out and I'll get her going.'

Without waiting for me to respond he flings the car door open and steps back, removing the only barrier between my mortal soul and the sheer drop below. He then expectantly looks at me. I look from his earnest face to the drop-off and start to wish he'd been more like a British teenager and just mugged me.

I get out of the car on shaky legs. 'Jamie Newman,' I introduce myself with a voice even shakier. 'We're quite high up aren't we?' He doesn't need me to point this fact out, but I feel he's not appreciating the gravity of the situation enough.

Milo looks over the precipice. 'Could be worse, mate.'

Yes, I suppose there could be a pack of man-eating kangaroos at the bottom to finish you off if you survive the fall. Milo squeezes past me. He has to do this because I refuse to let go of the car with both hands at the same time.

'G'day!' he says to Laura.

'Hello. Nice to meet you,' she replies and can't help but stare at his biceps.

I'm fine with this. Happy marriages are built on the understanding that this kind of thing goes on all the time.

'You too!'

'I do hope you can get the car going okay.' She might as well bat her eyelashes and point at her vagina.

'Yeah, it'll be fine.'

Milo turns the ignition key and starts to pump the accelerator pedal like he's Hendrix pounding his wah-wah on stage at the Isle of Wight Festival. The engine continues to sputter for a few moments, but Milo's natural Australian exuberance finally bullies it into life with an ear-splitting roar that echoes around us.

He exits the car to the sound of Laura's heartfelt and somewhat over-the-top thanks and slaps me on the back.

'There you go mate. Right as rain. Just keep your revs up and you'll be right.'

He then moves behind me, dancing on the edge of oblivion, before jogging back to the orange Ute and the two girls he's no doubt going home to have sex with.

'Thanks, Milo!' I call after him. He throws me a salute and jumps back in his car.

I crawl back into my seat and drive away from the heart-stopping hairpin. I'm still going about four miles an hour, but I'm also revving the engine like an idiot, guaranteeing the clutch will explode within the next few minutes if I'm not careful.

The split-second the road divides into two lanes again, Milo and the twins roar past with a blare of the car horn that fades out rapidly as they turn a corner ahead. My wife's horn isn't likely to fade as quickly, and I have a feeling I'll be servicing her requirements once Poppy has been put to bed for the night – and providing she doesn't tell me to rev her engine at any point we should be fine.

On the drive back to the apartment I reflect on what's turned out to be a fairly typical day in Australia: One part terror, two parts awe, three parts incredulity. Add two spoonfuls of emasculation and you're golden.

# Laura's Diary

## Saturday, June 10th

Dear Mum,

I don't know if you ever noticed this in your years on the planet, but human beings really aren't meant to be in the water. We may kid ourselves with flippers, masks, armbands and swimming costumes that advertise our sexual services, but the truth is that the water – particularly the ocean – is an environment we are poorly suited to. I speak from cold, hard experience, thanks to the events of today.

'You seen the turtles yet, Laura?' Alan says to me on Monday, during one of his frequent visits to the store.

'Turtles?'

'Yeah, down at Cooly where you're living? There's a reef system out round one of the islands where you can swim with the turtles. It's a glorious way to spend the afternoon.'

I guess I have to take his word for it. If anyone knows how to have a good time when they should be at work it appears to be Alan Brookes.

'I'd be happy to take you out there sometime,' he adds, once again showing how nice a boss he is once you get past the bluster and Australian machismo.

After the Beach Whore incident though, I decided it would be far better to take Jamie, who is well used to my blunders and won't bat an eyelid if I do something embarrassing with a snorkel mask.

I brought the dive company's website up on the computer at lunch and had a look-see. The whole thing appeared quite impressive to say the least. Lots of pictures of happy snorkelling tourists weaving their way through forests of brightly coloured coral while sleek green turtles frolicked around their legs. There was even one picture of a blonde girl feeding one of the cute little buggers from her hand.

That could be me. I could be the blonde feeding the cute little turtle as I bob around gracefully above the multi-coloured reef. All for seventy-five dollars. It sounds like a brilliant day out. Unfortunately the age limit is fourteen, so Pops will have to take an impromptu Saturday visit to Surf Tots. The trip will do my morose husband the world of good, though.

Things have gone from bad to worse with Jamie's work situation, Mum. He *still* hasn't managed to find a job yet and it's really starting to bring him down. I can tell because there are days I get in from work and he hasn't even taken off his dressing gown. Jamie can be a lazy bugger if you give him enough of a run-up, but he also has a very active mind and when it's not being properly exercised it can lead to a permanent hangdog expression and the kind of loud sighing that really gets on your nerves after a while. You can imagine how delighted I am to return from a hard day at work to find that Jamie has done bugger all with his day, other than sigh and bemoan his lot.

Going from a day with Alan Brookes – who not only grabs life with two hands, but strangles it until it turns blue – back to a husband who wouldn't have enough energy to grab life if it stood in front of him and jiggled around on the spot, is quite depressing. I hate making the comparison between the two, but it's hard not to.

Jamie has attempted to fill his spare time by writing a book. He even read a few paragraphs of it to me the other day. I'm not sure the world needs a novel about killer robot women with enormous breasts, but I didn't want to make his mood any worse so I just nodded and said it sounded quite well written. Which was no word of a lie. Jamie can string a sentence together – I'm just not sure he's stringing the *right ones* together at the moment. Good subject matter for a book or not, writing it only serves to fill a few hours of his day before he gets bored and starts surfing the internet.

To combat the malaise I've started leaving Poppy with him for a couple of days a week. I'm not too sure my daughter is particularly happy with this development. She loves her daddy, but the entertainment possibilities with him are severely limited when compared to all the fun and games she can get up to at Surf Tots. She also gets to come into the shop at lunchtimes to see me. This delights her no end, but I can't be sure whether that's because she gets to spend time with her mummy, or just because mummy works in a chocolate shop.

With Jamie poor old Pops is forced to sit and watch

bad Australian cartoons, play age-restricted games on the laptop and take long ambling walks along the beach until her feet hurt.

'Daddy's boring,' she said to me in the car on the way to work last week. 'He doesn't push me properly on the swings.'

To Poppy Helen Newman this is a grievous crime. My three-year-old maniac of a child absolutely loves to be pushed as hard as is humanly possible while on a swing. Anything other than your one hundred per cent commitment is met with a no-nonsense frown on her little forehead and a pout that will last the rest of the day unless you buy her an ice cream.

Nevertheless, her presence at home is keeping Jamie from permanently living in his dressing gown, so for the foreseeable future Poppy is just going to have to put up with some limp-wristed swing action.

It also means I have to contain a certain amount of jealousy that Jamie is spending a lot more time with Poppy now than I am. But I have to suppress that feeling as much as Poppy has to put up with being a bit bored every other day. It's all for a greater good.

I figured the trip out to see the turtles might cheer Jamie up a bit, and for once I'm right.

'Cool! I've walked past the place a few times down in the town and it looks great,' Jamie says with the first genuine excitement I've heard in him for a long time.

'I know. You can feed the little sods and everything!' I exclaim happily.

It's generally quite rare for Jamie and I to be genuinely

excited about something, so we both intend to make the most of our day on the water and take as many pictures of the aquatic little fellas as possible. Jamie doesn't even make a comment about being a pathetic and emasculated kept man when I call the dive company to pay for the tickets.

This is something of a miracle, as not as day has gone by recently without him making *some* reference to the fact I'm earning all the money. We can't do the weekly shop without him making at least one comment about the disparity between us, usually in a tone of voice replete with self-pity and barely concealed jealousy. I'm getting pretty damn sick of these comments, so I'm very relieved when I don't have to hear any of them this time around. It appears his enthusiasm for turtle watching is enough to make him forget his silly neuroses for one day at least.

'I'll go put the camera in the waterproof case and make sure everything's working okay,' Jamie says eagerly and skips into the bedroom to go track it down.

I sip my cup of tea and sit back feeling decidedly pleased with myself. Not only do I get to have a lovely day out on the water, I also get to put a smile on my husband's face for the first time in weeks. Two big fat birds with one expertly aimed stone, I'd say.

And I do like to make him happy, Mum. He can be a very frustrating man sometimes, especially when things aren't going his way, but he's still the man I fell in love with and still the man who gave me the most important thing in my life, our daughter Poppy.

Anyway, this situation won't last much longer I'm sure. Jamie will find some work soon and this problem will go away. Once he feels like he's contributing something again, I'll get the old Jamie back, I'm sure of it.

We were both up this morning at the crack of dawn. Standing out on the balcony and looking to the heavens I deduce that it's going to be another warm, sunny and thoroughly pleasant day, ideal for some frolicking with green turtles.

By eight o'clock we're at Diving Gold and meeting the crew who will be taking us out on the water. They are, in apparent order of boat seniority: Daffo, Wilko, Tommo and Spud. Spud is the only one who doesn't appear to be delighted with the nickname bestowed on him. I can only assume his surname is Murphy or O'Neil and the other members of the crew have made the appropriate connection between the Irish and potatoes and named him accordingly. I guess 'O'Neilo' wouldn't come across right and would skirt very close to sounding Italian, which just wouldn't suit Spud's ethnic background at all.

Daffo, Tommo and Spud take off in a VW camper van covered in pictures of turtles to go prepare the boat down in the harbour, while Wilko stays behind to help us choose wetsuits.

There is a grand total of eight people on today's excursion.

Alongside Jamie and I are a French couple, two lads from Arbroath and an American twosome who look well into their sixties. All appear to be fairly pleasant, although one of the Scots is very possibly mildly drunk at eight fifteen in the morning.

Of the group it's the pensionable Americans who seem to have the most trouble getting their wetsuits on. None of the rest of us jump into ours like we're Jacques Cousteau's cousin, but we don't have the indignity of realising we've put it on the wrong way round. Such is the unhappy fate of the husband, who neatly pinches his elderly penis in the teeth of the zipper before Wilko realises what is happening and has old man turn it round with the zipper running up the back as is right and proper.

I can see Jamie suppressing a grin throughout this pantomime. He obviously doesn't realise that the old American is basically him in thirty-five years, with a Yankee twang.

Once the wetsuit fitting is over and they've been stored away for the trip, Wilko packs us off with a map to the docks where our boat awaits. Diving Gold is a small operation, and the single camper van they own has already beetled off so we have to drive ourselves. Jamie is some-what put out by this, but I don't mind. I'd rather not have to force polite conversation with anyone at this time in the morning. I'd only get trapped by the American pensioner as he tells me all about how his scrotum is now a ball of fire thanks to the zipper fiasco. I don't know what it is about getting old, but you seem to lose most of the inhibitions you carry round with you when you're young, and are quite happy to discuss your most embarrassing ailments with a complete stranger if it'll pass twenty minutes.

As it is, Jamie negotiates with the sat nav for about three miles. It must be in a truculent mood this morning as we arrive at the boat dock without having taken one wrong turning. Spud greets us at the gangplank and helps us onto the boat by taking our rucksacks.

Jamie and I take up temporary residence on the bench at the back of the medium-sized pleasure craft that bears a slight resemblance to a modernized version of the one from Jaws that I try not to think about.

The docks themselves are about half a mile inland of the entrance to the broad Tweed River, which flows from up in the hinterland mountains, emptying out into the Pacific Ocean right on the border between Queensland and New South Wales.

'I could get used to this,' Jamie says, lolling his head back and basking in the sun with his eyes closed.

I have to say I agree with my husband as I look across the calm river, squinting a bit as the sunlight bounces off the gently rippling water. Then something happens that fair takes my breath away. The water is suddenly broken by the glistening back and fin of a dolphin coming up for air. Before it has sunk back beneath the waves, another one is cresting, followed by another, and a fourth.

'Jamie!' I cry and go to hit him to get his attention. I don't turn my head while I'm doing this for fear of losing the aquatic creatures so end up whacking him in the testicles.

'Ow! What woman?'

'Dolphins, Jamie!'

'Where?'

'There!' I point at where the first dolphin is coming up for another gasp, sending a fountain of water up from his blowhole with an audible expulsion of air.

'Fuck me,' Jamie says in awe.

My eyes start to tear up a bit. This is the first time I've ever seen a dolphin, other than on TV or in a movie. It's a rather special moment. Coming this close to the second most intelligent – and most playful – animal on the planet is quite incredible.

'Bugger off, you little sods!' I hear Daffo shout from behind me. He looks down at me and my shocked expression. 'This river's chock-a-block with bloody dolphins. It's a miracle we don't run 'em over all the time. They can be a right nuisance.'

A *nuisance*? These beautiful, smart, graceful creatures . . . a nuisance? I'm incredulous and tell him so.

Daffo smiles. 'You get used to them, believe me. The shine wears off the apple a bit when you've had to smack one on the nose for the hundredth time because he won't bugger off when you're trying to test your new scuba gear.'

'Really?'

'Oh yeah. They love irritating you.' He leans over the side of the boat. 'Smack your hand in the water like this. One of 'em might come over for a look.'

I do as I'm bid and watch the water closely.

I spend the next five minutes concentrating on this and am thus completely unaware that the rest of our gang of turtle watchers have boarded the boat and are now watching what I'm doing. The probably think the English woman has gone stark staring nuts, slapping the Tweed River like it's getting a harsh telling off for being too lazy.

I don't care though, I'm determined to attract a dolphin over. And yes! I see a fin break the water and come in my direction. I start to slap the water harder in excitement. I can't believe I'm about to get up close and personal with a dolphin! I don't care what Daffo says, these are majestic animals and the idea of touching one makes my heart hammer in my chest.

Underneath my hand I see a grey shape rise to the surface. A pointy grey head breaks the water and a clammy wet nose butts against my palm.

'Bloody hell, Laura, that's amazing,' Jamie says breathlessly.

'Jim, look, this woman's petting a dolphin!' one of the Arbroath lads says to his compatriot.

'Shit on toast,' Jim exclaims.

'Ooh!' squeals the French woman. 'Incroyable. Zat is amazing!'

'Harry, get your camera out,' the American lady says and I hear Harry rifling around in his rucksack.

'Stand back a bit, Myra, I can't get a good shot,' I hear Harry say to his wife.

I can feel the others crowding around me, but I can't take my eyes off my new aquatic friend. The cheeky way in which his mouth curls up at the ends makes me giggle, as does the way his eyes roll back and forth a bit, as if to suggest we're sharing some unspoken but hilarious in-joke that only he and I understand.

This is miraculous. Whatever else happens today, I have got my money's worth. What a beautiful, wonderful, brilliant creature. What a—

PHWOOOOSSHHH!

A healthy dose of Tweed River and dolphin snot hits me square in the face.

*Little sod!*

I jerk my head backward, connecting with the lens of Harry's camera. The old man stumbles back, caught by Jim before he has chance to fall to the deck and fracture a hip.

Nursing the back of my head with one hand, I wipe dolphinous bogey from my eyes and look back down at my waterborne assailant, who nods his head at me, rolls onto one side, waves a cheeky flipper that must be the equivalent of the middle finger and sinks back beneath the waves to join his friends.

'See?' Daffo says. 'A right bloody nuisance.'

I've finished cleaning myself up by the time the boat sets off from the docks. Jamie, who knows which side his bread is buttered, chooses not to comment. Jim and his Scots pal can't look me in the face without grinning. Harry and his wife are sat studying his camera lens for signs of damage so I'm spared their attention for the time being.

'Zat was unfortunate,' the French woman says and introduces herself as Sandrine. 'He seemed like such a nice animal before zat 'appened.'

'That's the problem with the smart ones,' Jamie says sagely. 'The more clever they are the more likely they are to take the piss out of you.'

'Yes indeed,' she agrees. 'An octopus hit my 'usband in the penis last month off ze coast of Cannes.'

This is greeted with stony silence. Frenchy realises she may have provided too much information and makes her apologies to go to the toilet.

'Good grief, that's a weird thing to happen to someone,' I say to Jamie. 'I wonder what he did to the octopus to make it that angry?'

'The dude's French, do you need anything else?'

'That's a bit unfair. It must have hurt. I wonder what he did about it?'

'Threw his hands up and surrendered I would imagine. The French tend to do that when confronted with physical violence. The octopus has probably been made president by now.'

The boat chugs up the river at a fairly slow pace, giving Wilko and Tommo a chance to take us all through the safety briefing. They explain how to use the snorkels, when to put on and take off our life jackets, and demonstrate the universally approved sign for being in distress.

'You throw your hands around over your head and scream *"Help, I'm fucking drowning!"'* says Wilko to a chorus of slightly nervous laughter.

The briefing successfully concluded, Daffo announces over the mic that he's going to speed the boat up and we're suddenly off like a rocket, spearing towards the river's entrance with the breeze and salty spray providing much needed relief from the baking heat.

'This thing's a lot faster than it looks!' Harry exclaims with exuberance.

He's right. We're clipping along at a speed I'm unaccustomed to in a boat. I was quite happy with the leisurely pace we were setting previously, but there are turtles to see and a limited to time to do it in. I grip the seat behind me and try to grin and bear it.

Grinning and bearing changes to clenching and suffering as we hit the Tweed's mouth. Our life jackets go on as a precaution at this point, given that the river has suddenly gone from flat as a pancake to a seething cauldron of crashing waves and rushing whitecaps.

'This is what it's like when the river hits the sea!' Wilko shouts at all of us by way of explanation. 'Don't worry. We'll be out beyond it in a few minutes.'

This is just as well. I've always been pretty good on boats, but this rollercoaster is bad enough for my breakfast to be considering a glorious re-entry to the world. Wilko is as good as his word though, and very soon we're out into the ocean proper and chugging along on waves that are half the size and much more manageable.

'There's the island where the reef is,' Jamie points out. 'The turtles should be right there.'

I spy the tiny grass-covered rock a mile distant and fix my gaze on it. This helps settle my stomach, so much so that I'm quite happy to munch on one of the cinnamon doughnuts Spud has produced from the boat's galley.

Daffo decreases speed back to a gentle chug when we're about a hundred yards off the island's rocky edge and swings her round so she's broadside.

'Okay ladies and gents, this is our mooring point for today,' he says over the mic. 'If you'd like to climb into your wetsuits and get your snorkelling gear we'll jump in the water and see if we can spot some turtles.'

I don't need to be told twice. I have the image of the turtle being fed firmly in my mind. I can't wait to jump in the crystal clear waters and float around the gorgeous multi-coloured reef as promised by Diving Gold's website. I'm the first to be ready and am standing at the rear of the boat with my flippers on before poor old Harry has had a chance to trap his scrotum in his zipper again.

'Right then, you ready?' Wilko says from my side.

'Yes!' I cry excitedly.

'In you go then.'

I take a deep breath, hold the snorkel mask as I have been told and take a step out into the unknown . . .

If you look at The Gold Coast on a map, you'll note it's far nearer to the equator than Antarctica. Nobody's told the sea that though. It's bloody cold. So cold that I'm very glad I elected to have a nice thick wetsuit on over my swimmers. I come up for air spluttering with my eyes goggling in the snorkelling mask. Jamie is still standing on the side of the boat. He gives me a thumbs up and jumps in. I get a face full of salty sea water when his head pops back out right next to me.

'Cold!' he wails.

'Yes, I'd noticed!'

Jim and the other Scottish lad are next to follow. I never did find out his name, so I'll just have to call him Drunky.

Neither seem too bothered by the frigid water. But then

they are Scottish and there could be icebergs floating by and they'd probably be fine.

Sandrine and her octopus-wrestling husband are next. He elects to dive in headfirst, the pillock. I think he's trying to look macho but all he succeeds in doing is nearly ripping his nose off when the mask hits the water.

Harry and Myra take an age to climb in, but then we really can't blame them for that. Rather than jumping in, both clamber down a steel ladder that drops into the water. This is just as well as the shock would probably have exploded Harry's pacemaker the second he broke the surface. In actual fact Harry seems to be the happiest one out of the lot of us once we're all bobbing around a few feet away from the boat.

'Woo!' he exclaims. 'That'll get your heart pumping!'

He's not wrong. Mine is trip-hammering away right now. This is partly because I'm doing more exercise than I have done in months in cold Pacific sea water, and partly because my excitement levels are reaching a crescendo. I am mere moments away from glorious reef-turtle feeding fun.

Last into the Australian ocean are Wilko and Tommo, our guides on this trip.

'Okay guys, listen up,' Wilko says. 'We're both going to snorkel towards the best areas of the reef and start pointing things out to you. Just follow either me or Tommo. You're welcome to swim between us, but please don't go beyond where we are. If you get into any trouble, give us a shout.'

Which is fair enough unless you're already twenty feet under and sinking – but I shake off that disturbing train of thought and take off after Wilko, who I've decided to follow as he has the nicer bottom of the two. Jamie in turn follows me. I'd like to think that's because he reckons I have the nicest bottom as well. Sandrine's athletic French behind looks like it could give me a run for my money, but I still think I'd just about edge it in the perkiness stakes.

The sea here is relatively calm, which is good as it means you can skim along on the surface of the water quite happily towards your intended destination using your flippers to propel you along. It also means that when I come to use the snorkel I can do so without worrying about waves crashing over my head and sending a dump of cold, salty water down the breathing tube.

I reach Wilko's bottom – and by extension the rest of him – where it has now positioned itself a good fifty yards from the boat.

'Right, this is one of the best parts of the reef to see the turtles,' he says to us. 'Just remember to breathe nice and calmly while you're snorkelling and watch out for one another. I'll shout if I see anything picture-worthy. Have fun!'

*Oh, I intend to, Wilko. Don't you fret.*

I put the snorkel into my mouth, take a deep breath and plunge my head under the surface.

Now, I am well aware that holiday brochures don't necessarily tell you the whole truth when it comes to the trips and locations on offer. I'm well versed in the concept of photoshopping, and always take those pictures you see in the glossy pages of the Thompson brochures with a pinch of salt. The sky is never really that bright cobalt blue and the sand is rarely that perfect shade of white. Clouds are banished by the delete tool, as are any surly looking locals that happen to walk through the frame when the photographer is taking the snap.

Brochures of that nature are designed to sell you a dream and therefore are likely to play fast and loose with the truth every now and again to tempt you in. I accept this. And I accept that the website for Diving Gold would probably use some of the same tactics to draw people in to their turtle-watching reef trips.

I say all this to reassure you that I wasn't expecting to lower my head into the water and see a fantasy land of colourful coral reef that looked *exactly* like the pictures I'd been gazing at the night before. I'm not that stupid. I was however expecting to lower my head into the water and see something *similar* to what the images on the website had promised me.

What I wasn't expecting was brown pointy things – and a lot of them. Don't get me wrong, there were lots of different brown pointy things down there. Some were thin and pointy, others were quite fat. Some were quite stubby, while others were long tendrils feeling their way out from the seabed.

There was a lot of variety in the shapes and sizes on offer, but – and I can't stress this enough – they were all fucking brown. Light brown, dark brown, mottled brown and streaky brown. Browns of every hue. Browns of every tone. Fifty shades of brown, in fact.

It's just as well the sea around me is dark green,

otherwise I might have felt like I was swimming around in a giant toilet bowl. This coral system is supposed to be at the end of the Great Barrier Reef. If so, it's definitely at the arse end, judging by the decor. I can't help but feel disappointed by this development.

Jamie doesn't seem too bothered though. He's happily snapping away with the underwater camera and we'll no doubt have a fun-filled evening showing Poppy pictures of a huge variety of blurry, brown pointy things.

Still, it's not really the reef we came here to see anyway, is it? Nope, the turtles are our main goal this morning, and surely they will make up for the monotone nature of their habitat, won't they?

It's just a question of finding some . . .

Wikipedia states that green turtles 'spend most of their time in shallow, coastal waters with lush sea grass beds. Adults frequent inshore bays, lagoons and shoals with lush seagrass meadows.'

What it completely fails to tell you is that they have the ability to turn themselves completely fucking *invisible*. I can only assume this is the case given the next twenty-five minutes of my life in an increasingly frantic underwater search off the coast of Queensland.

To begin with I just bob around more or less on the spot, confident that sooner or later I'll spy a turtle and can go in for a closer look. After a few minutes it becomes apparent that this tactic is a very bad one to employ as no turtles cross my field of vision even once. I do see one rather fat bored-looking fish pootling around on the seabed, but this isn't quite the same thing. In fact, it's a miracle I can even pick him out among the coral forests as the fucker is of course a healthy shade of brown.

It dawns on me that I should be surveying a larger area, thus increasing my chances of turtle success, so I start to flipper my way between where Wilko and Tommo are bobbing about on the surface of the water.

This takes up the next fifteen minutes, during which I spy the following:

A brown pointy rock covered in seaweed.

The fat bored fish again.

Jamie.

A brown flat rock covered in brown coral.

Sandrine's bottom, which looks even more annoyingly pert underwater.

The fat bored fish's mate, who is slightly smaller but looks equally fed up with his lot.

Jamie.

The underside of the boat.

The first fat, bored fish again, who is now starting to think I'm up to something.

Wilko's bottom, which is by far and away the best thing I've seen so far.

A brown coral that looks like a beach ball covered in dog fur.

Jamie.

A large crab negotiating its way through a thick patch of seaweed.

My friend the fat bored fish, who is now convinced I'm stalking him and is about to jump on the phone to alert the nearest authorities.

What I don't see hide nor hair of is a turtle.

By now my legs are tired, the skin on my fingers is pruning magnificently and I dread to think how much product I'm going to have to use in the shower to counteract the damage this cold, salty water is doing to my hair. I'm almost on the verge of tears. All I wanted was to pet the head of wizened-looking green turtle in his natural habitat, is that too much to ask?

Jamie surfaces next to me. 'Have you seen a turtle? I thought I did over there but it turned out to be a coral that looked like a furry beach ball. I took a picture of it anyway.'

'No. No turtles at all.'

'Elusive, aren't they?'

'Shoes that fit my toes properly are elusive, Jamie. What these buggers are is *non-existent*. I want my money back!' I shout and slap the water with one frustrated hand.

'Oh come on, there must be some down there somewhere. Have another go.'

And with that, Jamie's head disappears again.

I sigh.

It's pointless.

If I was going to see a turtle I would have done by now.

But I did pay quite a lot of money to come on this trip, so what the hell. Let's give it one last try.

I submerge my head and take another look around.

Even the fat bored fish is nowhere to be seen now. He's probably off warning all his friends about me.

Nope, it's no good. There's nothing else to see. Just large, pointy brown rocks and co—

*Bugger me!*

A flash of green flits across my field of vision. My head snaps around to follow it. I can see flippers. I can see a head. It looks wizened. God damn it, it's a turtle!

I take off in frantic pursuit and can see Jamie doing likewise from my left-hand side. Thrashing around in the water for all I'm worth, I pursue my quarry across the reef. He darts left, then right, but I keep him in my sights. My lungs are burning and my legs are screaming at me to stop, but I can't give up the chase now. This is my one and only chance to be friendly and caring with a turtle today, and if I have to catch the bastard and pin him against the nearest rock with my fist I bloody well will.

The turtle starts to descend into the depths and I try to follow him. In my headlong pursuit I forget that my head – including the snorkel – is now completely submerged under the water and I try to take a breath. This brings the chase to an immediate halt as I inhale an unhealthy amount of sea water. Choking and coughing I rise to the surface with ringing ears and a crushing sense of frustration.

I was so damn close. I nearly had the little sod where I wanted him. If only I'd brought a spear gun!

Jamie helps me back to the boat. He once took a life-saving course and is delighted to be able to put what he learned into action. This seems to consist of throttling the life out of me with one arm, while flailing the other and the rest of his extremities around in random fashion, in the hope that it will in some way propel us both to safety.

157

I'm still spluttering and coughing as I climb back aboard. To add to this is the unpleasant sensation of having swallowed several mouthfuls of briny Australian ocean. I wrench off the wetsuit in disgust and plonk myself back down on the seat with my head between my legs. Jamie comes and sits next to me, cycling through the hundreds of pictures of brown pointyness he's just taken.

'How are you feeling?'

I look up at him and give him the best expression of utter misery I can muster without sending myself off into another coughing fit. 'I wanted to see turtles, Jamie. They were supposed to gracefully weave their way around me. Why didn't they want to weave, Jamie?'

'I don't know.' A huge grin then appears on his face. 'I got a picture of one!'

'Really?'

That would at least give us something to show our daughter. She might not be so angry at us then for dumping her in daycare.

'Yeah, look!'

Jamie hands me the camera and I look at the display.

It's less a turtle, more a small greenish grey blur in the corner of a picture that is otherwise a murky sea green, with a bit of brown pointyness at the bottom. I've seen more convincing and clear photos of Bigfoot. But the look of happy achievement on Jamie's face is so adorable I don't want to ruin it.

'Well done. We'll show it to Pops later.'

The rest of the group have made their way back to the boat. I hear Drunky and Jim moaning that they didn't see many turtles either, but the others seem quite happy with their day's animal watching. I guess Australian green turtles must have an innate dislike for people from the British Isles. I can't think why – maybe we used to eat them during the days of the empire. I'll have to look it up.

With everyone back on board Daffo swings the boat around and we head back to shore.

While I'm deeply put out that the reef was predominantly brown and the turtles were predominantly missing in action, I've still enjoyed much of this trip. The sun above us is hot, the sea is a gorgeous shade of green and the warm wind that ruffles my hair as we motor along is extremely pleasant. And I got to pet a dolphin didn't I? Alright he did give me a snot facial, and I could have probably petted one without laying out a load of money, but I'm taking it as a win. The trip could have been a lot worse, all things considered.

Then we hit the rough water of the river mouth and the sea water I've swallowed interacts with the remains of the cinnamon doughnut in my stomach and I spend the remaining few minutes of our trip throwing up over the side of the boat. I can only hope that some of it landed on that sodding dolphin and gave him a dose of his own medicine.

I've banned oceanic pursuits for the foreseeable future. It seems the wisest course of action.

Still, this is by far and away the happiest I've seen Jamie look for a long time, making the queasy feeling I still have in my stomach more or less worth it. I'll take non-existent turtles and snotty dolphins over a miserable husband any day of the week.

Love you and miss you, Mum.

Your landlubber of a daughter, Laura.

xx

# Jamie's Blog

# Monday 17 July

Six months in Australia. It's quite unbelievable.

When I was a kid the prospect of a week in the Canary Islands sounded about the most exotic thing on the planet. The idea of spending half a year across the other side of the world would have completely blown my mind.

We've been in Australia long enough now to have dropped into a rather pleasant routine – pleasant that is, provided you forget about my complete inability to find work. *Still.*

Aside from the five hundred bucks I earned at the end of last month doing some *extremely* freelance advertising copy for the local youth hostel, I haven't been able to contribute to the family budget at all.

This means I'm getting ordered around a lot these days. As the breadwinner, Laura has naturally fallen into the dominant role and is the one holding the purse strings. Every morning now she issues me with a task, usually to go out and buy milk, or to make sure Poppy meets up with her friends from daycare at the right time and place. I grit my teeth and accept the situation, no matter how pathetic it makes me feel. I'm pretty sure Laura doesn't like the dynamic anymore than I do, but it's the one we're stuck with at the moment, and we both try to make the best of it until something changes.

I can tell Laura's starting to get really twitchy about the whole situation now, though. The air between us grows especially frigid whenever the subject of money comes up. Laura's just about managing to keep a lid on it, but I can tell her frustration levels are reaching a critical mass.

My priorities have therefore changed somewhat in my quest to find a job. It's now no longer a question of just boosting my self-esteem but a matter of keeping my marriage on the straight and narrow.

I think it's best if we gloss over those issues for now though, as the whole thing depresses me if I think about it too much – and will no doubt depress you too if I keep moaning about it. You're going to need your wits about you to cover the next few paragraphs with me and I need you alert and upbeat from the outset.

As I was saying, our daily routine as a family largely consists of the following: We get up around seven thirty and have breakfast together. Laura gets ready for work while I play with Poppy. If it's a day Poppy is going to daycare Laura leaves with her, dropping her off at Surf Tots before going to her job at Worongabba. I then fire up the laptop and write another couple of thousand words in the great Boobatron saga.

If it's a day I have Poppy we amble down to the swing park, before I load her up with sweets and we spend the rest of the morning playing on the beach. I can't tell you how much I enjoy this. This is the most time I've ever been able to spend with my amazing daughter and I'm loving every second of it.

I feel incredibly guilty that Laura is out working while I'm having a good time with Poppy, though. I want a job mainly for the money, but I won't pretend that getting the guilt monkey off my back is not a powerful motivator as well. There are times when Poppy will sit at the dinner table telling Laura all about what she and I have got up to that day, and I can see the regret in my wife's eyes. I would like nothing more than to swap places for her, even if it's just for one day, so she can spend the morning poking dead jellyfish and building sandcastles, while I sit at a desk in a shirt and tie doing something productive.

The days in the warm Queensland sun seem to fly by, and before I know it Laura is coming in through the front door at about four thirty. Sometimes she's tired and cranky from a hard day's work, but most of the time she's still quite bright-eyed and bushy-tailed. Working for Worongabba may mean she doesn't get to see much of her family, but Laura does love her job, of that there is no doubt. The most animated she ever gets is when she's discussing her day with me. I don't understand half of what she says, but I do my best to listen attentively. It's the least I can do.

Once Laura's got her work clothes off and had a cup of tea we either go for a walk along the beach, or if the temperature is still high enough we go for a swim. The latter pursuit is becoming rarer these days as it's winter here now, but every now and again we'll get a gorgeous sunny day, just right for a late afternoon dip before dinner.

Such was the case on Friday. We spent half an hour mucking about in the cool, crystal clear Coolangatta water, before towelling off and going back to the apartment for chilli dogs and salad.

When we go swimming, I always tie my front-door key into the cord around the waist of my board shorts for safe keeping. It saves having to leave my keys on the beach while we're in the water.

I've done this on many, many occasions and it's never proved a problem before. Once we're back at the apartment, I always put the key back on the key ring with the one for the car and all is well. This particular Friday, however, I neglect to put the front-door key back in its rightful place alongside the Magna's, an oversight that will cause many problems in the very near future.

After the chilli dogs we discover that we are running low on milk for our customary early evening cuppa.

'I'll just pop down to the shop on the corner,' I say and grab my keys, forgetting that the one to the apartment is still loosely tied into my shorts, which are now crumpled up in a heap in the bathroom.

'Okay, me and the Popster will come as well. I want some new hair bobbles and madam here wants the latest Wiggles magazine.'

Sidebar: If you're unfamiliar with The Wiggles, they are an extremely popular group of Australian children's entertainers, consisting of four middle-aged men wearing brightly coloured costumes that wouldn't look out of place on the Starship Enterprise. They are at the head of a global industry with a turnover of hundreds of millions of dollars every year and are in NO WAY really fucking creepy to look at.

So all three of us are now leaving the apartment. An apartment that has a very secure lock. The kind that when you slam the door it locks into place and won't open again unless you have the key. Which of course I don't. Sadly, I don't realise this until it's too late – by a few agonising microseconds.

I'm on the stairs that head down to the courtyard when the vision of my crumpled board shorts flashes across the front of my brain, desperate to get my attention before disaster strikes. I whip my head around to see Laura pulling the door closed.

'No, wait! I—'

But it's no good. The door slams with undeniable finality.

'I haven't got the key!' I cry and lunge at the door.

'What? Why not?'

'It's still tied in my shorts,' I tell her as I pointlessly bang on the door.

'Why? You normally put it back on the key ring. Why didn't you do it today?'

'Because I forgot, that's why.'

'Oh, you idiot, Jamie!'

'Sorry, I'm sorry!'

'What the hell are we going to do? It's six thirty on Friday evening. No one's in the office onsite.'

She's right. This is the absolute worst time this could have happened.

'Maybe Mindy's at home,' I say hopefully. 'She might have keys to let us in. Stay here and I'll go and ask.'

I leave my wife and daughter at the door and run down the stairs, across the courtyard and into the block on the far side of the swimming pool. Mindy is up in apartment 401 so I climb the stairs and bang on her door heavily, praying that she'll answer.

The door swings open and I'm greeted by the rather lovely sight of Mindy in Lycra shorts and bra top, holding a water bottle. Just behind her I can see a treadmill running in the corner and I can hear rock music playing from a stereo. She's got a sweat on and her hair is a right mess, but Mindy has the advantage of being young and Australian, so she still manages to look extremely attractive despite the sweat stains.

'Hello,' she says, a hectic blush across her face caused by the exercise.

'Hello, Mindy, sorry to interrupt your workout, but I've got a big problem.'

I proceed to explain the situation, hoping that Mindy can point me in the direction of a spare key.

'I'm really sorry,' she says, 'but that apartment is privately owned, so I don't have a key for it in my office here. They'll have one at the main offices, but no one will be there this time of night.'

My heart sinks. 'Oh.'

'I'm really sorry!'

'It's not your fault. We'll just have to think of something else. Maybe get a locksmith out if all else fails.'

'Yeah, we had to do that for Mrs Spelnik in number two thirteen. Cost a lot though.'

'How much?'

'It was in the evening too so it was about three hundred dollars.'

'Really? It'll be cheaper to stay in a hotel for the night.'

'Yeah, probably.' Mindy takes a long swig from her water bottle. This is entirely an unsuitable time for me to look at her breasts as she does this, but I do it anyway. 'I really hope you can get it sorted out,' she continues. 'You could have stayed here, but I have my friend Dan coming over later.' She holds out a hand. 'It's nothing serious, we're just close friends. But I know he wants to take it to the next level. I'm not sure it'll be a good idea, though.' Mindy cocks her head to one side. 'Do you think I should just stay friends with him?'

'I don't know, Mindy,' I say in disbelief. Here I am in dire straits and she's asking me about her relationships. 'I have to go now.'

'Oh, okay. No worries.' She actually looks vaguely disappointed.

*I'm sorry I can't sort your sex life out for you, Mindy, but I have other priorities right now.*

I trudge back down the stairs, across the courtyard and back to our place.

'Nope, she's no help,' I tell Laura when I get back. 'Though we're not getting a bloody locksmith out, they cost and arm and a leg.'

My wife is now crouched at the door handle, one of Poppy's hairpins inserted into the lock, another pressed firmly between her lips.

'What are you doing?' I ask.

''Rying to 'ick the 'ock,' she says.

'Mummy's being a spy!' Poppy adds.

'For God's sakes, Laura, this isn't *Mission Impossible*.'

'No, it isn't,' she snaps. 'Tom Cruise wouldn't get locked out of his bloody flat.'

She stands up again and picks up Poppy, whose mouth is staring to droop at either end in a sure sign that she's getting upset.

'Don't worry, Pops, Daddy will sort this out.'

Laura raises one eyebrow but remains silent.

Luckily, I have my mobile phone on me. I'd at least remembered to stick that and my wallet in my short pockets. I find our letting agent's number and call. My heart sinks when I get a message indicating that the office is now closed until nine o'clock tomorrow.

So Mindy is no help, and the rest of the letting agency have buggered off for the day. The only other person with a spare key is the landlady, but she lives in Brisbane and is unlikely to be impressed with the notion of driving two hours down here to let us back into the apartment.

We are – as the Aborigines would say – up shit billabong without a narawang. Disconsolately, we shuffle down the stairs and sit on a couple of sun loungers set up around the communal swimming pool.

'We'll have to check into a hotel then. I've got my wallet.'

'My pay's just gone into the account for the month so it should be okay. It's going to cost a good hundred dollars plus though,' Laura says, the accusatory tone in her voice very evident.

'Alright, alright. Give me a break, will you?' I can feel

myself getting angry out of sheer embarrassment. Not only have I got us locked out of our apartment, but it has to be Laura who bails us out because she's the one with the job. Bringing this sore subject up again won't help matters now though, so I look away from her and into the floodlit swimming pool, trying to calm myself down a bit.

'You folks alright?' a voice pipes up from the other side of the fence that runs around the edge of the pool area.

I look up to see Sandra the housekeeper. 'Hi, Sandra, we've locked ourselves out.'

'What's this *we* business?' Laura points out, which while factually correct, is not particularly helpful at this trying time.

Sandra looks aghast. 'Oh no, what are you going to do?'

'Check into a hotel I guess. The one across the park is nearest. Then we'll go get a spare from the agents tomorrow morning when they're back.'

Sandra makes a face. 'You don't want to stay at that place, especially not on a Friday night, it gets really rowdy and your little one won't like it.'

'Hi folks,' another voice says and Bob, Sandra's groundskeeper husband, appears from behind a thick palm tree. 'How you going?' Bob could be Alf's twin from *Home and Away*. Actually, scratch that, there's every chance this *is* Alf from *Home and Away*, doing a bit of moonlighting while he's not filming his ten millionth episode of the show.

'They've locked themselves out, Bob,' Sandra tells him.

'Oh really? That's a bugger,' Bob says.

'It is,' I agree.

A four-storey bugger with attractive sea views, in fact.

'They're going to spend the night at the Ocean Bay, Bob.'

Bob sucks his teeth. 'You don't wanna be doing that. Not a salubrious environment once the old beer gets flowing, if you take my meaning.'

'I don't think we have much choice,' Laura says, rocking a rapidly tiring Poppy in her arms.

'You could always come and stay with us,' Sandra offers, smiling broadly.

'Yeah! We've got room,' Bob adds.

*Oh dear.* Oh dear, oh dear. This could be problematic. This is undoubtedly a very generous offer on Bob and Sandra's part, but it puts Laura and I in something of an awkward position.

We're both big on privacy, and spending a night with these kind folks would probably end up being uncomfortable in the extreme. Given the jobs they do here at the apartment block I would imagine their house is pretty small for starters. And it hasn't been that long since our fateful night under Grant and Ellie's roof. If we had a repeat performance of that there's every chance I'll find myself on the other end of divorce proceedings in the not-too-distant future. I'd much rather find a hotel to spend the night in, even if it does cost us money.

But we've already discussed and more or less eliminated the idea of staying at the Ocean Bay and no other options are presenting themselves. There's not even an opportunity for Laura and I to discuss what we should do out of their earshot. They've got us pinned down and there's nowhere to run.

I throw a quick glance at Laura, whose expression plainly shows that she's thinking exactly the same thing I am. Time to throw up some classic British politeness. 'Oh, we couldn't possibly impose on you like that,' I tell them.

'Nah!' Bob waves his hand. 'No worries, mate, we're happy to help out.'

'But we'll end up ruining your evening. We'd feel awful,' Laura interjects.

'We've got nothing planned, love,' Sandra tells her. 'In fact, we'd be quite glad of the company.'

Fuck me, these bastards are persistent.

I decide to play the Poppy card. 'We'd need somewhere with room enough for Poppy though, it'll be too much trouble for you.'

'She'll be right, mate,' Bob argues. 'Plenty of room at our place, trust me.'

Oh God, he's being so nice, but I bet there isn't.

My brain tries to conjure up another excuse for us not staying with Bob and Sandra, but the only thing that presents itself is Laura's bowel problems, and I'd rather spend a night sleeping in a pit of radioactive snakes than use that one again. I chuck Laura a pleading glance to see if she can come in and save the day, but I get an equally pleading glance straight back at me.

Oh no. I'm going to have to accept the offer. We'll just have to hope the night goes quickly and eight o'clock in the morning comes around as fast as possible.

'Okay, well, thank you very much. We'd love to come spend the night with you.' I try to sound enthusiastic, but my tone rather suggests that this idea is actually right up there with having all of your teeth pulled. Sandra and Bob don't appear to notice, though.

'Great! I'll go home now and get the place tidy for you,' Sandra says.

Oh fantastic, now we're making the poor bitch do more housework, after she's just spent the entire day doing it here at the apartments.

'And if you folks don't mind, I just have a couple of things to finish over in the gardens at the back. When they're done I'll jump in your car with you and direct you home.'

'Okay, thank you,' I say with an apologetic tone.

This is just awful.

Both Sandra and Bob wish us a brief farewell and go to attend to their respective chores.

'That was very nice of them,' Laura says once they're out of earshot.

'Mmmm.'

'You don't think so?'

'Oh, it was very nice of them, but I still think I would have preferred a hotel.'

'Well why didn't you come up with a reason not to go?'

'I couldn't think of one.'

I know where my wife is going with this, and I wait for the inevitable.

'I could have just told them you have trouble taking a

poo anywhere within earshot of another human being,' she says snidely. 'That might have done it.'

Ah, I see. We're going to occupy ourselves with some banter while we wait. Well, why the hell not?

'True,' I agree. 'Or you could just turn up in your beach whore outfit, that'd probably give them second thoughts about inviting us in.'

'Funny,' Laura says with eyes narrowed. 'I know – you could suggest cooking them fajitas,' she says. 'Once they see you crouched over their bin that'll get us chucked out before you know it.'

I open my mouth to tell her she should bring around a copy of the Polish penis slapping movie for them to watch, but stop myself. 'Look, let's not go down this route. I've got no problem with a bit of banter, but it's all fun and games until somebody loses an eye.' I take her hand. 'I'm sorry I got us locked out, but at least we've got somewhere to stay for the night.'

'Yeah, I suppose you're right.' She looks down at Poppy. 'I want to get this one inside and into bed as soon as we can.'

It only takes Bob about ten minutes to square away whatever task he was finishing off and in no time at all we're in the Magna and he's directing us to his home.

'Sandra will have the place looking lovely, don't you fret,' he says in jovial fashion from the passenger seat.

'Sounds great,' I tell him, unable to completely wipe the disconcerted look off my face. I can just imagine Sandra right now, putting the finishing touches to their home, a half smile of expectation on her face.

*Oh God.*

'Take a left here, mate,' Bob says and I oblige.

'Keep going until the road splits. We're just on the left after it.'

We're certainly up in the hills by this point. I've had to rev the Magna hard to get us up at least one of the inclines. Bob and Sandra are in no danger of flooding any time in the near future, that's for certain.

I see what looks like another road just after the split in the one we're on and presume Bob's house must be after that.

Bob says differently. 'Left now, mate. Otherwise we'll be headed up into the boonies.'

'Okay.'

I turn into what I thought was another road, but turns out to be a driveway. Then something very strange happens. I drive the Magna into a vast courtyard. On my right is an enormous triple garage, and on the left is a three-storey house the size of my primary school.

Poor old Bob. He must be going senile. He's taken us completely the wrong way and now we're going to have the embarrassment of calling Sandra to help her befuddled husband get home.

'Right then, welcome to our house! Out you get.' Oh dear, Bob actually thinks he lives here. Look at him, poor old mentalist. He's actually walking up to the front door. This is going to be excruciating. The owners will come to the door and we'll have to lead poor senile Bob away before he shits himself and tells them he's a train driver.

Oh no, now he's getting a set of keys out. This just gets worse and worse. Look at him trying to get in the door. He's actually trying to turn the key. He's actually opening the door. He's actua—

Hang on a fucking minute.

Bob is standing in the doorway to what is patently his home, looking at us and wondering why we're not getting out of the car. 'You guys coming or what?'

Now, I've never claimed to be an expert at reading people, but I don't think I've ever got it as wrong as this before.

In my defence, what was I supposed to expect? Bob and Sandra seem like working-class types. You wouldn't normally think that someone in housekeeping and someone who is employed as a gardener would be able own a house this large and expensive.

'You have a very nice house,' Laura says in wonder as she carries Poppy across the threshold.

Beyond is an open-plan living area you could comfortably play a game of tennis in. They must have killed an entire rainforest to provide the material for the polished hardwood floor I'm now standing on.

An expansive lounge sits to our right, an equally impressive kitchen is off to the right and there's a dining table in the centre that King Arthur would get hard just looking at. And then there's the *view*.

The entire right-hand side of the house is paned with glass. Beyond this is a huge decked area, replete with a barbecue the size of a country house Aga and more patio furniture than you'd see on a brisk walk around Homebase.

Beyond *that* is the Gold Coast. All of it. A one-hundred-and-eighty degree night-time panorama takes in everything from Surfer's Paradise way up north to Tweed Heads just south of us. A starfield of such magnitude hangs overhead it makes my jaw drop in awe.

'Bloody hell,' I say breathlessly.

'Good, ain't it?' Bob replies with characteristic Australian understatement.

'Yes,' I gulp.

'That's why we had the place built up here. We like a nice view.'

'You giving them the grand tour?' Sandra says, walking out onto the decking.

'You have a very nice house,' Laura repeats. My wife seems to have got stuck in some kind of default loop-mode.

'Aw, thanks love. We like it.' She looks at Poppy, still in her mother's arms. 'I think we should get little 'un squared away don't you? She looks all in. I'll take you up to the second floor. It's where you'll be sleeping.'

Sandra leads the way up the mahogany staircase to an area roughly three times the size of the apartment I've just got us locked out of.

A super king-sized bed awaits Laura and me past a partition at one end, and Poppy has her own double bed to sleep in next door. There's every chance she'll want to be adopted by our hosts when we tell her she has to leave tomorrow.

I spy a fifty-inch television in what looks like a second lounge area. And the view from here is if anything better than it was on the floor below.

'Okay, guys. Get little Poppy to sleep and then pop

back downstairs for a drink,' Sandra tells us. 'Treat the place like it's your own. We have this whole floor for when our kids come to stay with their families so it's purpose built for folks like you!'

'We can't thank you enough for this,' Laura says as she lays the sleeping Poppy down.

'Oh stop it, we're more than happy to help.'

Sandra leaves us so we can get ourselves settled in. This doesn't take long as all we have are the clothes we're standing up in. The super king bed is so comfortable it almost makes me cry.

'I should get us locked out more often,' I say to Laura from my prone position. 'This is perfect.'

It turns out Bob used to work in the opal industry. 'Did pretty well,' he tells us, as we sit with the both of them out on the vast decking. To the tune of several million dollars, it transpires.

When he retired four years ago, they built this mansion in the hills at Coolangatta to be closer to their daughter Madison, who lives just north of here in a town called Currumbin. The second floor of the house, when not being used by the Newmans, is usually reserved for their other daughter Tamsin, who lives in Thailand with her rich husband and their two children.

'But why do you work at our apartment block?' I ask when Bob has finished explaining all of this.

'Well, you don't want to get bored do you?' he says.

No, I guess you most certainly don't.

'We like to feel useful,' Sandra continues. 'So when we saw the vacancies come up we jumped at the chance.'

'Yep, let's us keep our hand in.' Bob takes another swig of lager from his stubby holder.

It's funny. Back in the UK Bob and Sandra would spend their days with other oily middle-class couples discussing the latest Audi convertible and complaining about the people from the Housing Association. Out here though, you're hard pressed to tell the rich folk from the poor ones. Everybody acts, dresses and talks the same. There's none of that obnoxious superiority complex that seems to infect the British psyche once it's earned a fair bit of money. The class system here appears to be deader than the Australian music industry. I find the whole thing very refreshing – and in the case of my family this evening, also very convenient.

The next couple of hours are whiled away talking about life in Australia (it turns out Sandra is actually from Walthamstow and moved here when she was eight), the state of our respective governments, the state of our respective sports teams, the weather, tax, the Second World War, having children, getting older and invisible turtles.

At half ten Bob takes a look at his watch. 'Time to turn in I reckon. We've got an early start.'

'Oh yes!' Sandra joins in. 'We're off up to Brisbane to see my sister.'

I groan internally. We'll have to get up early as well then. I was rather looking forward to a lie-in.

'You folks don't have to get up at the same time as us though,' Sandra continues, as if reading my mind. 'You stay in bed for as long as you want and just make sure the front door is slammed shut when you leave. There's a shower in the en suite and feel free to raid the fridge for breakfast in the morning.'

'Thank you so much,' Laura says. I can tell from the relief in her voice that she was thinking much the same thing I was about the early start.

With that exchange, the evening is over and we retire to our bedroom . . . sorry, I mean our second-floor apartment.

'Unbelievable,' I say to Laura as we climb into bed. 'I get us locked out and it turns into one of the best evenings we've had here so far. What a lovely pair those two are.'

'Yes, dear. You're an accidental genius,' Laura replies in typical withering fashion. 'They are lovely, but I still think I would have preferred the night in my own bed.

'Where's your sense of adventure, baby?'

'Next to your door key on the floor of our currently inaccessible bathroom, pal.'

I smile and give my wife a kiss. This stirs things in the trouser department.

She catches the expression on my face. 'Don't be ridiculous, Jamie. We're in somebody else's house. They might hear.'

'In this place? It's enormous.'

'I'm not taking the risk. Try to hold on until tomorrow when I'm less sure we'll be putting on a performance for a middle-aged Australian couple.'

Laura kisses me back, not helping matters in the slightest. She then rolls over onto her side, leaving me looking down disconsolately at my erection and once again cursing my forgetfulness.

Laura's probably right though. The idea of Bob and Sandra hearing us go at it is awful. Best to let this one slide and attempt re-entry tomorrow.

Laura's reluctance to 'get jiggy wid it' is proved to be the right decision some ten minutes later when I hear voices coming from directly above us. I can't quite make out what's being said, but it's obvious Bob and Sandra are getting ready for bed themselves. It appears that while this palatial mansion has many, many good points, one of its less appealing characteristics is a lack of sound-proofing. They could probably do with slinging a few carpets down instead of all the polished hardwood.

'See,' Laura says sleepily. 'They'd have definitely heard us.'

'Yep. Good call.'

Bob and Sandra's conversation carries on for another few minutes. I hear the bed creak loudly as Bob gets in, and creak much more softly when Sandra joins him.

This is actually making me feel a bit uncomfortable. I feel like I'm intruding into their private life. I'm profoundly glad therefore, when I hear the click of a table lamp going off and the conversation above us stops.

I roll over onto my side and close my eyes, willing my penis to stop thinking about Laura all naked, sweaty and nibbling at my neck. I eventually win the battle and start to drift off into a half-sleep.

What brings me out of it is the soft moan of a woman.

*Hmmm. Interesting.*

Maybe Laura's had a change of heart. Maybe the lure of my undeniable sexual magnetism has overcome her reluctance and she wants to throw caution to the wind.

I roll over and disappointingly see Laura's back still facing me. I can hear her breathing in a deep, even way that's clear evidence she's asleep and in no way up for some rumpy pumpy.

I must have imagined her moaning. Damn my stupid penis and its ability to make me hear things. Then I hear the moan again. This time it's louder and longer.

Laura hasn't budged though, so where in hell can the sound be coming from?

Then, the light dawns. It's *Sandra*. I can quite clearly hear our female host in what sounds like the early throes of passion. Sandra moans a third time, this one ending in a throaty chuckle indicating that Bob has put something very important in *exactly* the right place.

This is confirmed when I hear Bob grunt in a self-satisfied manner.

The bed starts to creak in rhythmic fashion. I actually start to go a shade of crimson. They have no idea I can hear them at it, but it's still very embarrassing all the same.

The creaking gets a bit faster. Sandra moans again, this time joined by Bob. When he does it he sounds like a malfunctioning garden strimmer.

'Are they *fucking*?' Laura says from beside me in a voice half full of sleep, half full of incredulity.

'Yep. Bob and Sandra don't appear to be worried about being overheard,' I reply. 'I just hope he's a fast mover and it's over soon.'

'Agreed. I really need to sleep.'

So there my wife and I lie for the next five minutes or

so, waiting for Bob to arrive at his destination. We're expecting the creaking to speed up even more, climaxing in a fairly typical orgasmic series of grunts and moans before Bob rolls off and peace returns to the world.

This doesn't happen though. In fact, if anything the creaking is slowing down.

'I don't think Bob can cut the mustard,' I say.

'He is in his sixties,' Laura apologises for him.

'True.'

Then the creaking stops completely.

'Poor bloke.'

Turns out the festivities aren't over yet though. Our eyes both widen when we hear the unmistakeable sound of an electric buzzing device being turned on. If poor old Bob can't keep the fun going, then Sandra knows another way it appears.

Laura and I are now nearly frozen in combined mortification. We both subconsciously pull the duvet up under our chins in horror. The buzzing gets quieter . . . then louder. Quieter . . . then louder. Quieter . . . then louder.

I start to chew the duvet cover. Sandra, now really going for it, starts to moan so loudly there's every chance she's going to wake Poppy up.

She starts to say something to Bob. I can't quite catch all of it, but she's speaking loudly enough for me to pick up way more than I want to: '*Mumble mumble* on my back *mumble mumble mumble* up my arse *mumble mumble* jump on *mumble*.'

The bed creaks again, this time for longer, indicating

the shifting of bodies into a new position – a new position that I can only imagine all too well thanks to twenty years of watching porn.

What's playing across my mind's eye right now is not two healthy tight young porn stars assuming the position, but our good-natured middle-aged hosts, whose bodies probably haven't seen daylight in a good fifteen years. I don't want to see Sandra on all fours with Bob's beer gut resting on her bony bottom, but God help me I CAN'T STOP IT HAPPENING.

The creaking starts again, this time in a harder, sharper rhythm indicating that Bob is really getting down to business.

'What's he doing to her?' Laura asks in a small voice.

'Guaranteeing she won't be comfortable on their drive up to Brisbane tomorrow?' I whisper back.

Now Bob starts grunting in time with the creaking. Overlaid onto both sounds is the buzzing of Sandra's little friend, in a symphony of awkward I wish I was ten thousand miles away from. The whole thing gets louder, faster and more pornographic.

'Fuck me!' we hear Sandra spit quite audibly through the ceiling. 'Fuck me in that ass, you big strong bastard!'

I feel Laura take my hand in hers, seeking some solace from the terror. My wife and I are locked in this horrible moment together, one that we will never be able to forget, no matter how drunk we get.

'It's coming!' Bob exclaims, his voice muffled by creaking bed and roaring vibrator.

I'm hoping he means Armageddon, because after this

night I don't think I want to live in a world that would allow such horrors to be visited on me.

Laura grips my hand tightly. I let out a small squeak of fear.

Then finally, just when I think my mind is about to tip over into the chasm of insanity, Bob and Sandra let out a combined enormous grunt-moan, signalling the end of what would likely make the kind of porno only a very small, select audience would want to watch.

'Thank God for that,' Laura says.

The bed takes the strain of two spent middle-aged Australians flopping onto it in post-coital nirvana.

The buzzing noise abruptly disappears, proving that Sandra is most definitely satisfied for the night.

'That's going to need a wash,' I hear myself saying and instantly regret it.

A dreadful silence now descends across the house. It's like the aftermath of a particularly destructive tornado.

'Jamie?'

'Yes, Laura?'

'You know that we'll never be able to have sex again after that, don't you?'

'Yes, Laura, I know. It was fun while it lasted though.'

'It was.'

More silence. Then a horrible thought occurs: 'If that's the kind of sex they have when they know someone's in the house with them,' I say, 'what on earth do they get up to when they know they're alone?'

'I don't know.' Laura gulps. 'And I don't want to know, quite frankly.'

'They probably use a pedal bin.'

'Oh for God's sake, Jamie!'

'Sorry.'

'Can we just go to sleep now?'

'Yes, I think that would be a very good idea. Then tomorrow, we can pretend this was all just a dream.'

Our bedroom door creaks open. Poppy stands in the doorway rubbing her eyes. 'Mummy? Daddy? Is somebody doing nasty things to Sandra lady upstairs?'

Yes, poppet, they are. But the kind of things you're not going to know anything about until I'm dead in my grave if I get my way.

# Laura's Diary
## Tuesday, July 18th

It took us a good half an hour to convince Poppy that Sandra wasn't being murdered upstairs, Mum.

'You just dreamt it, Pops,' I lie to her unconvincingly. 'Sandra is absolutely fine, I'm sure. She was probably having a bad dream too.'

My daughter gives me the most suspicious look a three year old can summon in a half-sleep. 'Don't like bad dreams.'

'I know poppet.'

'Wanna sleep with you.'

'Okay, honey,' I sigh. When Poppy climbs into bed these days it usually means a restless night for all concerned. She's much like her mother in bed: a fidget. One night not so long ago she spun round a full one-eighty degrees. It was quite disconcerting to have tiny pink little toes waving around in your immediate field of vision at half-two in the morning.

Poppy yawns, climbs in between her mother and father, sticks one thumb in her mouth and promptly falls asleep.

'I guess I can look forward to getting kicked in the balls later then,' Jamie says, knowing what Pops is like as much as I do.

'Well, it's better that than she goes back to bed and has nightmares about Sandra being assaulted by a swarm of buzzing insects.'

'That fucker was loud, wasn't it? I've had washing machines make less of a racket than that. It must be a huge one.'

'I don't want to think about it, thanks.'

But now I have to, of course.

I'm a woman of the world, and I'm fully aware of what shapes and sizes vibrators come in. I can't help but picture Sandra holding one of the ones at the upper end of the spectrum, the kind that have complicated machinery going on inside them and in a pinch can be used as an effective weapon of self defence.

I don't know what to feel sorrier for – her lady garden or Bob's self esteem. Still, at least it sounded like they were enjoying themselves. I have to confess I'm quite jealous.

Thanks to my workload and the fact Jamie appears to be sinking further into an unemployed depression, our sex life is more dormant than a volcano that last blew its stack when sabre-tooth tigers were all the rage.

For the first time in the years we've been married, I have to actually try to remember when we last made love. It takes me a good minute or two to recollect the brief fumble we had last month after I'd put Poppy down for the night. And that was decidedly unmemorable for both of us.

The time before that was a further month back, and I have to confess that I was probably thinking more about

Milo the Ute-driving hunk of young Australian and his rippling biceps than I was my own husband.

This is a sorry state of affairs, Mum. I feel a combination of frustration that Jamie can't find work, and a severe feeling of guilt that I'm having such a good time in my job. I know damn well that he's feeling pretty emasculated by the whole thing. Coming to Australia is proving to be the best thing to happen to me since Pops was born and the worst thing to happen to Jamie.

These concerning thoughts keep me awake for another half an hour before I start to drift back into sleep. I only start to do that once I've resolved to put some time aside to helping Jamie find a job, while also reining in my enthusiasm about Worongabba when I'm at home. That's if we ever get back into our home of course.

I very much hope we can pick up a key to the apartment tomorrow with no problems. The idea of spending a second night listening to Sandra impale herself on her weapon of mass destruction fills me with dread.

In a half doze the next morning, I hear Bob and Sandra leave the house.

I lie in bed with an exquisitely strange and uncomfortable feeling. We're now completely alone, undressed and half asleep in the house of two people who were complete strangers twenty-four hours ago.

They're not complete strangers now, it goes without saying. Once two people have put on an audible sex show for you in the middle of the night, you probably know them in a more intimate fashion than you do your best friends.

'Do you think we should get up?' Jamie says from beside me, and over his daughter's wriggling toes.

'I suppose. This bed is very warm though.'

'I'm hungry.'

'Can't you wait until we get back to the apartment?'

'Probably not. The last thing I ate was tea before I got us locked out. If Sandra and her buzzing friend hadn't woken us last night, I think my growling stomach would have done it instead.'

'I don't feel right about eating their food.'

'But Sandra said help yourself. It'd be rude not to take her up on her kind offer.'

This is an argument I'm not likely to win. Men are quite happy to capitulate on any number of subjects if it means an easy life, but the state of their stomach is not one of them. It even seems to take precedence over their sexual appetite in terms of importance a lot of the time, which when you think about it must be some kind of miracle.

'Okay, we'll have a look what they've got but we're making sure we leave the place as clean as we found it, alright?'

'Yes, yes, of course.'

'You say that, Newman, but your idea of cleaning up and mine are completely different. We're going to do more than wipe a kitchen towel across the kitchen counter and half-fill the dishwasher.'

I shift in the bed and catch a whiff of myself. It isn't pleasant.

'But before all of that,' I say with a wrinkled nose.

'We're having showers. I may have to wear yesterday's clothes again until we get home, but I don't intend to spend another minute wearing the rest of yesterday as well.'

The shower is glorious and invigorating. It's one of those enormous walk-in ones that you usually only see in posh spas. Were it not for the fact Jamie is preoccupied with Poppy, I might have dragged him in here for some vigorous soapy sex, thus ending the recent drought. Then I remember Sandra ordering Bob around in bed last night and my desire is instantly extinguished. I may have only been half-joking when I told Jamie we'd never be able to have sex again.

If there's anything worse than having to put on dirty clothes after you've just had a cleansing shower, I don't know what it is. Yet this is my fate on this hot, sunny Coolangatta morning.

I grimace as I pull on my shorts. I frown as I slip the T-shirt back over my head. All I can say is thank God we're living somewhere hot so I don't have to wear much.

By the time all three of us have cleaned up and got dressed the day's heat is really starting to gear itself up. Having all these glass walls may look aesthetically very pleasing, but it does rather turn a house into something you'd usually grow tomatoes in.

We creep downstairs to the cooler environs of the kitchen and dining area. Why we're creeping I have no idea. We have permission to be in the house, but it still feels weird to have the run of a place you've only spent one night in at the behest of its owners.

The blast of cold air from the enormous double fridge is wonderful, as are the contents. I'd be amazed if there were any pigs left in Queensland, such is the amount of bacon Bob and Sandra have got stacked up on the shelves here. They also appear to have completely cleaned out the local farmer's market, given the piles of fresh fruit and veg on offer.

I've never looked into the fridge of a rich person before. It's enough to make you feel quite inadequate. I always like to think I keep ours pretty well stocked with a wide range of perishable foodstuffs, but when you're presented with a layout that resembles the entire refrigerated section of your average Tesco, you can't help but feel you might be letting the side down a bit.

My husband doesn't appear to be having any of my reservations about using Bob and Sandra's belongings as he's got the kettle on and has hunted down the tea bags before I've even got over the shock of seeing a whole watermelon the size of a basketball sat in the crisper.

'I wonder if they have any porridge?' he says, banging and clattering his way around the fifty or so cupboards that ring the kitchen area. 'Pops likes a bowl of porridge, don't you, Pops?'

'Yes, Daddy!'

God bless childhood. It's the only time in life you get can truly excited about oats.

'You want a bacon sandwich, Jamie?'

I can tell by the way my husband's eyes light up that he'd like nothing more in the world right now. I decide to have the same. We couldn't put a dent in the mountain of smoky back Bob and Sandra have collected at the rear of the fridge, so I feel a bit less guilty about eating their food.

I join my husband in the grand kitchen cupboard search, and am pleased to discover the frying pan just before Jamie lays eyes on the porridge. It's these small competitions that keep a marriage interesting, I find.

In no time at all, the kitchen is full of the smell of frying bacon and I'm already worrying about leaving a stranger's house stinking of dead pig. Poppy is happily munching her way through a bowl of hot, oaty goodness and Jamie is merrily burning some toast, adding to the stench that will greet Bob and Sandra on their return later that day.

I knew this was a bad idea. We should have just left straight away. Now I'll have to spend a good hour hunting through this ridiculously big house for the air freshener.

The bacon tastes wonderful though. Jamie wasn't the only one who woke up starving this morning, I realise, as I tuck into my second half. Such is our combined hunger that we decide to go back for seconds.

Now chez Bob and Sandra smells like somebody's firebombed a Walls factory. I would feel even more guilty, but I'm too busy eating Miss Piggy to notice that much.

With two bacon sandwiches in me I'm completely stuffed. I nurse my full belly with a second cup of tea while Jamie does his level best to fill the dishwasher. I know how bad he usually is at this, so I watch carefully as he puts the plates in the rack. He's doing it with an unusual level of delicacy, it has to be said. I give him grief a lot of the time for being careless, but he's treating Bob's and Sandra's belongings very well, to give him his credit.

The same can't be said for Poppy. 'Stop banging the spoon on the table and give it to Daddy, young lady.' I chide gently and take another sip of warm tea.

I then watch a game of wills between my husband and daughter for a few moments in a warm haze of bacon and tea. Pops has taken a real liking to that spoon, and is refusing to hand it over to her father. I'm assuming this is her way of berating him for getting her locked out of the apartment all night and having to hear Sandra being molested by a noisy battery-powered device.

'Come on, Poppy, give me the spoon,' Jamie says, holding out one hand.

'No!' Poppy shrieks, giggles and skips just out of her father's reach.

Jamie is trying his best to remain serious, but – as ever – our daughter's innate charm and downright cheekiness is hard to resist. He can't help but laugh as he pursues Poppy across the kitchen.

The War Of The Spoon comes to a climax over by the fridge, with the plucky young upstart being finally bested by her older, heavier opponent when he distracts her by turning a nearby oven glove into a puppet. This is a decidedly underhand tactic. No small child can resist it when an everyday item is given a silly speaking voice.

'Oooh, why don't you give me the *spooooon*, Poppy?' the oven glove says from Jamie's right hand. 'I eat *spoooons* and am very, very hungry . . .'

Pops giggles again and holds out the object of their

combined attention. It seems that her desire to see the oven glove monster fed overrides her need to retain the spoon for future usage.

Oven glove monster grabs the spoon and starts to make overblown chomping noises, causing further giggly emissions. I have to laugh myself. It's been a long time since I saw such a happy, silly thing and it warms me even more than the cup of tea, which I'm sadly getting to the bottom of. Time to leave, methinks.

'I'm going to write a thank-you note,' I say to both husband and daughter.

'Good idea,' Jamie agrees, slotting the spoon into the dishwasher and shutting door. 'You do that and Pops and I will go make sure we've got everything from upstairs.'

To the sound of the gurgling machine I start to construct a short but heartfelt note, using the pad and pen sat on the counter next to the fridge:

*To Bob and Sandra,*
*Thank you so much for letting us stay the night. We don't know what we would have done without you.*
*Best wishes to you both, and look forward to seeing you around the apartment complex.*
*We must take you out for a meal to show our appreciation properly.*
*Many thanks,*
*Laura, Jamie and*

Oh dear. I have to stop writing as I'm overcome by a rather insistent stomach cramp.

The combination of bread, bacon and hot brown tea appears to have woken up my bowels. They gurgle at me again in no uncertain terms, indicating that I should retire to the nearest convenience as soon as possible. I hadn't factored in this development in my decision to eat breakfast on Bob and Sandra's dime. The unlovely realisation that I'm going to have to take a poo in their house becomes apparent.

*Oh dear, oh dear.*

While I am not what you'd call a 'nervous pooer' (despite what my idiot husband may claim to any Australian hippies who might be passing) the prospect of having to go for a number two in Bob and Sandra's house is not one I take any pleasure in. Still, needs must and all that.

I leave my note having not quite finished it yet and head in speedy fashion over to the downstairs bathroom that sits just off to one side as you come in the front door. Inside, things proceed rapidly and in time-honoured fashion. So healthy are my bowels this morning that I deliver a single, large package to its intended watery destination. I clean myself and stand, flushing the toilet as I do so.

Embarrassingly, the flush in this toilet isn't all that effective and my contribution refuses to make itself scarce around the U-bend. I wait a few moments for the cistern to fill and press down on the flush again. This second attempt also ends in failure. As does the third.

*Oh good grief.*

'Er, are you alright Laura?' I hear Jamie say from beyond the door.

'Yes! I'm fine!' I snap back.

'Okay, well I've got everything. Pops and I will go wait out by the car for you until you're . . . you know, finished.'

'That's fine! Everything's fine! You go do that then!'

This is awful. No, it's more than awful. It transcends awful, dreadful, terrible and appalling – and is headed right towards cataclysmic at the speed of fucking light. I flush again, hoping and praying the end result will be different. Nope. There it floats, bobbing up and down gently without a care in the world.

Now we've even sped right by cataclysmic, out past the event horizon of calamity and into some hideous alternate universe where the laws of physics break down completely. What the hell am I going to do? I can't just leave my deposit where it is. The idea of Bob and Sandra returning home to find their house clean and tidy, but with my recent brownness happy to greet them the second they step into the bathroom is truly, truly stomach-churning.

But I repeat: What the hell am I going to do? Then hideous realisation dawns on me.

If I can't get it to flush away, I'm going to have to *remove it in some other fashion.*

The mere prospect of retrieving my poo from the toilet bowl makes me gag. But what other choice do I have? If I can get it out of here somehow, I can dispose of it elsewhere. It looks pretty damn solid – thanks to my healthy digestive system – so it shouldn't be too hard to . . . *oh God in Heaven* . . . pick up.

Not empty-handed though. Bugger that for a game of

soldiers. I have to find something to put as a barrier between me and it. Toilet roll is out, that'll disintegrate in seconds. I need something more robust.

Tentatively, I open the bathroom door. From here, I can see Jamie and Poppy playing outside by the car. Jamie has found a bright pink ball from somewhere and they're preoccupied with throwing it to one another while they wait for me to come out.

*Good.* The last thing I need is any attention from my family right now. I hurry back to the kitchen and start to look for something that can come to my rescue, banging the cupboard doors open in desperation.

Wax paper? No, too stiff. Kitchen roll? No, that'll go the same way as the toilet roll. A Tupperware container? No, Sandra will miss it. *Ah ha!* I see a roll of cling film and grab it. Perfect!

Jamie and Pops are still pre-occupied with their game so don't see me scuttle back to the bathroom, unravelling the cling film as I go.

Back inside, I tear off the large strip of cellophane I've gathered in one hand, gird my loins, and plunge towards the offending article. Trying my hardest not to regurgitate my breakfast I squidge my cling film-covered hand around my waste material and pluck it from its watery home. As quickly as possible I wrap it completely in the cling film, creating a small brown parcel of unloveliness that I can't wait to get rid of.

I walk back into the kitchen to find the bin. My plan is to drop the package into it, then take out the bin liner to the enormous refuse bin Bob and Sandra have sat next to the garage. That'll solve my problem, as well as making it look like we've gone that extra mile in tidying up the house before we leave.

The location of the bin is not immediately apparent. It must be one of those internal jobbies that fasten to the cupboard door. Jamie cleared away all the breakfast mess, so I have no idea which cupboard it may be behind.

Great, now I have to hold a cling-film wrapped poo in my hand while I search through somebody else's kitchen cabinets for what feels like the tenth time this morning.

I start the ritual of opening and closing once more, but am interrupted by a sharp child's scream coming from outside.

*Poppy!*

Without thinking twice, I fling my poo parcel onto the counter next to the thank-you note and run towards the front door, calling my daughter's name. Out by the car, I can see her held in Jamie's arms, wailing at the top of her voice.

'What happened?' I ask, taking her from her father.

'She fell over, that's all,' he explains. 'Got a little too carried away playing ball and went arse over tea-kettle.'

'Aw baby,' I console, and start to rock Pops back and forth in my arms. 'Don't worry, it's all alright. You're fine, sweetheart.'

I know I'm probably being over-protective, but that sharp, shrill screech of pain was absolutely horrible.

'Hurt my hand, Mummy,' Poppy says between the tears and shows me her newly scratched palm.

'I know sweetheart.'

Jamie really should be more careful with her when they're playing on a hard surface. I turn to berate him appropriately and see that he has gone from my side. I look round and to my horror I see him closing the front door.

'No, Jamie!' I bark and hold out one hand.

But it's too late. *Far, far* too late.

The door slams. 'Oh Christ no!' I shriek.

'What's the matter? You were all done, weren't you?' Jamie says. 'I got everything out okay.'

All thoughts of Poppy's scratched hand are gone. I may love my daughter, but even her misery has to take a back seat when her mother has just left a smelly brown present on a kitchen counter with no way of retrieving it.

'No, Jamie,' I splutter, my mind trying hard to comprehend the disaster that's just befallen me. 'I left something, Jamie . . . I have to get back in, Jamie.'

'You can't. They said the door locks behind when you close it. What have you left in there? We didn't have anything else, did we?'

I look from the door to my husband, back to the door again and for a final time back at Jamie. I open my mouth to start to explain, then immediately close it again.

How exactly *do* I describe the current situation? How do I explain that when Bob and Sandra return home later they will discover a thank-you note left by me, along with a very special gift? The kind they are not likely to forget in a fucking hurry?

And what's even worse is that I never got the chance to finish the bloody note by signing Poppy's name, so they're likely to get the impression that I'm including my poo parcel in the thank you . . . like it's a member of our bloody family.

I can picture their honest, hard-working faces as they discover their prize.

Actually, no I bloody can't. I doubt that anyone has ever returned home before to find faeces covered in cellophane on their kitchen counter. There simply hasn't been a facial expression invented yet to deal with such a bizarre occurrence.

I flap one hand at the front door and give my husband a distraught look. 'There's poo, Jamie.' Hand flap, hand flap. 'Poo, Jamie. There is poo.'

Now he really thinks I've lost it. 'What? Poo? What are you on about?'

I try to slow my breathing and come up with a coherent way of telling him why I'm so distressed, but the calamity of it all robs me of the ability to think straight. All I can do is flap my hand at the door again. 'Poo, Jamie. Poo.'

Now the word has ceased to mean anything. I've said poo so many times in the past minute that it's lost all connection to the real world.

'Poo, poo,' I repeat. I sound like a pigeon with a speech impediment.

'Laura, for crying out loud, stop saying "poo" and tell me what's going on.'

It takes me a good five minutes to calm down and make Jamie fully comprehend the horror of what's happened.

'Are you fu—*fudging* mental?' he says when I finish my

tale of woe, which doesn't really help matters. 'We're never going to be able to look them in the face again!' His face has gone very pale.

'I don't know what you're worried about, it was my poo.'

'Well they don't know that, do they? I hardly think it matters which one of us was responsible! Either way it looks like we're rewarding them for their hospitality with a lump of cling-filmed shit!'

'Daddy said a swear!'

'Sorry, honey.'

'I know, Jamie! What are we going to do?' I ask desperately.

'Move back to the UK? I can get us on flights by this evening if I go on Expedia right now.'

We both lapse into silence, trying to think of a way out of this horrendous state of affairs. Even Poppy has gone quiet, but I think that has more to do with inspecting the new scratch on her hand than her parents' current predicament.

'We're just going to have to leave,' Jamie eventually admits. 'And hope we don't bump into them any time soon.'

'I guess so.'

Then my blood freezes. 'What if Sandra tries to *unwrap* it?'

'I don't know. But if she has trouble and gets Bob involved it'll make the worst game of pass the parcel in fucking history.'

'Daddy!'

We drove away with our tails figuratively between our

legs, Mum. The car ride to our letting agents was conducted in silence. There simply weren't any words.

That was over three days ago now. We haven't seen Bob or Sandra since. I spotted the top of Bob's hat the other day from behind a bush and went and hid for twenty minutes in the outside loo by the swimming pool. Sooner or later we're bound to bump into them, though. It's inevitable. I haven't told Jamie yet, but if I do see them I'm going to blame the incident on his strange bathroom habits.

If he can lie about my bowel movements to get us out of Grant's and Ellie's house, I can sure as hell convince Bob and Sandra that my husband has a rare kind of OCD where he has to wrap his crap in cling film and leave it lying around the house.

If they don't believe that I'll just give them all my money and run away screaming.

Love you, miss you . . . and if there is a God, can you call him an utter git for letting this happen to me?

Your Bob-dodging daughter, Laura.

xx

# Jamie's Blog

# Thursday 21 September

Unbelievably, this is an actual conversation I had with a spotty, overweight teenage girl yesterday morning:

'Excuse me?'

'How you going?'

'Fine, thank you.'

'What can I get you? We've got a special on our winter flavours range, including rum and raisin.'

'Er, I'm not actually here to buy an ice cream.'

'Okay.'

'I came in because I saw your advert for part-time staff.'

'Oh, right.'

'Do you have any application forms?'

'Yeah . . . is it for your kid?'

'My *kid*? How old do you think I am?

'I don't know. Old enough to have a kid who wants a job in a Baskin Robbins?'

'My kid isn't even four yet. She'd just eat all the stock and then throw up. The application form is for me.'

'But why would you want one?'

'Because I'd like to apply for the job here.'

'*You* want to work *here*?'

'I'm not so sure I'd say *want to*, but I need a job so here I am.'

'Okay. I'm not so sure you're quite what the manager has in mind.'

'What's that supposed to mean?'

'Well, the rest of us are all . . . a bit *younger*. And we're kind of all, you know, *girls*.'

'So? All you need is someone who can scoop ice cream. I can do that.'

'Yeah, but . . . it might not give quite the right, you know, *impression*?'

'What do you mean? There's nothing wrong with me working here. Nothing wrong with a man in his thirties working alongside a load of teenage girls who—'

'You okay?'

'Not really. I've just realised what I'm doing.'

'Yeah?'

'Yeah. I sound like a sex offender, don't I?'

'A little bit, yeah.'

'Hmmm. Sorry about that. Can I just have a rum and raisin and we'll call it quits?'

I've reached a new low, it would seem.

There have so few jobs around that when I saw the advert scrawled on a piece of cardboard and placed in the ice-cream shop window, the sheer novelty of it over-whelmed me, so I went in to apply. I really am at the end of my tether. We've been in Australia now for nearly ten months and I've earned roughly what I could have accrued on a paper round back in the UK.

What work I have been able to nail down has been

patchy at best, and if it weren't for the connections I've made over at the youth hostel, work would be completely non-existent. They liked the first job I did for them so much that they asked me to write their promotional brochure copy for the summer season, which I was more than happy to do. That led to similar work with one of the local surf schools and a pretentious hotel in Rainbow Bay called 'Aquous' that caters for rich idiots who wouldn't know a tasteful colour-scheme if it bit them on the arse. I tried to point out that there was at least one too many letter 'U's in the name of the hotel, but nobody seemed interested.

And that's it. In over nine months that's all the gainful employment Jamie Newman has been able to conjure up for himself and his family. Only two and a half thousand dollars' worth of work in the same period Laura has earned over fifteen times as much.

It's quite pathetic.

It's also going to cause a divorce if I'm not very careful about it. Half the reason I made a fool out of myself in Baskin Robbins was down to the row Laura and I had over the breakfast bar at seven thirty before she left for work.

It started, as they all do these days, when the subject of money was brought up. It was one of my days to have Poppy and I wanted to take her to the cinema. Australian movie theatre prices are extortionate and my wallet was feeling pretty light, so I took a deep breath and swallowed my self-esteem by saying the following to my wife: 'Can I have some money, baby? I want to take Pops to see that new Disney flick about the singing beavers.'

If Laura had just nodded, said *No worries*, gone into her purse and handed over a few notes, we might have got through the emasculating exchange with no further difficulties. As it was, she said 'No worries,' went into her purse to look for some cash to give me . . . and *sighed*.

Now, there are many reasons why a person may sigh. Tiredness, boredom, remorse, loneliness and self-satisfaction are all good reasons for emitting a noise that sounds like a tyre being deflated. This wasn't any one of those kinds of sigh, though. *Oh no*. This was a sigh heavily laden with a cocktail of exasperation, resignation and *pity*.

'What's that supposed to mean?' I say in haughty fashion.

'I didn't say anything.'

'You didn't have to. You sighed.'

'So what?'

I cross my arms and sit up ramrod straight. 'If you don't want to give me any of your blo—*blooming* money, Laura, then don't. I'll just take Poppy to the swings again.'

'Oh give me a break, Jamie,' Laura says and shakes two twenties at me. 'Just take the money, will you?'

'Nope. You're obviously not happy about handing it over, so you keep it.'

'I don't mind giving you cash, Jamie,' Laura hisses from between teeth now firmly clamped together.

'Really? That sigh says otherwise.'

'Oh for fu—*fudge's* sake. I didn't even realise I was sighing.'

'No. I bet you didn't. Says a lot though, doesn't it?'

'What do you mean?'

'You think I'm a loser.'

'What?'

'You think I'm a loser because I can't get any work and need to come to you for handouts.'

Yes, I'm well aware that I sound like a spoiled housewife right now, but you have to understand that this wretched display on my part is the culmination of nine months of constant frustration. If I'm honest with myself it also comes from a place of deep insecurity and jealousy at the level of success my wife is experiencing in her career. My situation is not Laura's fault and I'm being very unfair. Hell, it's not my fault either, but when you feel like your back's against the wall you have to lash out at someone, and my poor Laura is the only target within shouting distance who isn't three and a half years old and watching cartoons.

'I don't think you're a loser,' Laura rebuts and gets off her stool in an attempt to end this silly conversation.

'Yes you do!' I snap, following her over to where she's retrieving her jacket from the cupboard. 'You hate the fact I haven't found a proper job yet, I can tell. I've had plenty of time to think about it.'

'I bet you have.'

'You see?! That was another dig!'

'Oh God, I'm *sorry*, Jamie. I just—'

'Just what?'

'I just wish you'd find *something*. Every morning I have to get up and go to work, while you just stay here in your pyjamas.'

'You think I *like* it?'

'I don't know. Maybe you *do*? Even if you don't want to admit it to yourself, it might be why you haven't found proper work yet?'

'Because I like sitting around on my arse doing nothing?!'

Laura throws her hands up. 'Oh, I give up!' She storms over to Poppy and gives her a kiss.

'Are you and Daddy mad at each other?' our daughter asks, her earnest little face drawn into an unhappy frown.

I hate having a child around when I'm building up a head of steam. When all you want to do is rant at someone it really puts you off your stride when somebody else empties a full bucket of guilt over your head.

'No, honey,' I say in a soothing voice. 'Mummy and Daddy are fine, we're just talking about things a bit too loudly because Mummy has a lot of wax in her ears.'

Laura throws me a look that would have chopped my head off if I hadn't ducked in time.

'Yes, that's right, Pops. Mummy has waxy ears,' Laura is forced to agree to maintain the fiction. 'That's why we're being loud. Now watch your cartoon and ignore us.'

Laura stalks back to the front door. 'You'd better stop blaming all our problems on things that are wrong with my body, Newman,' she says as she throws it open.

'Otherwise I'm going to do something to a part of your anatomy in the middle of the night that really will give you an excuse not to go out and find a fu—*fudging* job!'

The door closes loudly before I get a chance to respond.

I trudge back over to the breakfast bar and the two twenty-dollar notes crumpled up next to my half-eaten bit of toast. I don't want to pick them up and put them in my pocket, but I do anyway.

Poppy enjoyed the animated flick about the singing beavers. I really didn't. There was one song called 'Giving It Your Best' which just seemed to be mocking me throughout. I don't need a bunch of pixels rendered into the shape of a grinning beaver to remind me that I'm not living up to one hundred per cent of my potential. By the time the main beaver had learned a valuable lesson about hard work and trusting your friends I wanted to smash his big stupid front teeth in and burn down the family lodge.

I spent the rest of the afternoon trying to entertain my daughter, and thinking of ways to apologise to Laura when she got home.

To tell the truth I wasn't feeling all that apologetic, but anything for an easy life, eh? Laura took the apology with good grace I think, though the kiss I got that night before we went to sleep was perfunctory at best and cold at worst.

I lay next to her for a good twenty minutes before I drifted off, hating myself, hating her, hating Worongabba, hating Australia and hating myself again just to sandwich my bile in self-loathing.

You can imagine what kind of mood I was in when I woke up this morning. Not only did I have yesterday's fun and games to mull over, I also had the unlovely prospect of an entire day on my own as Laura was taking Poppy to Surf Tots.

Nine long hours of strangling out a few paragraphs featuring the Boobatrons, dolefully walking through the town centre looking for work, and masturbating bitterly in the bathroom while the washing machine cleans the underwear I was wearing last time I'd cracked one out.

Laura and I didn't argue before she left for work, but the kiss was just as abrupt as the one she'd delivered the night before, and even Poppy didn't seem all that bothered about not spending the day with her daddy. I can't blame her. Even at the age of three you know that yet another day with a depressed parent is going to be a right downer. The choice between that and occupying yourself drawing all over the face of another toddler with a marker pen is a no-brainer.

The front door closes with a slam – my absolute *least* favourite sound in the world these days – and I stare at the wall contemplating my next move. This only takes up about three seconds of my time, so I decide to go for a lengthy and satisfying crap.

Half an hour later I'm sat at the laptop trying to think of a way to get Max Danger out of his current predicament in the novel I'm still trying to piece together. He's backed up against the wall of a Moroccan hashish den by three heavily armed Smegma agents with nowhere to go. He's either going to have to shoot the light out above his head to plunge the room into darkness and make his escape, or kick that enormous bong full of water at his enemies as a distraction before shooting all of them dead.

I never got on all that well with marijuana when I was a teenager so elect for the black-out option. Max's bullet is finding its target successfully when I hear a knock at the door.

*Fabulous.* Just when I'm building up a head of creative steam someone has to come along to interrupt my genius. With a huff, I get up from the table and walk over to the door. I fully intend to give whoever is on the other side the royal stink eye for their dreadful timing.

My pre-prepared look of disgust disappears when I open the door to find the happy, open face of Mindy the twenty-year-old letting agent beaming at me from the corridor.

'Hi, Mr Newman, how you going?'

'Hi, Mindy. Fine thanks.'

Though I'd be even better if you could take your cute blonde head away from my door so I can get back to the tricky business of saving Max Danger's life.

'Stoked!'

I remember that this means 'good' in Mindy's odd parlance.

'What can I do for you, Mindy?'

I'm expecting her to tell me she needs to inspect the apartment, or that the rent is late again. The banking system in Australia is mired in the nineties and the direct debit we have set up has been late on no less than three occasions in the time we've been living here.

'Just wondering what you were up to today?'

'Er, not much. Just doing a bit of writing.'

'Cool! What are you writing about?'

'Um . . . it's a novel. A thriller.'

'Wow, that sounds great!'

I wish Mindy would tell my wife that. The only reaction I've had from Laura about *Max Danger and the Boobatrons* is a look of ambivalence and some brief noncommittal remarks that are obviously designed to humour me.

'Thanks very much.'

'You think you'll be doing that all day?'

'I wouldn't have thought so. I usually just write in the morning.'

'Oh right. You fancy coming for a swim in the pool later?'

'Sorry?'

'I just get a bit bored when there's nobody else around and I know you work from home so I thought I'd ask . . .'

'Ah. I see.'

Well this is all very strange. I've barely said two words to Mindy in the past few months. For her to come up to the apartment and ask me something like this must mean the poor girl is even more bored than I am. If your main source of potential company is a moody Pom in his thirties, it might be time to think about changing careers. Still, what the hell else am I doing today?

'Okay, sure. Give me another hour and I'll meet you after lunch at one?'

Mindy's bright, tanned and youthful face lights up. It's

nice to see I can put a smile on at least one female's face today. 'Great! I'm stoked! I'll bring a couple of beers along if you like?'

'Fine by me.'

'Okay, I'll see you later then . . . Jamie.'

'You will indeed,' I reply, a bit taken aback by Mindy's sudden informality.

She bobs up and down on the spot for a second before turning and walking quickly back down the stairs.

I close the door again in a slightly better mood than when I opened it. It'll be nice to have some adult human company for a while. Well, nearly adult, anyway. Mindy wouldn't be my first choice of conversation partner, but as the only other choices I have are the spotty girl in Baskin Robbins, the homeless guy who sits on the board-walk feeding the pigeons, and the customer services department at the National Australia Bank, I'm happy to while away an hour or two in her company. Besides, she'll be wearing a bikini, and with any luck and I can occupy my time in the mental pursuit of erection avoidance if the conversation does dry up.

With a slight spring in my step, I return to the laptop and the thorny problem of Max Danger's escape.

In the end I just went for brute force and in the half-light streaming from one shuttered window I had Max kick all the enemy agents in the knackers. Not the most subtle of tactics, but massively effective, I think you'll agree.

My waistline suggests I should have a light lunch, as do the old wives' tales about not swimming on a full stomach. But to hell with it, I'm a married man and never believed in anything an old wife has had to say, so I make myself a monster double-bacon sandwich with eggs, mushrooms and enough cholesterol to block the channel tunnel.

With that disposed of I throw on the board shorts, fling a towel over one shoulder, grab up the iPhone in case anyone rings about a job (ha! chance would be a fine thing) and make my way down the stairs to the pool area below.

Mindy hasn't arrived yet, so I stick the towel on a chair, drop the phone onto the small table next to it, step out of my flip-flops and dip a speculative toe in the water.

Today is a bright, sunny hot one so the pool's heater hasn't been turned on. This means the water is just about cold enough to be uncomfortable. Not freezing, *per se*. Certainly not chilly enough to prevent a swim, but still cool enough to make the process of entry into the water a tentative and unpleasant one, especially when the water-line reaches your testicles.

I'm just debating whether I should man up and dive in when I see Mindy walking towards me carrying a six-pack. She's wearing a bright red bikini that covers about two square inches of her golden body.

'Hey, Jamie!'

'Hmmm?'

'You okay?'

'Hmmm?'

'Jamie?'

'. . .'

'You want a beer?'

'What? Oh, yes please.'

Mindy hands over the six-pack and I wrench a tin from the plastic ring. At the same time I subconsciously attempt to suck in my gut, not a particularly comfortable thing to do when you're full of messy bacon sandwich.

The letting agency trainee – and part-time supermodel if she has any sense – takes her own tin and lays down on one of the sun beds that surround the pool. 'This is great. I'm normally out here on my own so I'm wrapped I've got some company.'

'Won't your boss mind you doing this while you're supposed to be working?' I ask, lowering myself slowly onto the sun bed next to her, which isn't an easy process with all the sucking in of stomach muscles.

'Nah. They never come down here unless they have to. As long as they think the place is running smoothly they're happy. Besides, if the phone goes I can hear it from here anyway.'

Mindy takes a sip of beer and I sneak a customary look at her boobs. I can see an awful lot of them as the red bikini she's got on is one of the tiny ones you'd usually find in your average copy of *Playboy*.

Thankfully, all the effort I'm employing to stop my gut from rolling out over my board shorts is preventing any blood from going to my penis. 'What about friends? I remember you talked about some guy called Dan?'

'Things didn't work out with Dan and my friends are all working. I wouldn't want to risk any of the tenants telling my boss I've had any of my girls over anyway.'

'That's a shame.'

Mindy dazzles me with a bright, open smile. 'Doesn't matter. You're here, yeah? And you're a lot cooler than most of my friends.'

*Oh, I see . . .*

Now I understand why Mindy asked me to join her today. She's stark-staring insane. That can be the only explanation for her last comment.

For some reason this revelation makes me feel better. Mindy's grip on the real world must be tenuous at best, so I figure there's no point in standing on ceremony. I slowly relax my stomach muscles and let my spare tyre free.

'What's your thriller about?' Mindy asks with genuine interest. I explain the brief plot details of *Max Danger and the Boobatrons* to her. 'Oh wow, that sounds really original,' she says.

This statement once again confirms my diagnosis of her poor mental state. Such a shame. Here she is, an otherwise incredibly attractive and bubbly girl with her whole life in front of her, and she's likely to end up in a padded cell before she's thirty.

'Thanks,' I reply and take another sip of beer.

'What's your wife's name again? I see her most mornings when she's going to work.'

'It's Laura.'

'She works a lot of hours, yeah?'

'Yeah. Too many.'

'Out all day it looks like.'

'Yep.'

'Takes your little girl with her most of the time as well.'

Boy, for someone who comes across as a bit of an airhead on first inspection, Mindy is an extremely observant girl. 'She does.'

'Leaves you on your own a lot then?'

'That's right.'

Mindy takes a long draw on her beer, looking at me over the neck of the bottle. 'You wanna take a swim, Jamie?'

Given the fact I can feel rivulets of sweat running down my back and into my arse crack, I'd say that's a terrific idea. I nod my head and put my beer on the ground. 'Don't try racing me though. I'm a lot older than you. You'll hammer me!'

Mindy stands up slowly. I can't help but watch how her leg and stomach muscles flex under her tanned skin, and the way her breasts strain at the bikini top when she stands fully upright and takes a long, catlike stretch.

'You're not that old, Jamie,' she says and pads softly past me towards the shallow end. 'I don't think you look a day over twenty-five.'

*Mad.*

Absolutely certifiable.

And possibly blind.

I follow her wiggling bottom down to the end of pool and my gut involuntarily sucks itself in again. Mindy walks down the steps into the cool water and with a squeal of delight starts to swim towards the deep end. I get as far as the first step down, with barely my ankles covered, before starting to regret the decision to get wet. If anything, it's colder at the shallow end than it is over by where I dipped my foot in halfway down. This section of the pool in the shade and the glorious mid-afternoon sun hasn't had a chance to warm it up. But I've committed myself now, haven't I? I'm going to look a right softie if I don't follow Mindy into the water.

'Come on, Jamie!' Mindy shouts from down at the deep end.

I smile, wave and take a deep breath.

With far more bravery than I'm used to exerting I march down the steps and into the water, submerging myself up to the neck.

'Hawoooofa!' I exclaim as the cold water sends the shock up my spine.

*Well done, Jamie. At least you don't look like a complete homosexual now.*

In fact, once the initial shock has worn off the water feels quite pleasant and I start to swim towards Mindy and into the sunny part of the pool.

'The water's really good today,' she says as I reach her.

'Yeah, it is.'

It's also doing a good job of hiding my spare tyre and doughy physique as well, which can only be a good thing when in the company of someone as lithe, brown and annoyingly fit as Mindy.

She giggles, splashes me and takes off back towards the shallow end.

'Come back here!' I shout with a chuckle and go after her.

No. I had *no* idea what was really going on at this point, in case you were wondering. I know that this whole situation has a very obvious undercurrent to it, but it wasn't one I could see at the time, okay?

Don't worry, Mindy will make me painfully aware of it very shortly. But first, there's some agonizing cramp to deal with . . .

I'm halfway to Mindy, intent on ducking her head under the water when I catch her, when searing, immediate pain rockets down my leg. It seems that the old wives' tale might not be so inaccurate after all. My right thigh feels like someone's jabbed a red hot poker into it.

'Aaargghh!' I scream and grab my leg. This is not the best course of action when still slightly out of your depth in a swimming pool, so my next exclamation of pain is swallowed up by the pool water as my head goes under.

Great. Now I not only have the cramp from hell, I'm also choking to death. Panic sets in and I start thrashing about, secure in the knowledge I'm about to drown in less than six feet of water. Then I feel Mindy's breasts against my back and everything isn't quite so bad after all.

'Are you okay?' she asks, one arm clamped around my chest.

'Cramp!'

'Where?'

'Right thigh. Really painful.'

'Okay, hang on. I'll get you to the shallow end. Just relax, I used to be a surf lifesaver.'

And I bet all her skills and experience are coming into play now, as she has to manhandle a fully grown man through the treacherous shallow waters of a medium-sized swimming pool on a bright, sunny day.

*Good grief.* How embarrassing.

Mindy helps me back up the pool steps and onto dry land. The cramp is so painful I have to lean on her as we make our way back over to the sun beds.

'Here, lie down and I'll take a look at it,' Mindy says. With a wince I sit down and stretch myself out on the plastic bed, trying hard not to groan in agony too much.

Then Mindy kneels next to me and grabs my thigh with both hands. She starts to massage the muscle in an attempt to release the cramp. Initially, I have to throw my head back in pain – body ram-rod straight, but as the massage begins to take effect I start to relax as the cramp dissipates. I close my eyes and rest my head on the back of the sun bed.

'Wow, you're good at that,' I tell Mindy.

'Thanks. Dealt with a lot of cramps like this in my time, so I've had a lot of practice.'

'I'm very grateful,' I murmur, still with my head back and eyes closed.

'No worries. I'm just going to move up your leg a bit. It still feels stiff.'

'Okay.'

'How's that?'

'Great. The cramp's almost all gone.'

'Just a bit higher . . .' Mindy says and I feel the sun bed move as she lowers her bodyweight onto it.

This girl really is thorough. She's not going to stop until that cramp is well and truly—*Hmmm.* I'm pretty sure the cramp doesn't go quite that far up. I open my eyes and lift my head. The sight that greets me would have been all my Christmases and birthdays rolled into one when I was eighteen.

Mindy is now straddling me. I can see right between her boobs thanks to the way she's leaning forward. Her hands are right up my board shorts and more or less in my groin. All at once, I become fully aware of what Mindy's intentions have been since she knocked on my door this morning.

My mind plays out the last couple of hours in a split second and comes to the stupendously obvious conclusion that Mindy the twenty-year-old letting agency trainee wants a piece of Newman. Specifically, the piece her hands are getting closer and closer to by the moment.

'Okay if I go a bit higher?' she says in a low whisper.

I stare at her, struck dumb.

*Jamie?*

*Jamie?*

*This is your conscience.*

Afternoon, conscience. How are you?

*Perturbed.*

Why's that then?

*Well, Jamie, for some reason, you haven't as yet said 'no' to the delightful Mindy's proposition.*

I see.

*As your conscience I must point out that you are married to a rather lovely, intelligent and beautiful woman, with whom you have an equally beautiful daughter.*

This is very true.

*And yet, here we still lie, not telling Mindy to get away from us, as is right and proper in the situation. Can you think of why this is?*

**I know why.**

*Go away, penis, this doesn't concern you in the slightest.*

**Doesn't concern me? This is all about me, pal. She's only a couple of inches from wrapping one hand around me and making this afternoon end with a bang.**

I wish both of you would leave me alone.

**I agree. You just lie back and let me do all the heavy lifting.**

*No. This is wrong. Tell her so, Jamie!*

Mindy's speculative look would be enough to turn any man's bones to water. But then I see the combined faces of my wife and daughter and self-preservation kicks in.

'Um . . . I don't think so, Mindy. Thanks for the offer, though.' I gently pick her hand up and remove it from my thigh.

Mindy looks decidedly disappointed. I get the feeling that it's rare for any man to turn down her considerable charms. 'You sure?' she says, batting her eyelashes and breathing in deeply to push out those fabulous breasts. This one doesn't give up without a fight.

'Yeah. I'm very flattered, but I've got a wife who I love and—'

'Okay, no worries.' The look of disappointment is gone and Mindy is all smiles again. 'You want another beer?'

It's like the last thirty seconds never happened as far as this particular letting agent is concerned.

'I'd better not. I promised Laura I'd clean the flat before she got home, so I'd better get back upstairs.' As excuses go, I could have picked one that didn't emasculate me quite as much. I might just as well have said *'I can't let you give me a handjob because I am my wife's little bitch. Now unhand me, my good lady, for I have dusting to do!'*

'That's a real shame, Jamie. I was having a fun time with you.'

In an instant my mind throws up several different sexual positions I could engage Mindy in during the next couple of hours, and then compares this experience to vacuuming the bedroom carpet. Sometimes life just isn't fair.

'Yeah, it was nice to hang out with you too,' I say. Then, my stupid innate sense of British politeness rears its ugly head. 'Maybe we could do it again sometime?'

*Why did you say that, you idiot?*

I'm trying to be nice!

*Fuck nice! You're just leading her on!*

**Lead her on, baby! Lead her on!**

Shut up!

Mindy smiles and climbs off me. 'I'd like that Jamie . . . very much.' She sits herself back down on the sun bed next to me and sighs. 'I suppose I'd better get back to the office myself. I'm sure I've got some work I could be doing.' Mindy then looks up into the glorious blue sky. I try very hard not to look at the gentle curve of her neck as she does so. 'It's just so lovely out here though.' She lies back down and stretches herself out on the sun bed provocatively. 'A few more minutes can't hurt.'

Not for her maybe, but if I spend any more time in her company I'm likely to explode. I have to leave *right now.*

'Well, see you later, Mindy,' I say in a strangled voice and start to hurry away.

''Bye, Jamie,' Mindy replies in a husky voice that is no doubt deliberately targeted at my libido.

I slam the front door behind me and lean against it, thinking long and hard about what's just happened. A bloom of intense guilt has flowered in my chest, making it hard to breathe. I don't know why I feel so remorseful. Nothing happened after all. I did the right thing and put Mindy off the massage way before it had chance to turn into a happy ending, so why do I still feel so shitty?

*Because you should never have been in that situation in the first place?*

I try my best to ignore my conscience but there's every chance it's right. I should have been a bit more alert to Mindy's intentions, but who'd have thought someone like that would have been interested in somebody like me?

A rather disturbing thought then occurs: what if there was a part of me that knew *damn well* what Mindy was up to, and was quite happy to let it happen? If so, what does that say about the state of my relationship with Laura? Before we came to Australia I'd never so much as looked at another woman, and yet here I am today getting offered a handjob by one after agreeing to take a swim with her and her pneumatic breasts.

Either I've become so socially inept that I can't detect when a woman is overtly coming on to me, or my marriage has reached such a bad stage that I subconsciously welcome that kind of attention.

I spend the next ten minutes leaning against the front door playing all these dreadful thoughts in my mind, and am only moved from the spot when the doorbell rings and frightens the living shit out of me. I open the door to once again see Mindy the temptress standing there in her bikini with a speculative smile on her face, holding out my iPhone in one hand.

I forgot to pick the fucking thing up, which she probably thinks was a deliberate ploy on my part to get her up to the apartment. Her sexually charged smile widens.

'You left your phone by the pool. I thought I'd better return it.'

'Thanks.'

'You should really be more careful. This is a great phone. I love the camera on it.'

'Yep. Great camera!'

*Christ, this is excruciating.*

'Anyone would think you wanted me to—'

'Great camera. Great phone. Thanks for bringing it back. Bye now!' I snatch the phone out of her hand, shut the door in her face and run into the bedroom to hide myself under the duvet. I'm fairly sure I hear Mindy's footsteps going back down the stairs almost immediately, but decide that discretion is the better part of valour and stay hidden for another twenty minutes.

I spend the rest of the day suffering from an inexplicable pain in the penis. I'm sure this is entirely deliberate on its part.

# Laura's Diary

## Tuesday, October 6th

Dear Mum,

Why is it that men never seem to grow up?

No matter what success they have in life, or how many years of adult experience they've had, they can still revert to being little boys at the drop of a hat. This doesn't happen all the time of course. If it did, they couldn't have fought all those wars, built all those cities and gone to the moon.

To be fair, acting like a little boy can be endearing in the right circumstances. A fully grown male hunched over a half-finished Airfix Spitfire model, with tongue stuck out in intense concentration as he tries to stick the wing to the fuselage, is something you can take a great deal of pleasure in.

Most of the time though, the reversion back to childhood can be intensely irritating. They can turn into emotionally unstable, petulant little idiots at the drop of a hat. In my experience of such matters, I've come to the conclusion that this only tends to happen when there is a vagina in close proximity to them. Usually mine, but I'm sure any vagina would have much the same effect on their fragile psyches.

First case in point – my husband. He's always had his moments in the past (the reaction he had when I told him about Mike when we first started dating springs to mind) but Jamie is one of the more level-headed men I've met in my life.

That was until we arrived in Australia and I became the main breadwinner of the family. Since then we've descended to the stage where I feel like I have to look after two three year olds instead of one.

I'm *convinced* that things would be very different if I was a man. If Jamie lived with a male friend and he paid most of the bills, my husband probably wouldn't give two hoots. Oh, he might feel a bit out of sorts, but not the ridiculous extent I'm faced with each and every day, thanks to the fact I am the proud owner of a neatly trimmed lady garden.

There's something buried deep within every man that just cannot accept it when a woman is perceived to be more successful than him, even when it's his own bloody wife. Rather than dealing with the sense of inequality in an adult fashion, the little boy inside Jamie has come out to play more and more frequently in the past few months.

'Jamie? Are you actually throwing a tantrum in the frozen food aisle?' I ask my husband in a calm voice. It's tinged with a degree of disbelief, as I can't believe I'm witnessing this display – stood as we are in the middle of the local Woolworths supermarket on a warm Sunday afternoon in October. I only told him I didn't want to eat burgers again, before asking him to put the packet back in the freezer.

'But I want burgers,' he scowls at me.

'We have them every week. I'm bored to tears with burgers.' I'm also developing a tension headache. We've been in here for a good hour and a half and the strip lights overhead are brighter than the ones they have on the runway at Heathrow. 'Just put them back and get something else.'

'But I want burgers!' he repeats emphatically.

'Put them back!' the headache snaps.

'Fine!' Jamie snatches the frozen bag of meat from the shopping trolley, throws open the freezer door with such vehemence that the handle nearly smashes into the next door along, chucks the burger bag so hard it bursts, and then slams the door shut again, making the whole cabinet rattle. This is when the disbelief kicks in.

'Don't you think you're being just a bit childish?' I say to him as he stands there seething. 'Even Poppy here doesn't act that way when I tell her she can't have more sweets.'

'Well, you do sound like my fu—*fudging* mother, Laura,' he replies with a sneer. 'Perhaps if you didn't control the purse strings quite as much I wouldn't feel like I was your second child.'

'And perhaps if you—'

I stop myself. What I'm about to say won't help the situation one bit. Besides, I know Pops is starting to get a bit upset from her seat in the shopping trolley. She's heard her mummy and daddy snapping at each other too much recently, which pierces my heart. I know Jamie hates it too.

'Perhaps if I what?' he says, leaning forward.

'Nothing, Jamie.' My eyes flick down to our daughter. Jamie gets my point.

'Alright, we'll have something else instead.' He leans down to Poppy's height. 'Why don't we let Pops decide? What do you want, sweetheart?' His tone of voice is light, but I can tell that the anger is very much still there and bubbling just beneath the surface.

'Can we have turkey dinosaurs?'

She says it in such a sweet, little lost voice that I hate myself and my husband for the way we're acting around her these days. Jamie and I both despise turkey dinosaurs, but our combined, unspoken guilt means we come home with three bags of the bloody things today.

The argument we end up having once Poppy is in bed is the same one we've been having for weeks. We're both so bored by it now that we can only muster about ten minutes of vitriol before giving up on the whole thing.

The sex we have on the couch an hour later is perfunctory and unromantic. I'm not sure whether this is better or worse than if we had continued the argument.

I'm well used to Jamie's occasional regressions into his teenage years, but I was taken completely by surprise yesterday when my boss Alan Brookes developed the same worrying behaviour.

Yesterday started with a lie-in until eight. This is a particularly pleasant way to start your working week and came about because I was due to be in the office until late that evening. Alan had emailed me at the weekend to say he wanted a meeting with me at seven p.m., which made me nervous. When that kind of request comes out of the blue from your boss it usually means you've done something wrong and they mean to chastise you for it. Anyway, the prospect of a meeting with the boss didn't exactly fill me with much joy, even if it did mean I could get up at a reasonable hour for once.

By the time five p.m. rolled around I'd worked myself into a deeply foul mood, partly thanks to the inclement rain that had turned the usually beautiful Gold Coast grey and unpleasant, and partly due to the selection of annoying distributors I've been on the phone with today trying to sort out new transport links to the north of the state. You'd think one person would be enough when attempting to arrange stock delivery dates, but it transpires that you have to speak to at least five before you actually get somewhere.

By seven, the store was empty and closed, so I had the slightly disconcerting sensation of being completely on my own in a place where I'm usually surrounded by people. People are in and out of my first floor office all the time during the day, and the permanent low murmur of passing foot traffic is a constant during opening hours. Once that all disappears it's quiet enough to hear the surf crashing from across the street.

I'm in the middle of an email to my counterpart down in Sydney when I'm frightened out of my skin by Alan appearing at my office door with his usual bombast.

'Evening, Laura!'

'Aaiiee!'

'Strewth, Laura, you're a bit jumpy this evening, aren't

you?' Alan comes and sits in the chair across the desk from me and flashes a grin full of expensive white veneers.

'It's just a little strange being here all on my own.'

'Yep, it's like that round here. Place empties out faster than a tinny with a bullet hole in the bottom when it gets dark.' He leans round to look at my computer screen. 'What are you working on?'

'Just emailing Julia down in Sydney.'

'Pfft. That woman's got a stick up her arse. Gets on well with the wife though, I'll give her that. I just wish I could hold a conversation with her when she doesn't look like she's sucking a lemon.' Alan leans even further over the desk. 'Not like you, Laura. You're an absolute diamond. I don't know what I've had done without you running the show around here.'

'Thank you, Alan.'

'My pleasure!'

I send the email off to Julia – who I've never met, but now have an impression of someone who permanently suffers from pursed lips and a pained expression – and close my email down. 'So, what exactly did you want to talk to me about this evening?'

Alan waves a hand. 'Oh good grief, not here! Let's go somewhere a bit more comfortable. You hungry?'

'Um . . . yes, I guess so.'

Alan stands up. 'Great! Let's get out of here then. There's a nice Italian place about a five-minute walk away.'

'Do you mean Ambrogio?'

'Yep, that's the one.'

Ambrogio is the type of restaurant us mere mortals

walk past as quickly as possible so we don't inadvertently see any prices on the menu and instantly suffer a shock-induced heart attack. Even a glass of water would likely bankrupt me. I can't think of anywhere worse to hold a meeting.

'You like Italian, Laura? My treat!'

*Oh well, if he's paying ...*

'Yes. Love it! Shall we go?'

Now, at this point, the klaxons should have started going off in my head. It is not typical for your boss to invite you to dinner at a costly restaurant if he just wants to talk shop. In my defence, I haven't eaten anything since the chocolate bun I had at about three, so I'm ravenous. The prospect of a bowl of delicately seasoned pasta is enough to make me ignore any warning signs that might be parading in front of my mind's eye. Besides, we are both married to *other people*, which precludes any funny business, doesn't it? I know, I know. I have no idea how I've lived into my thirties displaying that kind of naïvety either.

I'm the first to enter the restaurant so am treated to the full force of the maitre d's stare of disapproval.

I'm in my work suit, which by now is rumpled and creased thanks to the fact I've been dressed in it for ten hours. I look like someone who's just done a full working day, which is to say, pretty damn rough around the edges. The officious little sod can't completely hide a sneer that curls one lip up like it's tied to a piece of string being pulled by a small child from above.

It seems that the good-natured Australian way of not

worrying about class and social standing based on appearance doesn't extend as far as the threshold of Ambrogio. The maître d' is no doubt about to call security when Alan steps through the door behind me and his look of derision turns into one of abject smarm. My extremely rich boss is obviously a regular here.

'Mr Brookes, so nice to see you,' the maitre d' says in an accent thick with Sicilian charm.

'G'day, Baldo,' Alan replies. The guy has a full head of hair, so I can only assume that Baldo is actually his name, or that Alan is shortening it Australian style from something more poetic like Baldallini.

I'm guessing the latter from the rather pained expression that fleetingly crosses the maître d's face.

'A table for two?' he suggests.

'Yep, thanks, Baldo,' Alan agrees and pats him on the back.

Thinking about the way in which I was greeted with a sneer, I smile at the little Italian man. 'Yes, thank you so much, *Baldo*. This really is a lovely restaurant, *Baldo*.' I take no small degree of pleasure from the way he flinches imperceptibly each time I say the name.

Baldo leads us over to a table near the back of the restaurant. There are only three other patrons this evening, so it's lovely and quiet. There's nothing worse than trying to enjoy your food than when there's a constant clamour of voices all around putting you off your linguini and conversation in equal measure.

Baldo has the good grace to hold out the chair for me. 'Thank you, Baldo,' I tell him, savouring the pained expression on his face one more time.

He gives us both a leatherbound menu, tells us our waiter will be over shortly, and retreats to the safety of the front entrance.

I watch him go and then take my first proper look around the restaurant. It's quite exquisite. There are no red and white checked tablecloths and bad paintings of the Leaning Tower of Pisa in sight. This is a classy establishment, decked out in a tasteful mixture of dark blue and cream. The only hints that the theme here is Italian come from the national flags embossed on the front of the menu, and the bistro music being quietly piped into the room. It takes me a minute to recognise that I can hear Dean Martin singing 'That's Amore'.

As soon as I do, I am instantly transported back five years to my old flat and the birthday surprise Jamie laid on for me that day. The memory is so instantly powerful that I have to blink back unexpected tears. I'm not sure whether they're ones of happiness at the memory, or sadness that it seems so long ago.

'You okay, Laura?' Alan asks.

'What? Yes, yes, I'm fine. Just a little tired.' I pick up the water jug and pour myself a glass. 'So Alan, what business would you like to discuss with me?'

'Let's order first, shall we? I'm starved.'

I nod my head, pick up the menu and open it. I groan inwardly as I do. It's all in Italian. I should have expected as much. Any restaurant with a pretentious maitre d' like Baldo was bound to have an incomprehensible menu. The assumption must be that poor people are less likely to speak a foreign language, and by having the menu in

Italian it will likely frighten them away and send them scuttling to the nearest Kentucky Fried Chicken. Hmmm. I could murder a bargain bucket right about now.

Alan obviously catches my look of panicked incomprehension. 'Why don't you let me order? I come here a lot so I know what's good.'

'Okay,' I say with relief and put the menu down. I'd rather have a bit more control over what I eat, but leaving Alan to decide is still infinitely preferable to stumbling my way through an order for 'moscardini lessati alla Genovese', while the waiter rolls his eyes and resists the urge to correct my horrendous pronunciation.

Over comes said waiter and Alan looks up at him with a smile. He then starts to speak in fluent Italian. Well of course he does . . .

Why wouldn't he? It often seems to me that you either need to have enough time to give over to learning a foreign language, or enough money to throw at it. I wait patiently in a complete lack of linguistic understanding as the two men babble back and forth about the order.

This whole thing feels extremely awkward, and I really wish I was back home right now with my husband and daughter. They're probably settling down to a nice dinner of burger and chips, while I'm sat here about to eat God-knows-what on a bed of green pasta.

Eventually the waiter disappears and Alan turns his attention back to me. 'I ordered us some white wine to go with the meal. One glass is okay when you're driving, right?'

'Yeah, I guess so.' I don't normally drink anything when

driving but have to admit that one glass of the glorious white stuff will probably calm my nerves a bit. I am feeling decidedly jumpy right now, for reasons I'm not able to fathom thanks to a combination of hunger and fatigue.

The waiter returns and pours me a glass of the sweetest wine I've ever tasted in my life.

'Good isn't it?' Alan says when he notices how wide-eyed I've gone.

'Yes, *very*,' I reply, taking another sip. There's every chance a bottle of the stuff costs as much as it would take to feed a small African village for a year.

Alan puts his elbows on the table and laces his fingers. 'So, how are things going with you then, Laura?'

'Fine thanks.'

'Everything okay at home, is it?'

'Yes. Why do you ask?'

'Well, I was chatting to Jake the other day and he mentioned you might be having a few problems.'

*Blast.* I knew I shouldn't have confided in my shop manager. Jake is a nice guy, but he couldn't keep a secret if his life depended on it. During several idle conversations at work over the past few months, he's ruined three movies for me by giving away the endings, told me all about Kathy the shop assistant's predilection for sex with strangers, and disturbed me greatly when describing his mother's bowel problems.

I've made the mistake of off-loading my troubles at home onto him, and my tales of marital distress have obviously got back to Alan Brookes. I should learn to keep my mouth shut, but when I'm having a problem with

237

something I like to talk about it, and Jake's the only person around most of the time at work who I can do that with.

If I were back in the UK Mel and Tim would have been getting an earful about my relationship with Jamie, but as they're ten thousand miles away Jake has become an unwitting substitute – and not a very good one apparently, thanks to his loose lips.

'Um, well, my husband's had some problems finding a job,' I tell Alan, fiddling with the stem of my wine glass.

'Gotcha. A writer isn't he?'

'Yes. We thought he'd find more freelance work, but there's not been much about for him.'

'Yeah, sounds about right. A lot of you Poms come over thinking work is easy to get, but if there's any Australians who need the job, they'll always get picked over a foreigner. Not many jobs going round the Gold Coast area in general, to be honest.'

'That's right. It's really not Jamie's fault, but it's still hard for him . . .'

'With you bringing home the bacon and him out of work? Yeah, I can understand that. A fella likes to be the one in charge, doesn't he? Still it must be hard on you as well, Laura.' Alan provides me with the softest, most sympathetic smile I've ever seen him produce.

'It is, Alan, it really is.' I bang my hand on the table in frustration. 'I just wish he'd stop being such a child about it all. It's not my fault if he can't find work is it? But all I get is him moaning at me nearly every day. It's really starting to—' Aghast, I realise what I'm saying. Here I am at a business meeting, whining about Jamie and my personal life.

It's completely inappropriate. 'Sorry, Alan, you don't need to hear all of this.'

'No worries, Laura.' He extends a hand and covers mine for a moment. 'My employee's happiness is very important to me and I always like to know if they've got a problem.'

The warmth of his hand is initially comforting, but when he doesn't remove it again straight away I begin to feel awkward. I have to withdraw my hand from under his instead, going for my wine glass a little quicker than is strictly necessary.

Alan sits back again and sloshes wine around in his glass, before necking the rest of it like he's swigging from a beer bottle. 'Yep, relationships are a bugger sometimes. The wife and I have our moments, I can tell you.'

*Please don't, Alan. This conversation has skirted into some very personal territory and I'm starting to get weirded out by the whole thing.*

'Not about me earning more than her, of course.'

*Oh bugger it.*

'As far as Valerie's concerned my bank balance is my most attractive feature.' Alan pours himself more wine. 'I sometimes think she'd prefer it if I was just a walking ATM that produced money out of my arse whenever she needed it!'

*Oh boy.*

Now we're swimming in some rough waters. I try to think of something positive to say. 'I'm sure it's not just about your money, Alan. She's your wife, I'm sure she loves you.'

Alan snorts derisively. 'Yeah, loves our landscape

gardener Charlie as well, if my next-door neighbour is to be believed.'

*Oh fucking hell.*

'We're barely speaking these days,' he continues. 'She lives down there in Sydney lording it over the social scene and spending all my money, while I stay up here in our holiday apartment in Burleigh Heads, wishing divorces weren't so expensive. I don't know how things got this bad between us, but I can hazard a few guesses.'

*Good grief.*

I think he's about to give me a blow-by-blow account of his marriage break-up. And there was me worried about mentioning the grief I'm having with Jamie.

My bacon is saved by the waiter coming back with our food. He plonks a bowl of ring-shaped tortellini pasta down in front of me, which is topped off with what looks like mushrooms, red pepper and some other unidentifiable vegetables in a rich, red sauce. It smells divine.

Alan has ordered spaghetti with a similar coloured sauce on top. 'Hope you enjoy yours, Laura. It's got a bit of a kick to it, so I hope you don't mind your food a bit spicy.'

This could be tricky. I'm not a fan of spicy food. My digestive system just doesn't get on well with it.

I'd better be polite and give it a go though. The meal probably cost a week's salary. 'I'm sure it's lovely,' I tell him with a doubtful smile and gather up a forkful. Praying to whatever benign deities may be watching, I put the food in my mouth and chew . . .

Sighs of relief all round. It's a little spicy, but also very tasty. I can easily cope with this, providing I eat it nice and slow, chasing it with water when the taste of the chilli gets a little too much. Alan tucks in to his food as well, with none of the care I'm putting into the process.

'This is great,' he says after his first few mouthfuls. 'I can't remember the last time I had such a nice time with a woman in here.'

*Oh strewth, he's about to bring his wife up again.*

I can see him working up to saying something else about her. From the way his eyes have gone all doe-like I can only assume it's going to be emotional for him – and cringe-inducing for me. I fork some pasta into my mouth and baton down the mental hatches.

'You really are a beautiful woman, Laura.'

*What?*

'What?' I say round my mouthful of tortellini.

'Yeah, absolutely stunning, I'd say.'

I start to chew very quickly and look down at my plate. Suddenly its contents have become *extremely* interesting and worthy of constant study.

'You're a free spirit as well. There aren't many women who would be brave enough to wear a swimming costume like the one you had on when we went down the beach.'

*Oh for fuck's sake. I can't believe he remembers that.*

'That day really showed me what an incredible person you are,' Alan continues. 'You remind me of Val when we first met.'

*My, this tortellini really is wonderful.*

'She was a free spirit back then, full of life. Not any more though. Now she's just old and bitter.'

*I wonder how they get the meat stuffed into it like that?*

'You remind me so much of her when we were young.'

*It must be quite a tricky process.*

'But you're even better than her, Laura! You mix that free spirit with a strong head for business.'

*You wouldn't want to put too much in because it'll burst the pasta, but then if you don't put enough in, you won't be able to taste the meat properly.*

'I wanted to tell you all this, Laura. That's why I invited you to dinner tonight.'

*Oh look! A lovely big bit of pepper on this piece of tortellini. Let's see what it tastes like shall we?*

'The truth is, Laura . . .'

*Crunch. Crunch.*

'You see the truth is . . .'

*Crunch. Cru—hang on, this isn't pepper.*

'I think I'm falling in love with you.'

*It's a bit of fucking chilli!*

As the intense heat hits the roof of my mouth I instinctively spit what remains of the chilli and pasta out, spraying the man who's just declared his undying love for me in half-digested food.

Coughing like a lunatic I throw water down my gullet in an attempt to quench the fire.

Gasping, I see Alan clean off his grimacing face with a napkin. 'Christ. That wasn't the reaction I was hoping for.'

'Sor—sorry!' I say and take another gulp of water.

Sadly I also manage to gulp a load of air at the same time, causing me to then produce a chilli-flavoured burp of Homer Simpson-like proportions. Well, if you want to put a man off you romantically, spitting food at him and then belching in his face is as good a way of doing it as any, I suppose.

Alan waves a hand in front of his face. 'Strewth. Better out than in!'

Pushing the plate away from me, I take a deep breath, another gulp of water and attempt to sit up as straight as I can. 'I think it might be best,' I say, mustering what remains of my dignity, 'if I went home now, Alan.'

'Oh, okay,' he replies sullenly.

'I apologise for gobbing my food onto you.'

'No worries. I shouldn't have ordered something so spicy.'

'Quite possibly.'

The doe-eyed look returns. 'You will think about what I said though, won't you? About my feelings for you?' His heart-felt, romantic tone is ruined somewhat by the blob of masticated pasta still stuck to his forehead.

'This is all . . . all very strange.' I actually manage to produce a scowl. 'I thought this was going to be a business meeting.'

'I know, I should have been honest with you months ago. I really do love you, Laura.' His voice has gone up a couple of octaves.

'No you bloody don't!'

'Yes I do.'

'You only think that because I remind you of your wife when she was younger. You just told me that.'

Alan stamps one foot under the table. 'That's not it. I love you!'

243

Oh for crying out loud, now I'm dealing with a love-struck teenager, rather than a multi-millionaire businessman. My tone of voice changes into what can only be described as 'parent mode'.

'Now you look here, Alan Brookes,' I say, waggling a finger. 'You brought me here under false pretences. You can't just spring this kind of thing on a girl. You're my boss.'

'Sorry, Laura.'

'What?'

'I said I'm sorry, Laura. I just couldn't think of any other way to come out with it.'

'You shouldn't have come out with it *at all*. We're both happ—We're both married!'

'But I can't help the way I feel.'

I look at his puppy dog eyes and frustration boils over. This is *completely* unfair.

If this was a man who didn't write my monthly cheques, I'd be able to deal with the situation easily. I'd simply make it bloody clear that I wasn't interested in him in that way and show him my heels.

But Alan Brookes is my boss, and apparently a sixteen-year-old boy again. Teenage boys don't take well to rejection. If I storm out of here, I could be cooking my own goose. Alan can fire me at a whim if he so chooses. Therefore, despite the fact that I'd like to just tell this lovesick idiot that I have no interest in him, I'll have to soften my approach a bit – unless I want to join Jamie huddled over the job ads every day.

'Look, Alan,' I say in a softer tone. 'I'm very, very flattered by all of this. You're a wonderful, handsome man.'

*That's good, girl. Massage his ego a bit.*

'But I have a husband and a daughter to think about.'

He hangs his head. 'I know. This is totally wrong of me.'

'No, it isn't.'

I see a spark of hope in his eyes.

*Shit.* That was the wrong thing to say. I may have gone a bit over the top here in my desire to keep him sweet. 'I mean, it was a lovely gesture,' I say, trying to back track.

It's no good though, the damage is done. That light in his eyes isn't going out now. I figure I'd better get out of this before I bury myself in an even deeper hole.

'I'm going to leave now, Alan. This is all very confusing and I need some time on my own. Will I see you at the meeting with the distributors on Friday?' I add.

'Yes, I'll be there.'

'Good.' I stand up. 'Well, I hope you enjoy the rest of your evening.' I point at his forehead. 'You may want to check your face in the mirror. Goodnight.'

With that, I walk off towards the exit, passing Baldo without so much as a glance.

By the time I get back to the car I'm fully in shock. My boss has just told me he's in love with me. I have responded by pebble-dashing his face with red hot pasta and chastised him like he was a naughty schoolboy caught setting fire to worms in the back yard with a magnifying glass. Then I have changed tack completely in an effort at self-preservation and managed to lead him in on. Talk about your mixed signals.

Where does this leave me now, Mum? I have to keep

working with this man, but how am I supposed to after what transpired this evening?

I know, I'll do what any self-respecting woman would do in similar circumstances: completely ignore the issue and hope it goes away. Yeah, that's constructive, isn't it? The next time I see Alan I will be all business, and pretend like today never happened. With any luck he will do the same thing. As long as we're never in the same room together alone everything should be fine.

Everything should be absolutely *fine*.

Love and miss you, Mum – as always.

Your apparently free-spirited daughter, Laura.

xx

# Jamie's Blog
## Sunday 12 November

If I were a religious man – which I'm not, otherwise this blog wouldn't be quite so full of swearing – the phrase *'The Lord giveth, and the Lord bloody well taketh away again'* would be one very close to my heart at the moment.

Last month my luck finally changed for the better. I found some work! Well-paid work at that. Nothing permanent, but it was still a fortnight of copywriting that paid me as much money as I would expect to earn from two months' hard graft back home. And I got to do it from the comfort of our apartment. The best commute to work in the world is the one you take from your bedroom to your living room, wearing nothing but your pyjamas and a dressing gown.

The job was with a boat company up in Brisbane, run by the brother of the guy who owns the badly spelled Aquous hotel. He was apparently so pleased with the copy I'd written for him that he told his sibling all about it – who then offered me a gig extolling the virtues of his new speedboat range for the 2013 catalogue. It's not what you know, it's who you know, eh?

'Baby, I've got an idea,' I say in a sleepy voice to

Laura, as we lie in each other's arms on a balmy Gold Coast evening after my first day of work in what felt like forever.

We'd just had sex for the first time in a month. It really is amazing what a boost in your self-esteem can do for your libido.

'An idea?' she replies, idly running a finger across my chest.

'Yep. Your birthday's coming up.'

'Yes, don't remind me.'

'I want to do something nice for it.'

'Like what?'

'Well, this job is going to pay me quite a bit of money, so I can afford to treat you to something nice – if you can get the time off work, that is.'

'To do what?'

'I want to pay for the three of us to have a long weekend up in Cairns. We can do all the touristy stuff like go on the Great Barrier Reef and see Cape Tribulation. It'll be my birthday present to you, if you can get the time off. I know it's really short notice.'

'That sounds lovely, Jamie. I'll book a few days off when I get in tomorrow.'

'Your boss won't mind?'

Laura's eyes narrow. 'No. I'm sure he'll be *fine* with it.'

'Fantastic. You get that sorted and I'll arrange the flights and accommodation.'

'You sure you want to do this? It'll be quite expensive.'

'Absolutely. Things have been pretty crappy between

us, and I want to make it up to you. I really want to do this, Laura.'

'You're quite the romantic when you want to be, Newman,' Laura says and kisses me. Things stir down below. Laura's eyes widen. 'And as horny as a sixteen year old as well, it seems.'

Yes indeed, earning some cold hard cash really does return your mojo to full working order.

And so it was that family Newman boarded a plane from the Gold Coast to Cairns last Thursday, intent on a few days of sun, fun and relaxation. Which we got. For the first thirty-six hours anyway.

Cairns, like a microwaved cucumber, is green and hot. Up in the tropics, the city itself stews uncomfortably in thirty-degree heat most of the year, while stretching beyond it north up the coast are a series of gorgeous beaches that towns have grown up around in the past few decades, mainly for all the tourists that come here from all over the world.

Taking a holiday here is rather like visiting some of the incredible beach locations across South East Asia, without having to worry about learning a foreign language or getting a shot in your arm to protect you from a variety of water-borne diseases. The Cairns area is famous for its wildlife, too, including wild saltwater crocodiles that occasionally pop up along the rivers and creeks, scaring the bejesus out of the locals and taking a bite out of the odd passing dog.

Then there's the small matter of the Great Barrier Reef, which is trying its level best to remain beautiful, despite the best efforts of mankind to kill it off as soon as possible thanks to our relaxed attitude to climate change.

We landed at Cairns airport at lunchtime on Thursday, drove the hire car to our boutique hotel in a lovely beach resort called Palm Cove and proceeded to do fuck all for the rest of the day, apart from sit on the beach and eat Thai food.

Friday was Great Barrier Reef day, and what a fantastic experience it was. I didn't even mind getting up at six in the morning to catch the enormous catamaran that sailed from Cairns harbour, for some six or seven miles off the coast. We snorkelled on the reef. We sunbathed on a nearby island. We paddled in water so blue it looked like it had been touched up in Photoshop. Laura saw her turtles (at last), Poppy tickled a clown fish and I didn't make a fool of myself once, not even when transitioning from the catamaran to a small rubber dinghy and back again no less than *three* times. It was the best day we've spent in Australia so far and I paid for every penny of it.

Lovely.

Then came yesterday. Thanks to which, I have decided to contact the tourist board and suggest a new strap line for the area: CAIRNS – *it's bold, beautiful, and absolutely bastard terrifying*!

This was Laura's birthday, so I had planned a whole day of fun exploits. First Laura would go for some treatments at a local spa in Palm Cove, while I entertained Poppy elsewhere (i.e. watching *Finding Nemo* – *again*). Then after lunch we'd take a ride on the Skyrail, an enormous cable car that takes you up the mountains and into the ancient rainforest beyond. For dinner, I'd arranged a rather special meal for all of us via our hotel, which consisted of sampling some tasty Australian cuisine at a table set up on the beach. Then to conclude the birthday we'd take a slow, relaxing walk along the beach as the sun went down, offering ample opportunity for the kinds of holiday snaps that make your friends insanely jealous of you.

Sounds great, right? I thought so too. Then came the breakfast spider . . .

I'm up and out of bed good and early, intending to make Laura breakfast in bed. I only manage some toast and marmalade, but it's the thought that counts, right? After I've delivered the breakfast into my wife's grateful mitts and wished her a very, very happy birthday with some kisses and the biggest hug I can manage, I make myself a cup of tea and saunter out onto our first-floor balcony to soak up some early morning sun. This has become something of a ritual for me down on the Gold Coast, and it's nice to continue it up here where, if anything, the weather is even better.

Our large holiday apartment is at the end of the building next to a collection of trees, some of which have branches that droop close to your head on your left as you stand at the railing, surveying all before you with a feeling of intense smugness.

The view is wonderful. I take a sip of tea and look out onto sparkling clear blue waters, happy locals taking their morning jog along the beach, swaying palms, singing kookaburras, and A FUCKING HUGE SPIDER RIGHT NEXT TO MY HEAD.

The tea goes into the air as I skip out of range of the crouching monstrosity. I'm not usually scared of spiders, but this bugger would terrify Jesus himself if he decided to begin the Second Coming on my hotel balcony.

It's a good seven or eight inches across and would quite easily cover my palm if I was dumb enough to pick it up. He's quite a colourful little bastard, with spindly brown and black legs, a bright yellow and black abdomen, and a shiny patina across his whole body that almost glints in the sun.

The blighter has spun his web between two of the afore-mentioned hanging branches that have grown out over our veranda. Quite why he's done this is beyond me, unless he knows something about the local fly population that I don't. Maybe the last tenants of this particular apartment were a disgusting bunch, and the insects congregated over huge piles of rubbish, leading to my big black friend here setting up shop in the flight path. Whatever his reasons, the spider is way too close for comfort for my liking.

Laura appears from behind me. 'What time is it, honey? I don't want to be late for my—*Oh fucking hell, what the fuckity fuck is that?*'

'That would be a spider, my darling wife. One of the ones they warned us about before we came here.'

'It's bigger than my head!'

'Quite possibly.'

'Urrggh. I don't like it! Do something, Jamie!'

'What? Put a lead on it and take it for a walk?'

'Get rid of it!'

'I would, but I don't have a bazooka on me right now.'

'Stop messing about! It's my birthday and I don't want it ruined by that horrible, ugly thing.'

I look back at the spider, who shows no signs of distress at being insulted in such a manner. It must be used to this kind of treatment. 'I'll go get the mop.'

I scamper back into the kitchen to retrieve the damp mop from a kitchen cupboard and return to the balcony holding it out in front of me. My intention is to whack our multi-coloured friend with it until he either dies, or at least gets pissed off enough to move to another postal code.

'Shoo!' I say effeminately, poking the mop at the spider.

'Shoo!' I repeat, waggling the mop ever closer.

All this manages to do is give the now irate arachnid something to jump onto and crawl down in order to launch his attack.

'Yaaarrggghhh!' I screech, throwing the mop in the air.

'Muuurrggghhh!' Laura then cries, as the spider is catapulted from the mop handle onto the front of her dressing gown, just below her face. '*Getitoff, getitoff, getitoff!*' she begs me.

I do the only thing I can – I pick up the mop and smack her with it. This results in the spider being success-fully dislodged – and Laura receiving a face full of damp mop that had last been used yesterday evening to clean up Poppy's spilt chocolate milk.

Our arachnid adversary decides that this whole situation is for the dogs, and scuttles over the side of the balcony and out of our lives as swiftly as he entered it. I spend the next five minutes apologising to my wife while trying to ignore the smell of sour milk emanating from her body. As starts to the day go, this one has not been the most successful.

The shower Laura had was much longer than normal – understandably so, I guess. She went off happily to the spa for the morning, leaving Poppy and me with *Nemo*, after which we went and ran around on the beach until we both felt sick. By the time I'd recovered from entertaining my hyperactive daughter, Laura had returned with a blissful look on her face.

'Good, was it?' I ask her.

'You have no idea, Jamie.'

I'm sure I don't. Spa treatments and men go together about as well as alcohol and working heavy machinery.

'We're going up high, Mummy!' Poppy says happily to her mother over lunch. I'd shown Pops pictures of the Skyrail last night and she'd been beside herself with excitement ever since.

'Yes we are, poppet,' Laura agrees. 'Nice and high above the trees, where there are no spiders and dirty mops.' She shudders involuntarily.

'Let's go then,' I say, before Laura can berate me for throwing an angry gigantic arachnid at her.

We drive the few kilometres to the Skyrail station, park up and make our way inside.

I'm stunned to see that there are hardly any queues between us and getting to a cable car. For a Saturday morning the place doesn't seem all that busy. Of course I'm used to tourist attractions in the UK, where you can't move for Japanese tourists and Beefeaters ninety per cent of the time. Up here in the remote tropics of Queensland, 'busy' doesn't quite mean the same as it does at the entrance to Madame Tussauds on a Saturday morning in the height of summer.

The cableway is a pretty serious feat of engineering. It takes you up the side of the mountains, skimming above the canopy of thick rainforest that covers the entire range. Once you've gone over the summit, you descend under the canopy to a waypoint, before travelling all the way to the main station at the other end of the line in the rainforest village of Kuranda, which sits atop the mountain plateau – and does a roaring trade in didgeridoos, hats hung with corks and over-priced sandwiches.

Laura is all smiles and Poppy is virtually beside herself with excitement by the time the cable car door closes behind us. I'm slightly more apprehensive as it's just occurred to me for the first time that I'm now trapped in a small glass and metal bubble, suspended from a wire, and about to travel several hundred feet up the side of a mountain.

In my desire to create the most fun-filled day for Laura's birthday that I could, I may have neglected to actually think about the nuts and bolts of this particular activity. It's nuts and bolts that weigh most heavily on my mind as the small six-seat gondola starts to move up and out of the station towards the treeline. I'm really hoping that they are very strong nuts and bolts, built by efficient people in the western world who have sanitary working conditions and a professional attitude to their jobs.

Poppy giggles with pleasure as we get higher and higher,

passing through the trees and into the open air. My knuckles tighten on the seat and I do that thing everyone does when they're nervous – I grin like a maniac and go stiffer than a day-old corpse.

'You okay, Jamie?' Laura asks me as we rattle over the first pylon and start to ascend on an even sharper incline.

'Yes, yes, I'm fine,' I lie through gritted teeth. 'How about you?'

'It's lovely. Just look at the view.'

This is something I'm happy to do as gazing at the horizon means I'm not looking down at the ever-increasing space between us and mother Earth. Poppy has no such qualms, has her nose pressed right up against the gondola's glass wall, and is peering down into the canopy below us.

'Look, Mummy!' she squeals and points a finger. 'Look at the birds!'

'Shall we see how many we can count?' Laura suggests, to Poppy's absolute delight.

I'd be delighted right now if this excursion were soon coming to an end, but I have well over an hour of this shit to put up with before we reach Kuranda. There are stops along the way thank God, but it's still over sixty minutes of watching the green world slide by beneath us as the gondola clatters and rattles its way over the pylons set at regular intervals towards our destination. And of course, we've still got to come back as well.

As the minutes drag by slowly I start to fantasise about things I'd rather be doing than sitting here a couple of hundred feet in the air, rocking back and forth in the warm tropical winds. Having elective bowel surgery, for instance. Or inserting my head into a cow. Masturbating with sandpaper. Listening to a Cliff Richard album. Cleaning corpses in a morgue. Watching an entire season of *Downton Abbey* in one day . . .

Actually, forget that last one. Now I'm just being silly.

Regardless of what I'd rather be doing, the cold hard fact of the matter is that no matter how much I wish it were not so, I am still trapped in the bubble with my wife and daughter on an inexorable climb into the clear, blue November skies.

'Daddy, come and look at the trees!' Poppy demands.

'I think Daddy would rather just look out of the window at the view, sweetheart,' Laura tells her, picking up on my obvious distress.

Poppy's eyes go wide. 'Are you scared, Daddy?' She clambers over to me, climbs onto my lap and gives me a huge hug. 'Don't be scared, Daddy.' She says this with such genuine compassion I nearly burst into tears. My daughter's warm and comforting presence makes the ordeal about a thousand times more bearable. It even gets to the point where I'm able to look down into the trees with her to spot birds without wanting to retch violently and claw my own eyes out.

While I've relaxed a bit, and am less terrified for my mortal soul, I'm still extremely glad when we reach the first way station and take a ten-minute break from the journey.

'Are you sure you want to carry on?' Laura asks me as I sit down on a convenient – and blessedly solid – bench just outside the station entrance.

'Yeah. I'll be fine. As long as you're having a good time, baby.'

'I am. Pops is too.' Laura looks over at where our daughter is attempting to have a conversation with a passing lizard. 'But if you're not happy we'll go back.'

'No, no. I'm more or less used to it now.' I offer her a lopsided smile. 'It can't get any worse, can it?'

NEVER SAY THIS.

Never, ever say this in any situation *ever*. It will guarantee that things will indeed get worse. Far, *far* worse. I discover just how wrong I am on the second leg of our journey when we hit the Barron Gorge section.

Let's examine that word 'gorge', shall we? It automatically implies size, doesn't it? You've never heard anything small described as a gorge, have you? It's a big, round word with a very strong vowel sound, giving you a clear indication that it's being used to describe an object of considerable volume and depth. Such is most definitely the case here.

I've just about got used to sailing above the treeline, so it comes as a dreadful shock when the trees suddenly disappear from view beneath us and we're propelled out over a drop of such magnitude you could probably fit the Empire State Building in there with headroom left over for Nelson's Column. The river that runs through Barron Gorge cuts its way right through the mountain range, creating a spectacular waterfall that roars over a billion years' worth of geology, before plunging hundreds of feet to the basin below.

I have no idea who Barron was, but if he were in front of me right now I think I'd pull his ears off.

I'm not even able to summon a scream when we fly out over the gorge. My body has frozen solid.

'Wow!' Poppy cries and presses herself up against the window again.

Laura starts snapping away with her camera with equal excitement.

I try very hard not to shit my pants.

The human body is a wonderful thing. When presented with a horrifying situation such as this it takes steps to thoroughly occupy your mind, thus getting you through the torment without losing your marbles completely. Such is my desire to prevent a repeat of Fajita Night that by the time I've wrestled my bowels back under my complete control, we've passed through the gorge and come out the other side into the relative safety of the rainforest canopy again.

I don't go so far as kissing the ground when we alight at the Skyrail station in Kuranda, but I do pat the nearest gum tree as I emerge from the bubble into the sun on very shaky legs.

Laura gives me a hug. 'Well done, sweetheart. You were very brave.'

'I don't think you could call it brave, baby. Any time a three year old is absolutely fine with something and you're terrified of it, brave isn't even in the same post code.'

'Well never mind, we're here now. Let's look around for an hour before we go back.'

I groan. I'd temporarily forgotten that you have to go back down on the sodding thing again. I don't think my sanity or my underpants can take another trip over Barron Gorge today.

In the next hour Laura buys a series of tacky souvenirs for the folks back home, including two didgeridoos, several fridge magnets, four tea towels and a key fob made from kangaroo testicles. Poppy gets her hands on a stuffed koala bear that she may not let go of again until she hits twenty-one. I spend the entire time sourcing local taxi firms.

There's no way I'm getting back in that cable car, even if it means spending an extortionate amount of money on a cab. There are perfectly serviceable roads between me and the base of the mountain, so I see no reason to risk brown trousers again on this excursion.

I kiss both wife and child before waving to them as I watch the hateful green bubble rise into the trees again. Never in my life have I been so glad to be separated from my family.

While the taxi journey doesn't have the horror of severe vertigo, it does feature a lengthy conversation with my friendly aborigine taxi driver about the state of his bathroom. I usually hate getting into small talk with cab drivers, but am more than happy to listen to Terry's U-bend woes as he drives me back to sea level. Anything beats having your arsehole pucker more times than a trumpet player's lips during a jazz solo.

Back at the main station Poppy sees me waiting by the exit, squeals with her customary levels of happiness, and runs over with the koala bear still clamped firmly in her grasp. 'We spent most of the ride down coming up with a name for it,' Laura says as I gather our daughter into my arms.

'And what did you decide?' I ask Poppy.

'Pumbaa,' she replies.

'Isn't Pumbaa a warthog?'

'Not this Pumbaa. This Pumbaa is a koala bear.'

Having been put in my place, we make our way to the car and drive back to Palm Cove and the dinner I've arranged on the beach for my wife's birthday. All that fearing for my life at a great height has made me ravenous, so I'm looking forward to a relaxed evening in the company of my two favourite women.

So far today I've been scared by a spider and terrified by a cable car, but the day is rapidly coming to an end. So it can't get any worse, can it?

The set-up on the beach is fantastic.

It bloody well should be – it cost me enough.

Under a collection of neat, straight palm trees that stand just in front of the hotel and at the edge of the beach is a square glass table covered by an expensive cloth and three comfy chairs.

'Thank you very much,' Laura says as the waiter holds out her chair to let her sit down. 'This is incredible, Jamie,' she says to me with an enchanted expression on her face.

I have to agree. I've done alright here folks, and no mistake. If the food is anywhere near as good as the view, it's likely to be the best meal we've ever had.

I'm feeling decidedly pleased with myself as the waiter returns with the menus. My organisational skills are usually blunter than a set of steak knives from Poundland, so the fact I've managed to pull all this off in one day is an achievement of no small proportions on my part.

The food on offer does indeed look wonderful, with a selection of dishes that all sound mouth-watering. I spot one particular main course and look up at the waiter. 'Crocodile steaks?'

'Yeah. They're great. Taste fantastic. Made from crocs locally sourced.'

I knew this area had wild crocodiles, I didn't know the residents caught and ate them too.

'Eewww!' Poppy exclaims. 'You can't eat a croccy.'

'Pops is right, Jamie, you can't eat a crocodile.'

This of course makes my mind up for me. 'Oh no?' I look back at my waiter friend. 'I'll have the crocodile please, mate.'

'Jamie!'

'Daddy!'

I do love to wind my womenfolk up sometimes.

Laura elects to keep it simple with braised beef and Pops chooses the chicken nuggets from the children's menu. We really are going to have to modify that girl's diet at some point.

The food arrives and my crocodile steak is everything the waiter promised me it would be. It's delicious – kind of a cross between chicken and fish taste wise. It shouldn't work judging from that description, but by golly, it does anyway.

The belch that erupts from my stomach at the meal's

conclusion is testament to how much I enjoyed it. Poppy giggles. I waggle my eyebrows at her.

'Snappy tasted really nice, Pops.'

'You named your meal?' Laura asks with a roll of her eyes over her last bite of beef.

'Yeah. Snappy tasted wonderful, so I only thought it fair to give him a name as a tribute.'

'Can I have a stuffed crocodile called Snappy?' my daughter asks.

'Of course you can, gorgeous.'

All three of us barely have room for pudding, but we force the chocolate ice-cream sundaes down us with remarkable fortitude. Laura and I can do little else other than sit back and puff our cheeks out when the plates are taken away, but Poppy – who has the typical constitution of someone rapidly approaching the age of four – is up and building sandcastles down in the surf before the after-dinner drinks have arrived.

'Shall we go for a walk as the sun goes down then, sweetheart?' I suggest to Laura.

'That'd be lovely.' She takes my hand. 'Today has been wonderful, Jamie. Thank you so much.'

'My pleasure.'

I couldn't be more smug right now if I'd had lessons from Simon Cowell.

We give it another twenty minutes, during which I savour my third seven-dollar cocktail. It's called a Sin City and is a coffee lover's idea of heaven, a perfect mix of strong liquor and equally strong Java. It's got quite the kick as well, so I'm rocking a distinctly pleasurable buzz

by the time we stand up and amble down to where Poppy
is still playing near the shoreline.

'C'mon Pops. We're going for a walk up the beach.'

'Oh, Daddy, I'm building castles!'

'Yes, I know, we watched you, but there might be even
better sand up there along the beach.'

Poppy gives me another one of her most disbelieving
looks. Nevertheless she's quite happy to clamber up onto
my shoulders as we begin to walk along Palm Cove beach.
If we had a mind we could hike a good four kilometres
along the crescent shore all the way to Kewarra Beach in
the south, but this is more a light bit of exercise to walk
off the thousand calories we've just consumed than an
expedition, so I doubt we'll make it much further than
the creek that divides Palm Cove from Clifton Beach
about a kilometre away.

My smugness reaches a hitherto uncharted altitude as
we stroll along, given that the timing couldn't be better.
The sun is going down in a glorious shade of orange and
red that blazes its way across the azure sky, and the warm
sea gently laps at our feet.

Seriously, this is what they mean when they talk about
a picture postcard moment. I'm so full of myself I'm
amazed there's any room for the meal I've just eaten.

'Daddy, look at the wa'er!'

'Water, Poppy, not *wa'er*.'

My daughter climbs down from her perch on my shoulders and runs over to where the creek flows out over the
sand and into the ocean. There are many of these creeks
all the way along northern Queensland. Running down

from the mountains to the west. They tend to be slow moving and lined with mangrove trees for the most part, unless it's the rainy season, when they can become proper rivers that carve out large, impassable runnels in the sand as they empty out into the sea.

This is November, so the rains haven't yet arrived and the water in this creek is barely more than a trickle by the time it reaches the surf. Poppy is already throwing sticks into it by the time we catch up with her. Laura and I are both in whimsical moods, so instead of telling Poppy off, we join her in her stick-throwing fun.

Then I spot some coconut husks sitting in the roots of a palm tree. In my happy drunken haze they look positively *designed* for being thrown into creek water. The tree hangs right out over the creek, but I'm pretty sure I can gather up a couple of the husks without getting more than my flip-flop-wearing feet wet.

'What are you doing?' Laura asks as I make my way around the creek and grab the trunk of the palm tree.

'Getting a coconut. I just need to reach down a bit and I should be able to grab one of these—*URK!*'

I lose my grip and fall into the water with a tremendous splash. Luckily it's only about three foot deep, so I'm all laughs and spluttering coughs as I stand up.

'Oh, Jamie,' Laura says in a long suffering manner and crosses her arms.

Poppy is beside herself. She's laughing so hard her shrieks of hilarity carry right across the beach. It's incredibly infectious and I find myself joining in as I start to wade my way back to them, a coconut husk clasped under one arm. Laura is laughing hard now as well, doubled over with her hands over her belly.

'Yeah, yeah. Very funny,' I say, looking up into my wife's smiling face. She doesn't really need the amazing sunset behind her to highlight how beautiful she is, but it's happy to add the effect anyway.

Laura looks up just behind me and her expression immediately changes from one of hilarity to wide-eyed terror.

'What?' I ask and turn to follow her gaze.

There's no easy way of saying this, people. And there's no way of saying it without swearing, I'm afraid. On the creek bank beyond the palm tree I've just fallen off is a fucking crocodile.

Let me repeat: On the creek bank beyond the palm tree I've just fallen off is a FUCKING CROCODILE. If I thought my run-in with the spider and the Skyrail were scary, they completely pale into insignificance alongside finding yourself less than ten feet from one of nature's most aggressive and deadly predators. It's not the biggest crocodile in the world – probably only about four feet long – but by Christ that's big enough for panic stations, thank you so very much.

The crocodile is not moving. *Not yet*, anyway. It's probably in shock. I'm sure it's quite rare for the crocodile to have his evening meal delivered up to him in such an easy fashion and he's probably still processing the happy and unexpected development in his life.

I go rigid with fear. The important thing right now, the *vital* thing right now, is not to make any sudden movements or loud noises.

'IT'S A CROCCY!' Poppy screams behind me.

The croccy's head moves. So do my bowels.

'Jamie, get out of there!' Laura screeches.

*What an excellent idea. I'll be sure to give it some careful consideration.*

I will my legs into some backwards movement, but my motor functions seem to have taken the night off. Croccy slides a couple of inches down the bank nearer to the water. You can tell he's weighing up his options.

A sudden, horrible thought occurs: *I've just eaten a crocodile steak.* In my belly are the half-digested remnants of one of this bugger's relatives. It's probably his mother.

When the crocodile shifts its bulk ever closer to the water I affect the most hang-dog expression I can. 'Sorry, croccy. I'm really, really sorry I ate your mum.'

The apology falls on deaf ears and the snout goes in water. This seems like ample time to panic.

'AAARGGH!'

With an instinct borne of a million years of evolution I do the only thing I can right now that could possibly save my skin. I chuck my coconut at the crocodile with all my might. The sodden husk bounces off his nose.

*Congratulations, idiot. Now you've annoyed him.*

Croccy provides me with a look that suggests the imminent loss of my legs. This makes my recalcitrant lower limbs finally wake up to the seriousness of the predicament I find myself in, and they start to power me back to the creek's edge. In a maelstrom of kicking limbs, screaming lungs and splashing water I clamber up the bank with Laura dragging me along by the back of my T-shirt.

Croccy can't be arsed to give chase, it seems. He just sits there on the sand watching us flail around like idiots. If crocodiles could laugh, this one would be doubled over, holding his belly.

It takes family Newman roughly three micro-seconds to get back to the hotel. Such is our turn of speed on the return journey we bring a cloud of sand into reception with us as we rush towards the safety of our room. I manage to take my first proper breath since falling into the creek as I turn the security locks on the front door and lean my head against it with relief.

'Yes, I think that's the last walk along the beach we're likely to take while we're here, don't you, Laura?'

No answer.

'Laura?'

Still no answer.

I turn to see why she's gone so quiet, and am presented with an arrangement of flowers so large it should probably have a cable car suspended above it. A mixture of multi-coloured roses and crisp white lilies, it just about covers the entire dining table.

'Oh, Jamie,' Laura says with tears in her eyes. 'They're beautiful.'

'Um . . . yeah. Beautiful.'

'You shouldn't have. You've done enough today.'

'Don't worry, I didn't.'

'What do you mean?'

'These flowers aren't from me, Laura.'

I walk over to the table and search for a card. I find it nestled in the middle of a bunch of pale blue roses at the centre of the display. I pluck it out and read, 'Happy birthday, Laura. With all the love in my heart, Alan.'

I look up at my wife with confusion and dismay etched across my face. Laura has turned very pale.

'Is there something we need to talk about?' I say in a voice that comes from about a million miles away.

# Laura's Diary
## Tuesday, November 14th

Dear Mum,

I have no idea how to start this entry. It's the most difficult one I think I've ever had to write, and part of me just wants to shut this diary and throw it in the nearest rubbish bin. If it weren't for the fact I'm writing to you, I'd probably do that very thing right this moment.

I've never felt quite so awful in my bloody life and I know I'm partially to blame for it. The look on Jamie's face when he read that stupid card from Alan was just so, so horrible. My husband had spent the entire weekend making my birthday as fantastic as he could, and what reward does he get for his troubles? He finds out that not only is another man in love with me, but that I've kept this fact from him for weeks.

What started as a lovely birthday ended up being one of the worst nights I can remember having for a long time.

Jamie just about managed to keep a lid on his emotions long enough for us to put Poppy to bed, but as soon as he closed the door on our sleeping child I was subjected to the full force of his unhappiness. It was horrible. I've never seen him look so hurt, worried and confused in all the years we've known each other.

I tried my best to explain what had happened – or rather *not* happened – between Alan and me, starting with the meal at Ambrogio, but this only seemed to make things worse.

'This has been going on since *October*?' My husband says incredulously.

'Yes, but there's *nothing going on*, Jamie. I told you that.'

'No? Then why keep all this a secret? Why not tell me that your boss is in love with you and is sending you gifts like this fucking botanical garden over here?'

I should have said something to him before this, but I just wanted to put the awkward dinner with Alan Brookes behind me and move on. Not that my boss seemed able to do so. I stupidly hoped that Alan would forget his pronouncement of undying love over pasta, but I couldn't have been more wrong. Not a week has gone by since that he hasn't brought it up again in one way or another. If he isn't popping into my office for no apparent reason other than to see me, he's having gifts delivered by hand right to my desk. Jewellery, perfume, items of clothing – you name it, I've been sent it. About the only thing he hasn't tried is chocolate, for what should be obvious reasons.

I've been getting more and more worried that at some point Alan might send a present to my home address, but thankfully so far that hasn't happened. He's displayed that much self-control at least, confining his public displays of affection to the work environment, and I've let him get away with it because he's my employer.

I *should* have shut him down weeks ago. I *should* have been stronger and told him to stop. But I love my job and I didn't want to do anything to piss him off. That isn't so wrong is it?

Frankly the whole situation has become highly stressful, so I was delighted when Jamie suggested the trip to Cairns. I thought I'd be out from under Alan's nose for a few days and therefore wouldn't have to worry about his unwanted attentions.

How wrong I was. How was I supposed to know he'd go out of his way to track down which hotel we were staying at and get that ridiculous display of flowers sent to my door?

And why *didn't* I tell Jamie about all of this sooner, Mum? Why have I kept it to myself all this time? Is it because I know I screwed up and didn't handle things well at Ambrogio, leading Alan on in an effort to keep my job? Or is it because secretly I'm *enjoying* the attention?

Alan Brookes is a powerful, attractive older man, after all. Maybe a part of me is actually *revelling* in his constant declarations of love. Given the strain on my relationship with Jamie recently, my ego has probably craved the boost Alan's relentless campaign has provided. Maybe I've kept things as sweet as possible with Alan for more reasons than just to stay his employee.

I can't tell Jamie any of this. It would break his heart. It's certainly in danger of breaking mine.

In the end I just fudged a response and told Jamie I kept it all to myself as I was embarrassed about the whole thing. I'm not sure he believed me, but it more or less puts an end to the argument, for the short term anyway.

To be honest, *I'd* have trouble believing me. I know there's nothing going on between me and Alan, but from Jamie's point of view it's plain I've been keeping secrets from him for weeks now and no matter how hard I protest my innocence it's totally understandable that he wouldn't trust me completely.

When we turn in for the night, Jamie immediately rolls onto his side and does not even attempt to give me a goodnight kiss. I woke up that morning full of happiness. I went to bed that night with tears drying on my cheeks.

Needless to say things are very strained the following day. While we don't flat out argue again, Jamie and I are snappy and waspish with one another.

There are no walks along the beach today. I spend the morning cleaning clothes while Jamie busies himself on the laptop. As mutual avoidance tactics go these are the best we can come up with. Poor old Poppy is plonked in front of the cartoons, wondering what the hell she's done to deserve such a crappy morning when it's bright and sunny outside.

'Want to go bowling,' she tells us after a lunch of cheese on toast and extended silence.

'Not today, Pops,' I tell her. I just can't muster up any kind of enthusiasm for anything. Frankly, I'll be glad when we get up tomorrow morning to catch the plane back home to the Gold Coast.

'But 'm bored!' she snaps.

'You can watch your cartoons this afternoon, honey,' Jamie adds from over the laptop.

Poppy's eyes narrow in anger. It's an expression I'm very familiar with given that it's also one of mine. 'I've watched them all, Daddy,' she says in a flat, short voice. 'Want to go bowling.'

Both Jamie and I instantly get the message. If today is already bad thanks to last night's revelations, it will be made a thousand times worse if we don't do something to entertain Poppy. The girl has a set of lungs on her only rivalled by her stamina. If we let her build up a head of steam she'll likely scream the whole hotel to the ground.

'I don't think there's a bowling alley in Cairns, honey,' I say as a last ditch attempt to avoid an afternoon of screaming children and neon.

'Actually, I think there's one next door to the cinema in the city,' Jamie says.

This is deliberate. He knows I hate tenpin bowling with a passion. I sigh and try my hardest to stop my eyes from narrowing.

'Alright, let's go bowling then.'

Poppy claps her hands together and even Jamie produces the first smile I've seen on his face since before yesterday's encounter with the crocodile.

Before my cheese on toast has fully settled in my stomach we're in the car and driving the twenty minutes down to Cairns City towards the bowling alley and one hell of a tension headache.

In Britain bowling alleys are usually full during the

day when it's raining outside and people want to entertain themselves undercover in a building that has heating. In Australia people go bowling for precisely the opposite reason. It is blisteringly hot today and the air conditioning provides a much-needed escape from the high temperature.

Looking up into the clear blue sky just before entering Cairns Bowl, I can't help but think that thirty-four degree heat is still vastly preferable to the constant sound of bowling pins crashing into one another. This kind of weather would have murdered me when I first stepped off the plane in Brisbane nearly a year ago, but now it just feels extremely good on my tanned skin. What I wouldn't give to spend the next hour or so lying out in it, rather than breaking a nail on a bowling ball.

When you'd rather risk skin cancer than take part in a sporting activity you know you're on to a loser.

Inside it's as bad as I feared.

It appears every family in the Cairns area has decided to bowl this afternoon.

Then I realise this may be a very good thing. If all the lanes are full, we'll have to leave and maybe I *can* spend the rest of day cooking myself by the public swimming lagoon while Jamie takes Poppy shopping.

'You got any lanes free?' Jamie asks the tall young lad behind the service counter.

'Just one mate, down the end there. Number twenty-four.'

*Shit.*

'Great. Two adults, one child then please,' Jamie says and looks round at me.

'What?'

My husband cocks his head and gives me the old stink eye.

Realisation dawns. 'Oh, you need me to pay.'

The funds from Jamie's recent work dried up with last night's beach meal, so I've returned to my role as the local cashpoint.

I try to avoid the look on my husband's face as I pay. I know exactly what he's thinking right now: *'I spend all my money on this cow's birthday yesterday, only to find out she might be having an affair with her boss. I hope she gets cellulite in both thighs.'*

Actually, I doubt he's thinking that last part. Men have no idea what the potential horrors of cellulite can bring.

Still, I can't help but feel guilty. Jamie arranged this trip and spent all that money as a way of rekindling our love . . . and I wreck it all with one giant bunch of flowers.

I try to contain my revulsion as I'm handed a pair of bowling shoes that are probably jam-packed with bacteria from the sweaty feet of those who have worn them previously. This must be the only pastime in the world where you pay for the privilege of walking round in the skin flakes and impregnated foot odour of a hundred other people.

It would help if they were even the least bit fashionable, but the only statement you're making in these flat, badly stitched monstrosities is that you've probably just escaped from the special needs bus and need someone to help you get your finger out of your nose. Neither Jamie nor Poppy seem worried about their new footwear in the slightest, but this is to be expected as one is a man, one is a small child, and both are idiots.

We march past a collection of noisy families down to our lane at the end of the alley. This puts us directly underneath the speaker that's fixed to the side of the wall above our heads, so not only will I be deafened by the sound of balls meeting pins, I will also have my eardrums excoriated by the pounding of over enthusiastic pop music. Currently Pink is belting out her hit, 'Perfect', at a volume usually reserved for air-raid sirens. That song seems to follow me around in life like a bad smell.

Jamie sits at the computer and punches our names in. I'm amazed to see 'LAURA' pop up underneath his own name. I was rather expecting to see 'CHEATING WHORE' instead.

'Put me last, Daddy!' Poppy cries.

This is not an uncommon request for my daughter when taking part in a group activity of this sort. Some might say it shows a remarkable amount of politeness and patience in one so young, but I have a feeling it's just because she wants to size up the competition before taking her turn.

Jamie is first to bowl and does a respectable job, knocking all ten pins down in two goes to earn himself a spare. I'm still trying to choose a ball that's not heavy enough to wrench my arm out of its socket when he sits back down.

'Come on, Laura, hurry up,' he snaps.

I count to ten under my breath and grab hold of a bright pink ball that's the lightest I can find at eight pounds. As I walk over to the lane to have my go I discover that I've already broken a nail. At this point I should just fling the ball down the shiny strip of wood and not give a shit where it ends up. I don't like bowling and am in a foul mood thanks to Alan Brookes and Jamie Newman, so this course of action would be perfectly understandable. However, there's something about being at loggerheads with someone that brings out the worst of my competitive spirit. I've apologised to Jamie and told him there's nothing going on with my boss over and over, yet still he snaps at me and maintains his surly attitude. It would no doubt give him great pleasure to add to my misery by beating me at bowling. Therefore, this must not happen.

I take careful aim at the pins, compose myself, and bowl the most carefully placed shot I can manage. The ball immediately veers off to the left and drops into the gutter. I hear Jamie snigger behind me. *Fuck it.*

The next bowl is a bit better and I hit three pins. This is likely to be a long afternoon.

'Never mind,' Jamie says as I return. 'Maybe your boss can buy you some bowling lessons.'

I'm tempted to smash my bright pink eight-pound ball into his face but resist the urge as somebody has to bring Poppy up until she's eighteen. Speaking of whom, my daughter wheels over the children's bowling aid from where it sits just off to the side and lines the metal frame up with meticulous precision.

'You want us to put the gutter bumpers up, honey?' Jamie asks.

Poppy turns with a look of deep insult on her face. 'No thank you, Daddy,' she says with her hands on her hips, before turning back to the job at hand.

She picks up her purple bowling ball, pushes it down the ramp with all her might and hits a strike on her first go. Poppy's reaction is absolutely priceless. She gives a delighted whoop and starts to wiggle her bum around in a victory dance. Both Jamie and I burst out laughing.

'Next time she does that, make sure you've got your camera phone out,' I tell Jamie. The camera on my Nokia gave up the ghost ages ago, so we both now rely on Jamie's iPhone for moments such as these.

'Yeah, okay,' he replies and fishes the phone from his pocket, placing on the side ready for his daughter's next performance.

I'm pleased to say I do not snigger when Jamie scores a paltry five on his next go. Nor do I become smug after I hit a spare. Poppy is inconsolable at only knocking down eight pins on her next go.

'Have to line it up better,' she tells me as she sits down with her arms folded and a pout on her face.

Jamie once again hits a spare on his third attempt and I do the same. We are now bowling to a similar standard, which pleases me and probably disgusts him. Poppy takes about three hours to line up her third go.

'Come on, honey,' Jamie says. 'You'll want to go to university at some point, so you need to get a move on.'

'Leave her alone. She likes to take her time over things.'

'Bit like her mother,' he replies with a bucketful of snide.

With her tongue stuck out in concentration, Poppy pushes the ball as hard as possible. It rockets down the metal frame, bounces onto the lane, flies straight and true down the centre and hits the ten pins dead on, toppling every single one of them.

'Camera, Jamie,' I order.

He doesn't need telling twice. As Poppy proceeds to wiggle her bum again in celebration Jamie starts snapping away with the iPhone, trying his hardest not to ruin the shot from laughing so hard.

The next five rounds of bowling go a similar way to the first three, so by the time we reach the tenth and final frame Jamie is beating me by eight points and Poppy has murdered the pair of us with a total of six strikes.

It'd be highly embarrassing were it not for the pleasure derived from Poppy's victory dance. As the game has progressed it's become more and more outlandish, culminating with her spinning around and around with her arms out wide, until she had to stop or be sick all over her bowling shoes.

Jamie has managed to capture all of this on video as well as in still-photo form. As he goes up to take his final bowl, I pick the iPhone up and begin to cycle through the images he's caught.

A huge smile spreads across my face as I look through the multiple shots of my happy, celebrating daughter.

Here's Poppy jumping in the air.

Here's Poppy waving her hands above her head.

Here's Poppy spinning round on her bum.

Here's Poppy holding a bowling ball above her head in triumph.

Here's Mindy the letting agent with her tits out.

My jaw goes slack. My eyes widen in shock.

The pictures of my gorgeous daughter have ended, to be replaced with three shots of a blonde Australian woman wearing red bikini briefs, a suggestive smile and nothing else.

Obviously taken by Mindy into a mirror, they each demonstrate a different sexually alluring pose. In the first image she's standing face on, head cocked and breasts thrust out. The second is taken from over the shoulder, her back arched and her bottom stuck out. The third is the worst. This one has been taken lying on a bed, her legs open with the camera held off to one side. Her other hand is between her legs.

My heart starts to race. My vision starts to blur. I find it hard to catch my breath.

'Mummy?' I hear Poppy say. 'Are you okay?'

'Laura? What's the matter?' Jamie asks and sits down next to me. He puts one arm around my shoulder.

'Get your hands off of me,' I hiss.

'What's the matter?' he repeats.

'I said get your hands off of me!' I shrug my shoulders, shaking him off.

Jamie sits back startled. 'What's got into you?' he says.

I hand him the iPhone. 'Would you like to explain this?' I say in a level voice. All I really want to do is scream and start hitting him as hard as I can, but I have a daughter to think about, so keep a lid on my rage.

Jamie takes the phone and looks at it. His face goes ashen.

'Are you okay, Daddy?' Poppy asks him. Now she's worried about both of us.

I force a smile. It's the hardest thing I've ever done. 'Why don't you go take your turn, sweetheart? Daddy and I are just talking. We're fine though, I promise.'

Poppy turns away and goes to warm up for her seventh and final strike of the day. I clench my fist and warm up for a strike of a different kind.

'I . . . I . . .' Jamie stammers. 'I don't know how these got on here.'

'Really? You don't know how pictures of a naked girl got on your phone?'

'No.'

'Have you been fucking her, Jamie?'

'What?'

'When I've been out at work and you've been swanning around doing bugger all, I mean. Has little Mindy been keeping you company?'

'No! I told you I have no idea how—' Jamie stops talking, looks into the middle distance for a moment and then groans. 'Oh shit, I do know how these got on here.'

'Do you? Was it before or after you had sex with her?'

'I never had sex with her!'

While Poppy occupies herself with two more strikes to finish her game, Jamie spins me a story about how he was by the swimming pool back at our apartment complex with Mindy one day back in September. He then goes on to explain how he left his phone by the pool in his rush to get away from Little Miss Handjob, who returned it to him shortly after.

'That must've been when she took the pictures!' he tries to convince me. 'She must have done them at her place before bringing the phone back to me.'

'And you expect me to believe that?'

'It's the truth!'

'Oh, like the way you called yourself Glen Artichoke at the speed dating? Was that the *truth*? Or how about the time you said you were sure you knew the way back to the campsite in Wookey Hole? Was *that* the truth?'

'Why the fuck are you bringing those things up, you maniac?!'

'Don't call me a maniac.' I waggle my finger danger-ously close to his eye socket. 'You spend the whole of last night having a go at me for keeping what happened with Alan a secret, when you've been keeping this shit secret from *me*?'

'Oh, it's completely different, Laura!'

'Different? DIFFERENT?' I spring to my feet in barely controlled fury. As I hear my daughter whoop with delight thanks to her final strike of the day, I ball up one fist and stare at my husband's stupid face. 'You know what you are, Jamie?'

'What?'

'You're a cunt.'

His face goes slack. Mine does too. I *never* say that word. *Ever.* But here I am using it to describe the closest person in the world to me. It feels like the universe has shifted on its axis. We stare at each other for a moment, digesting the magnitude of what's just happened. I lick my lips, which have suddenly gone very dry.

'I'm going back to the car,' I say in a dull voice. 'You finish here with Poppy, and then we are going home.'

I don't wait for a response. I can't stand to be in his presence for another second. I don't cry either. That will come later tonight when he's snoring his head off out on the couch in the living room, and I'm sat in bed with a pillow clasped to my chest.

The flight back to the Gold Cost was conducted in uncomfortable silence all the way. Jamie and I haven't spoken to each other at all since Sunday, other than when Poppy is around and we're putting a brave face on the situation for her sake. She's a clever little girl, though. She knows that something is very definitely up with Mummy and Daddy. The look of worry on her face makes me sick with guilt.

The atmosphere between Jamie and me has been palpable since we got home to our apartment, and I find myself on the verge of tears whenever we're in the same room together. From the glassy look in his eyes I think he's in much the same state.

I tried to talk to him about it all last night, but he refused to engage with me and left to go out for a walk. I didn't see him again for nearly two hours. A dark, scared part of me thought he might have gone to see Mindy the letting agent.

Oh Mum, what am I going to do?

For the first time I feel like my marriage is actually going to end. Jamie doesn't trust me. I don't trust him. We've kept secrets from another and there may be no way back from that.

God, I can't stop crying. And I can't shift the cold, dead feeling I have in my heart. I wish we'd never come to Australia.

I love you and miss you so, so much, Mum.

Your daughter, Laura.

xx

# Jamie's Blog

## Wednesday 22 November

The worst week of my life was also Poppy's first, when she caught pneumonia. Coming in at number two is the past seven days I've had to endure since we got back from Cairns.

Laura and I only speak to argue and I'm sleeping on the couch. My wife and I have had our disagreements in the past, but it was always between just her and me – there were never outside influences like love-struck Australians in the mix.

I had no idea Mindy had taken those bloody pictures. I barely use the camera on that stupid iPhone so had no reason to go through my photo album at any point. I would have surely deleted them the *second* I saw them . . . after having a wank.

Laura's reaction when she got a look at them was entirely understandable. I'm amazed she didn't ram one of those bowling balls up my arse. Finding pictures of a woman prostrate on a bed, about to send her fingers into the promised land is just about the worst thing you could find on your husband's phone. Unless it was a *man* prostrate on the bed, I suppose.

Mindy could have at least made her divorce-worthy shots a bit more artistic and run them through Instagram.

I tried over and over again to convince Laura of my innocence. But how is she supposed to believe me about this, when I'm struggling so hard to believe her about what's been going on with her boss? I know I should trust her, but I just can't get the fact that she's been showered with all these gifts for months without telling me about it once! Why do that unless you've got something to hide?

Alan Brookes is a rich, successful, handsome older man, who could give Laura the kind of lifestyle she can only dream about married to Yours Truly. Is it totally unreasonable for me to suspect something might be going on? I'd certainly be tempted by his rugged charm and enormous bank account if I was her, especially given how pathetic my contribution to our relationship has been over the past year. I bet Alan's never thrown a tantrum in a supermarket over a bag of frozen burgers, or forced his family to spend the night under the roof of a couple of sexual deviants in their sixties.

Speaking of whom, I spoke to Bob for the first time since the adventure we had in the winter. We'd been successfully dodging both him and his vibrating wife for the past few months, but I was caught with nowhere to run the other day. I can blame Mindy for this, along with the imminent break-up of my marriage.

After another one of my long, miserable walks (which are becoming customary as the days go by) I was returning to our apartment, trudging along the path, when I see Mindy trotting down a set of stairs on the opposite side of the courtyard. I do the mature and sensible thing by jumping into the nearest bush and hiding like a little girl until she's moved away.

'You alright down there?' Bob says from beside me, where he's been cutting the bushes back.

I look up into his weathered face and sigh. 'Afternoon, Bob. I could spend the next five minutes stuttering at you, trying to come up with a reasonable explanation as to why I'm hiding in this bush, but we both know it'd be a lie, don't we?'

'I guess so.'

'Right. Therefore, I'm going to do something totally out of character and just be bluntly honest. How would that suit?'

'Sounds good to me, fella.'

'Excellent. I'm in this bush to hide from Mindy, because she wants to have sex with me. Does that make sense?'

Bob rubs his chin. 'If you were single, no. But as you're married? Perfect sense, mate.'

'Thank you.'

Bob looks over the bush. 'Looks like she's gone. The coast is clear.'

'Good.' I stand up and brush myself down. 'How are you Bob?'

'Fine thanks.' He regards me carefully for a moment. 'I've got a question for you mate, if that's alrigh—'

I hold up a hand. 'I'll stop you there Bob. I know what you're going to say. We didn't mean to leave it on the counter like that. It wouldn't flush and it was supposed to go in the bin, but we got distracted, locked out of the house, and had to leave it there.'

'Aaah, right. Sandra thought you were a pair of bloody mentalists.'

I provide Bob with a heartfelt look of dismay. 'We *are*, Bob, just not that kind of mentalist. Have a nice rest of the day won't you?'

'Yeah, you too, mate.'

I step back onto the path and make my way home in a reflective mood. If only sorting my problems out with the wife was as easy as that had been.

Sadly there was no way of avoiding Mindy today. Not when she turned up at the door dressed for business and holding a clipboard, asking to carry out an inspection of the apartment.

'Is it due again already?' I ask.

'Yeah. Been three months since the last one, Jamie.'

'And you couldn't have given us any more notice? I mean, the place isn't that clean or anything right now.'

'Well, I could do it next week, but I saw you were in today so thought I'd try. Do you want me to come back in a few days then?'

'No, no. Let's get it over with,' I sigh and let Mindy in. Given the circumstances, I'm sure this isn't a good idea, but with Laura at work it's probably best to get the inspection out of the way here and now. I can only begin to imagine how awkward it would be if my wife was here while Mindy poked around the bedroom looking for areas of wear and tear.

'So how have you been, Jamie?' Mindy asks as she makes a few notes about the state of the kitchen on her clipboard.

'Fine thanks,' I lie.

'You haven't spoken to me recently.' A small smile plays across her lips. 'Did I do something *bad*?'

*Oh good grief.*

'I think you know what you did, Mindy.'

'The photos?' she says coyly and nibbles on the end of her pen.

'Yeah. My wife saw them.'

'Oh! I'm so sorry!' She has the decency to look horrified. 'They were just meant for you.'

'Yes, I assumed that.'

'I thought you'd look at them straight away.'

'Well I didn't. Laura found them, so now I sleep on the couch.'

'I didn't mean for that to happen, Jamie.' The coy look has returned. 'I just wanted to make you horny for me.'

'Did you really? I hadn't realised . . .'

Mindy throws the clipboard onto the kitchen counter and slowly runs her hands down her body. 'Yeah. I've wanted you ever since I first saw you. You're not like all the other guys I know.'

'You're into men with crow's feet and a slight paunch, are you?'

'No, I'm into sexy older men, just like you.'

Now she's lifting her skirt to let me catch a glimpse at the black lingerie she's wearing underneath. The stockings have tiny red bows on them.

'Stop that, Mindy.'

'Why? Don't you like it?'

One part of my anatomy does, but I'm resolutely ignoring the little sod.

I move over to Mindy and grab her hands. 'Stop doing that, Mindy. I don't want you to carry on.'

She pouts and raises her chin. 'Not even if I do this?' One hand goes to my crotch. 'Fuck me,' she whispers breathily into my ear.

I back away like I've just been hit with a cattle prod. My heart beats a mile a minute.

'I think you need to leave, Mindy,' I say in a shaky voice. 'This inspection's over.'

Her hands go to her hips. 'You're really going to turn me down?'

'Yes.'

'You could have me in every room, you know.' She bites her finger. 'You can have me anyway and *anywhere* you like.'

*Oh sweet mother of God.*

I open the front door. 'You . . . you really should leave.'

Mindy picks up her clipboard and flounces over to me. 'You don't know what you're turning down.'

'Yeah . . . I really do. But I'm a married man.'

'So what? I've seen the two of you together. Neither of you look happy.'

I'm taken aback. The idea that people on the outside can detect problems in my relationship with Laura really stings. 'That's not true.'

'Isn't it? Then why did you let me in today?'

'You wanted to carry out an inspection.'

'Oh come on, Jamie. That was an excuse.' Mindy pouts again. 'I want you to be inspecting *me*, not the other way around.'

'Well I can't.'

'Can't? Or just won't?'

'Both.'

I expect the pout to get bigger but instead Mindy offers me another seductive smile. 'Well I'm not giving up, Jamie. I know you want me as much as I want you.' She cocks her head in thought. 'I finish work early on Friday afternoon, about two o'clock. By half past I'll be wearing the sexiest lingerie set I own. All you need to do is knock on my door and come in. I promise you that by the end of the day, you won't be thinking about your wife.' Before I can stop her, Mindy plants a firm kiss on my lips. 'Half past two on Friday, Jamie. Be there.'

I'm too stunned to respond.

Mindy leaves the apartment without looking back and walks down the stairs out of sight.

I remain standing at the open door for a few moments until my wits return and I remember how to close the thing.

I'd like to say that I've dismissed the idea of taking Mindy up on her offer completely. But when Laura got home this evening we argued for what felt like the hundredth time about money and she took herself off to bed early, leaving me sat on the couch alone with my thoughts. Thoughts that are largely full of the whispering sound Mindy's skirt made as she pulled it up over her thighs and the urgent feel of her lips on mine. I could do it . . .

I could spend an afternoon in the kind of carnal gymnastics I dreamed about as a teenage boy, and Laura would be none the wiser. There's every chance she's already having an affair with Alan Brookes anyway, so why shouldn't I take this opportunity to have a really fucking good time before my life completely falls apart?

Mindy definitely wants me, which is more than I can say for my wife these days. My mind strays back to the brief flash of Mindy's stockings I got this afternoon. Then it strays even further back in time to an exciting glimpse of a similar pair of stockings under a tight skirt – those worn by Laura as she makes her way up the stairs of my old house and into the bedroom so we can make love for the first time.

What I wouldn't give to be back in that bed with Laura right now. Ideally without Mittens interrupting every five seconds this time around.

The past is the past though, and things are very different now. I have a choice to make. Do I try to patch things up with Laura? Or is the damage too much to repair? Do I say sod it and give in to temptation with Mindy? Or do I do the 'right thing' and spend Friday afternoon staring out of the window, all by my lonesome?

I need to sleep on it. Which I won't do very well, because I'm stuck on this bloody couch.

# Laura's Diary

# Thursday, November 23rd

Dear Mum,

Today, a man opened his heart to me in a way that brought me to tears. He told me things I needed to hear. He made me feel very, *very* special. Sadly that man wasn't my husband, hence the fact I'm writing this diary entry with a hand that won't stop bloody shaking.

'Laura? Can we talk?' Alan Brookes says walking into my office.

'Can it wait? I'm in the middle of checking last month's sales figures.'

'It is important, Laura.'

I eye him suspiciously. 'Is it about work, Alan? Because I don't want to talk to you about *anything else*.'

'Yes, of course it is!'

'Alright.' I turn away from the computer keyboard and watch him sit down across the desk from me. 'What's up?'

Alan hesitates, and then leans forward in his chair. 'I can't stop thinking about you, Laura,' he says in a near whisper.

'Oh for God's sake!'

'I know I shouldn't, but I just can't help myself.'

'You need to stop this! I can't deal with it anymore, Alan. You need to stop trying to seduce me with expensive presents and just let me get on with my job.'

'Did you like the opal necklace?'

'Yes . . . I mean no!' I open my drawer, retrieve the plush long blue box containing the necklace and slam it down on my desk in front of him. 'Have it back and stop buying me things.'

'But I love you, Laura.'

He says it with such a look of hurt on his face I can't help but feel awful despite myself. 'Alan, what do you want me to say to you?'

Oh dear, this has obviously given him an opening and he intends to take full advantage of it. Alan is up out of his chair, round the desk and on his knees in front of me before I can do anything about it. 'Alan, stop it! Somebody might come in.'

'I don't care if they do. This is my company and if I want to kneel in front of the woman I love, I will.'

'You *do not* love me,' I hiss.

'Stop telling me how I feel, Laura,' Alan snaps. 'I do love you and you just have to accept it,' he says with authority in his voice. This takes me by surprise. I'm so used to having this man act like a lovesick little boy these days that I've forgotten the kind of man he actually is.

'I don't really know what to say.'

'You don't have to say anything, Laura. I know this is

wrong and I'm crossing a line, but being around you makes me very happy and I'd like to make it a more permanent arrangement.'

'I don't know how many times I have to tell you this, Alan. I'm married!'

He leans forward and takes my hand in his. For a brief second I have the terrible notion he's about to propose.

'He's not being much of a husband though, is he? You're doing all the work, while he just sits around writing.'

'It's not his fault.'

'Isn't it? Really? You've been here nearly a year and he's still got no job.' Alan puts a hand to his chest. '*I've* never been out of work that long. There's always a job out there if you're willing to look for one – even if it's cleaning floors. I'd resent anyone I was married to, if I was the one out working myself into the ground while they sat around doing nothing all day.'

Oh God, I don't want to agree with Alan, but in my heart of hearts I'm afraid I do. I *do* resent Jamie and his long lie-ins, walks down the beach and all the time he gets to spend with Poppy during the day. How many times have I come home dead on my feet to find he's still moping around in his jogging bottoms; his major accomplishment of the day being the carton of milk he bought for half price from Aldi and three hundred words of unreadable rubbish on the laptop? Oh, he's managed to score two or three very short contracts in the last year, but in all that time, surely he could have got some kind of *permanent* work? He could have made some effort to find a nine to five, even if it was something a bit menial.

If there's one criticism I could level at Jamie it's that he thinks some things in this life are beneath him. It's a trait he definitely picked up from his overbearing mother – and I don't like it one bit. Put all that together with the fact he's probably been fucking a twenty-year-old girl and yeah, I'd say resentment doesn't begin to cover it.

'I've heard enough about your husband to know he's no good for you, Laura,' Alan continues. 'I can give you everything he can't.'

My eyes fill with tears. 'You need to stop, Alan. Please.'

'I can't. I won't. I love you with all my heart, Laura. Have since the first day I saw you. If you wanted me to, I'd leave Valerie straight away and do everything I could to make a home for you and your daughter here. Neither of you would want for anything again, I promise. I'd love you and take care of you in a way James never could.'

'His name's Jamie,' I mumble.

'Just give me a chance, Laura. Please?'

Now I'm crying my eyes out, mainly because there's part of me that's actually contemplating Alan's offer. He leans forward and plants a kiss on my lips. I hesitate for the briefest of moments before I push him away.

'Please, Alan. Please just leave me alone. I can't . . . I can't deal with this. I don't know what to do.'

He stands up. 'I'm so sorry if I've upset you, Laura. That's the last thing I wanted to do.'

'I know.'

'I'll give you some peace now, but please think about what I've said. Sleep on it. I'll be at my place in Burleigh Heads for the whole of tomorrow. Take the afternoon off work and come see me. It's on the beach in a building called Beach Plaza. Mine's the penthouse on the fourth floor.'

'I'll . . . I'll think about it.'

*Oh fuck me, what am I saying?*

Alan smiles. 'Great. Have a nice rest of the day, Laura.' He turns and goes out the door.

I immediately leap out of my chair, run over and slam it. The last thing I want to do is see anyone else given the state I'm in.

My legs suddenly feel very shaky and I collapse to the floor, my back sliding down the office door until my bum painfully hits the carpet. If my legs hadn't given out from under me I would have probably fallen over anyway, thanks to the dizzying whirlwind in my head.

I have a husband who might be cheating on me, a boss who's offering me a dream lifestyle and a daughter whose welfare I care about above everything else. Alan Brookes can certainly offer her a more stable future than Jamie right now, whether my husband is sticking it to another woman or not.

*What in God's name am I supposed to do?*

I wish you could answer that question for me, Mum.

Would you tell me to stick with Jamie despite everything that's happened recently? Or would you tell me to grab the opportunity Alan has presented and make a clean break here in Australia with him?

I can hear Jamie coming back from another one of his bloody walks, so I'll have to stop writing now so we can have tea in silence together before putting Poppy to bed for the night. Tucking our daughter in is the only thing we do with each another anymore.

Love and miss you, Mum.

Your daughter, Laura.

xx

# Jamie's Blog

# Friday 24 November

It's two thirty in the afternoon.

My legs barely feel able to support my weight as I walk past the swimming pool, up the flight of stairs and along the corridor that will lead me to the apartment. My heart hammers in my chest so loud it's a wonder the other people in the complex don't throw their doors open to see what all the fuss is about.

I can't believe I'm about to do this. This isn't like me. I'm not this kind of man. But I've been forced into it, haven't I? What else is a man supposed to do when his wife has been keeping secrets about another man's affections? When she's hidden the truth from him?

Does he just turn a blind eye? Or does he do what he thinks is best for *him*?

Does he go into the apartment at the end of this corridor and do something he'll probably live to regret in the long run, but will make him feel *so much better* in the short term?

*Yes* is the answer. After much agonising I know this is absolutely the right thing to do. My hand still pauses before I knock on the door though.

I draw in the deepest breath I've ever taken, rub my eyes, breathe out slowly and grit my teeth. Here goes nothing.

*Knock knock.*

# Laura's Diary

## Friday, November 24th

I'm sorry Mum, but I can't do this any longer.

I can't carry on living the way I have with Jamie recently. The mutual deceit. The new-found distrust. It just has to end – and end *now*.

I can feel your look of intense disapproval on the back of my neck as I walk along the corridor to the lift. If you were here in front of me you'd be ordering me to turn around and leave *right this minute, young lady*. But you're not, so I get into the lift and ride it to the fourth floor.

The ping the lift makes when it arrives nearly makes my heart jump out of my throat. I will my legs to stop shaking and walk out of the lift towards the apartment door in front of me.

This is it then. Major life-changing moment ahead. Here goes everything.

*Knock knock.*

# Jamie's Blog
# Friday 24 November Continued . . .

I hear footsteps beyond the door.

Someone's obviously in a big hurry to see me. If this goes the way I think it's going to, I know I'm going to have to get pretty damn physical. This may be a problem as I'm decidedly unfit, what with the slight paunch and everything.

I just hope and pray I can give a good account of myself. Doing this is hard enough without having to worry about the embarrassment of poor performance. The door starts to swing open. I take another deep breath and prepare myself.

'About time you got here,' an amused voice says as the door opens. 'I was beginning to think you weren't com— Hey, you're not Laura! Who are you?'

Alan Brookes stares at me from the doorway, confusion writ large across his face.

# Laura's Diary

## Friday, November 24th Continued . . .

I hear the door being unlocked on the other side.

*This is it, girl. This is your last chance to leave and avoid doing something you* will *regret for a long time.*

I ignore the voice. It can't help me now. This is going to happen. I want it to happen.

Damn it, I *need* it to happen! The door flies open. Mindy is dressed in the most beautiful lingerie set I've ever seen in my life.

'I'm so glad you came, I can't wait to—' She immediately falls silent when she realises who's at the door.

# Jamie's Blog

# Friday 24 November Continued . . .

'Sorry, pal. Laura couldn't make it.' I stand as straight as possible, but I'm still a good four inches shorter than this bastard. 'I figured you and me should have a word, though.'

'I'm sorry, mate, who are you?'

I roll my eyes. At least he could have the decency to know the guy he's trying to cuckold. 'My name's Jamie Newman. As in *Laura* Newman. I'm her husband.'

Brookes goes suitably white. 'Oh.'

'Yeah . . . *oh.*'

'What are you doing here?'

'Well, Alan, me and the missus have been chatting. It's something we've not been doing much of recently and that's made things very bad between us. You and a horny twenty year old certainly haven't helped matters, but when you get right down to it the problem has been about our relationship with one another, not anybody else.'

'I don't understand.'

'No, from what Laura told me last night about your own marriage it sounds like you probably don't, do you?' This is good. I'm warming up now. 'We're not like that, though, Laura and me. At least we weren't until we moved here and things got complicated.'

Nick Spalding

'Look, I don't think we should be having this conversation, mate. I'm going to close the door and—'

My arm shoots out and stops it closing. 'Oh no, Alan, this *is* a conversation you should be having. You've tried your hardest to steal my wife from me over the past few weeks, so I think the least you can do is hear me out, what do you reckon?' The last is delivered in a low, menacing hiss.

This boy can pull out the tough bastard act when he really needs to, you know.

'Okay, mate,' Alan says, hands going up. 'I don't want any trouble.'

His conciliatory body language warms the cockles of my heart.

'Excellent. Now, as I was saying, Laura and I weren't speaking. We were keeping things from one another. And that's *never* a good way to maintain a happy relationship, is it?'

Alan gawks at me.

'*Is it?*'

'No?'

'No. It isn't. But we fell into the trap anyway. Mostly because of work and money and stress and bruised egos . . . you know, all that superficial crap that shouldn't matter for shit, but seems to anyway, no matter how hard you try to prevent it.'

'I see.'

'No, I don't think you do, otherwise you and the lovely Valerie might be getting on better.'

Alan goes wide-eyed. I *love* it.

'Oh yes, Alan, Laura and I are really talking now. About *everything*. We spent the whole of yesterday evening chatting after we'd put Poppy to bed.'

'Poppy?'

'Our *daughter*, Alan. The one innocent person in all of this.' I have to pause for a moment to let the anger and guilt subside. 'It's because of Poppy that I'm the one here with you now, and not Laura. You see, it's her birthday next week. The most important day of the year.'

*Hold it together, Newman. This berk doesn't need to see tears running down your face.*

'My wife and I should have spent the last week planning how to celebrate it. Instead, we haven't spoken at all. Because of you, because of a girl you don't know, but mainly because of each other.'

I don't really need to be telling Alan Brookes all of this, but I'm finding the experience more cathartic than I can possibly describe.

'Laura and I only realised we hadn't even thought about our gorgeous daughter's birthday while she was cleaning her teeth before bed.' I can't help the anger returning to my voice. 'Do you have any idea what that felt like, Alan? How *guilty* we both felt at that moment? No, don't bother answering. I don't actually care what you think.'

This statement is rewarded with a look of bafflement. I'm probably the first person to say they don't care what Alan Brookes thinks for a decade.

'That guilt is what started us speaking again. It made us realise how much damage we were doing to Poppy and to each other with all the secrets and lies. And you know what, Alan?'

'What?'

'That's when Laura and I remembered why we love each other; why we got married and why we had Poppy in the first place.'

'Why?'

'Because we *like* to talk, Alan. We love to *communicate*. Not just with one another, either. You should see how many diaries she gets through in a year, and how much bandwidth my blog uses.'

'A lot?'

'A fucking *shitload*, Alan. Enough to fill the pages of a book.' I wave my hand. 'But I'm getting off my point, which is that once we did start communicating with each other again, we realised that the situation wasn't as bad as we thought it was. In calm, rational voices, we managed to get everything out in the open at last. All the frustrations, worries, neuroses and bitterness that have built up since we stepped off that plane in Brisbane nearly a year ago. And you know what, Alan? Laying it all out like that just made the whole thing sound so *stupid*. A catalogue of mistakes, bad timing and worse coincidence that had all made one hell of a mountain out of what should have resolutely stayed a fucking molehill!'

It comes to my attention that I'm shouting and clenching my fists. Alan Brookes is looking like he's going to call security any minute. I make a conscious effort to relax my posture and step back. I need to get this lot off my chest and don't want to scare this man into getting me thrown out of the building before I'm done.

'The one thing Laura and I can do is look at ourselves objectively,' I continue in a calmer tone, 'if we're given the time and encouragement to do it. Once we did, it became far easier to forgive, if not actually to forget. The upshot of it all is that Laura and I have gone a long way to patching things up. Oh, it'll take more than one evening to completely mend what we very nearly broke into a million pieces, but I'm confident that it'll work itself out, and so is Laura.'

I square myself up to Alan Brookes. This is where things could get ugly. He looks fairly timid right now thanks to the way I've steamrollered over him thus far, but I'm about to descend into veiled threats – which may provoke a very different reaction.

'But for it to all work out, Alan, we don't need any outside interference. Get my meaning?'

One of his eyes twitches. I can tell he's sizing the situation up. 'I think so,' he says in a flat voice.

'Good. Because I know you're richer, taller, more successful and probably a lot harder than me, Alan, but you know what I've got that you don't?'

'What?'

'A wife and daughter to protect who I love with all my heart.' Eyes narrow, teeth grit, fists clench. 'And I'll bury anyone who tries to take them from me.'

Alan Brookes does the best thing he can do in the circumstances for us both. He steps back. 'Message received. I'll leave Laura alone from now on.'

I can tell he's not happy about it, but the man's no idiot. He's wise enough and old enough to know I mean what I say. You don't provoke a man blinded by love. You never know what kind of crazy things he'll do.

'Great!' I'm all smiles again. 'Then I'll do the same thing right now and leave you in peace, Mr Brookes. There's just one more thing . . .' I fish a piece of paper out of my pocket and hand it to him.

'What's this?'

'A phone number. Her name's Mindy. She likes older men. You two should get on like a house on fire.'

And with that, I take my leave of Alan Brookes, desperately hoping I never have to see him again in my life.

# Laura's Diary

## Friday, November 24th Continued . . .

'Expecting somebody else, you slut?' I say and deliver what can only be described as the mother of all bitch slaps.

'Ooooww!' Mindy screeches and holds a hand up to her red, stinging face.

The slap must have been painful, because it sure as hell hurt my bloody hand.

Not enough to prevent me raising the pointy finger of doom, though. 'If you come *near* my husband again,' I say with more venom than every snake in the outback, 'if you so much as *look* at him, I will come back here and kick your pert little Australian arse so hard you won't be able to waltz Matilda for a fucking decade. Do I make myself clear?'

Mindy nods her head once, tears brimming from her gloriously blue eyes.

'Good!' I go to leave, but turn back for a moment. 'That's a very nice bra. Where did you buy it?'

'Victoria's Secret.'

'Really? In store?'

'No, online.'

'Well, it looks very good on you. I may have to buy one myself.'

'Thank you.'

'Pleasure.'

The pointy finger is back. 'Remember what I said, Mindy. Leave Jamie alone, or this is one Pom you'll bloody regret crossing.'

Having finished my impression of a Mafia enforcer, I stalk away from Mindy's doorway nursing my poor hand. It may need hospital attention, and I may find myself up on an assault charge very soon, but this is the best I've felt in days.

I know we're supposed to sort our differences out as mature adults without resorting to physical violence, but when someone's tried to steal your husband away from you there really is no substitute for a good hard right-hander.

Sorry, Mum, I know you abhorred this kind of attitude, but it seemed an appropriate response once I looked in Mindy's eyes. All the anger I'd had bubbling away in me since I saw the photos she'd taken just burst to the surface all at once and I had no real choice in the matter.

I'm not really surprised, though. Once Jamie had told me everything about her campaign to get into his board shorts, I knew my confrontation with her wasn't going to be much fun.

Still, it was nice to be mad at somebody else, rather than at Jamie and myself.

What a couple of fools we've been, Mum. I'm sure

you've been tutting and shaking your head this entire time about how stupidly we've behaved.

Why did it have to get to the stage of potential divorce proceedings before we realised that keeping secrets is a recipe for disaster? When did we forget to trust one another? A marriage can survive anything, as long as it's built on a foundation of truth. The second you start keeping things from one another the foundation starts to weaken – and before you know it the bathroom has slid off the side of the house and you're standing naked in next door's garden with only a loofah to cover your embarrassment.

*Hmmm.* I may have lost the thread of that analogy there a bit. Blame the stress I've been under. Thank *God* Jamie and I started acting like adults at last, and got it all out in the open last night, otherwise he'd currently be stuttering his way through some awkward sex with a twenty year old, and I'd be about to throw my lot in with a man who thinks it's appropriate to wear a tatty vest and shorts when he's in his fifties.

By the time I've walked across the complex and back to our apartment the pain in my hand has almost gone, negating the need for any ice that may be lingering in the freezer.

A note on the dining table tells me that Jamie and Poppy are down on the beach, so I pop on my sun hat and walk across the road to join them, wondering how much a bra from Victoria's Secret costs these days.

I find my husband and daughter looking for fish in the

rock pools. Poppy is up to her knees in sea water, poking a rather defenceless crab who just happened to be passing at the wrong time. Jamie sees me coming and looks up, a hesitant smile on his face.

'How did it go?' he asks tentatively.

'Not well. For her anyway.' I put my hands on my hips. 'Mindy won't be giving us any more trouble.' I only feel a *little bit* like a superhero, honest.

Jamie smiles. 'That's great, honey.'

'And how did it go with Alan?' I ask, as tentative as Jamie was.

'Well, I'm pretty sure he knows the score now.'

'Good, good.'

'Work might be a bit awkward on Monday though.'

'Yeah. You're probably right.'

'You think he'll do anything nasty?'

'What? Like fire me?'

'Something like that.'

'Possibly.' I look out to sea, contemplating my potential unemployed status. 'You know what? I don't care either way.'

'You don't?'

'Nope. I don't think the Worongabba Chocolate Company and I were meant for a long-term relationship. If Alan doesn't fire me, I'm going to quit. I'll miss the big fat pay cheque and fantastic working conditions, but I won't miss the long hours and constant unwanted attention from a man old enough to be my father.'

Jamie laughs. 'You know what I miss?'

'What?'

'Marmite.'

I let out an involuntary moan. 'Oh God yes . . . that Vegemite stuff just isn't the same, is it?'

'And I miss Asda.'

'Really? Are you feeling sick?'

'No. I miss it – the prices, the selection. I even miss that surly shop girl with the lazy eye who stands at the entrance pretending to care how your day is going.'

'I miss having seasons. What I wouldn't give right now to be bundled up in a thick coat walking through an autumnal forest.'

'Yeah, yeah. That'd be good. Then we'd get home, stick on the central heating, order a chicken tikka and watch *Top Gear*.'

'*Downton Abbey*.'

'*Top Gear*.'

'*Downton Abbey*.'

'*Top Gear* then *Downton Abbey*?'

'Agreed.'

We both look out over the sun-kissed water lost in homesick contemplation. What with everything that's been going on we haven't had the time or the inclination to think much about our homeland, but now the thought of it hits with full force. So much so that I feel my bottom lip start to wobble.

'Jamie?'

'Yes, Laura?'

'Can we go home, please?'

Jamie puts his arms around me. It's the best feeling in the world.

'Of course we can, baby, of course we can.'

I put my head against his chest and look over to where my daughter is still engaged in her new-found hobby of crab-tormenting. 'We're going to be alright, aren't we, Jamie?' I ask my husband.

He doesn't respond for a moment. But then I feel his arms tighten round me.

'Yeah, I think so, Laura.' He sighs and looks around us in contemplative fashion for a moment, before a grimace appears on his face. 'You know what? I'm really fucking sick of the beach.'

'Yeah, I know what you mean,' I reply and giggle.

'Time to go home,' he says softly.

'Time to go home,' I repeat.

Jamie thrusts his chin out, puts one arm up and starts to sing. '*And did those feet, in ancient times . . .*'

'Jamie!'

'*Walk upon England's mountains greeeeeen . . .*'

'Jamie, stop singing.'

'*And was the holy thing of God . . .*'

'Jamie, stop singing or I will divorce you.'

'*On England's dum de dum, can't remember the words . . .*'

'People are starting to stare at us.'

'*BRING ME A BOW MADE OF GOLD!*'

'Oh, good God. Poppy, come here! We're leaving before this idiot gets us arrested.'

'*BRING ME A LOAD OF ARROWS I CAN FIRE!*'
'Daddy stop!'
'*DUM DE DUM, DE DUM DE DUM!*'
'Run, Poppy, run!'
''TIL WE HAVE BUILT . . . JERUSALEM . . . ON ENGLAND'S GREEN AND PLEASANT LAAAAANNNND!'

# Jamie's and Laura's Facebook Message

## Sunday 10 December

Hi everyone, Laura and I wanted to send you a quick message to let you know that we're coming home!

**Quick message? This is us we're talking about. Everyone knows we both suffer from chronic word diarrhoea, so let's not pretend otherwise.**

A fair point well made, wife of mine.

**Thank you.**

No problem. We wanted to drop you all a message to say that you'll be seeing us very soon. We plan on flying out of here at the beginning of January, more or less exactly a year after we arrived.

**That's right. I received a very healthy severance package from my job, for reasons which I won't go into now, but they'll curl your toes, I promise you.**

Don't be a tease.

**Sorry. It's just that I haven't seen any of our friends for months and am looking forward to a good gossip once we get back.**

Oh wonderful . . .

**Don't fret, you won't come out of it looking *too* bad.**

**Anyway, we have a bit of spare money so we're**

going to spend Christmas and New Year down in Sydney before flying home and the job of putting our lives back together in the UK.

Yes. I am hoping and praying it's easier to find a job there than it has been here.

**I'm sure it will be. Maybe the paper will take you back.**

Um . . . doubtful.

**Well I'm sure as hell not going back to Morton & Slacks. My ex-boss has been very nice—**

Hmpf.

**Leave it . . .**

**As I was saying, my ex-boss has been very nice and given me some names of people in the chocolate industry back home and I'm hoping to speak with them in the New Year. My experience at Worongabba should help me get a foot back in the door, if nothing else.**

And I'm going to do some writing!

No, don't make that face. I don't mean *Max Danger and the Boobatrons*. I have an idea for a romantic comedy that I'm going to have a crack at. Even Laura thinks it's a good idea.

**I do. I'm shocked.**

Be nice.

It's hard to believe that eleven months have flown by so quickly, but our extended Australian adventure is now coming to an end, without one spider, crocodile or snake bite, it has to be said.

**Only just on that second one.**

We've also avoided being stung to death by box jellyfish, have not been eaten by a dingo in the outback, and we steered clear of a slow agonising death due to heat exhaustion.

In fact, the only pain we've gone through has been the emotional kind. This country may be replete with all manner of horrible creepy crawlies that can bite your face off, but the damage they can do doesn't compare to what us human beings can inflict on each other if we're being stupid enough. I'd take a nip from Croccy any time over having to go through the past few weeks of my life again. A *small* nip, mind you. The kind that wouldn't do any real damage and would make a great anecdote at parties.

**Alright, Jamie, you don't need to tell everyone about our recent bust-up. Those that want to know more will ask when we get home and the rest probably have their own problems to worry about and aren't interested.**

Yes, dear.

**I knew you'd see it my way.**

**Other than some fairly fraught marital issues we've now managed to resolve, this has been a good experience and one we shall never forget – thanks to some breathtaking scenery, the extremely friendly people here, and the constant glorious heat. My little digital camera is chock-a-block with pictures of all manner of gorgeous locations that we will bore you with once we're home, until you wish for a swift and painless death.**

We're also coming home with a four-year-old daughter

who has developed a noticeable Australian twang that I hope she gets rid of before she starts school next year. I don't think she'd appreciate the nickname 'Kangaroo' Poppy all that much.

**No, probably not.**

Poppy's accent isn't the only thing that's changed. Laura and I are coming home with a much better understanding of how our relationship works.

**Very true. Our marriage has been well and truly tested in recent times, but sometimes you need to find out what your weaknesses are before you can fully appreciate your strengths.**

Oh great. I'm supposed to be the bloody writer here, and you're coming out with all the best lines.

**It looks like you've rubbed off on me, Newman.**

As long as I can rub up and down on you later.

**Stop it. This is supposed to be a nice letter to our friends back home, not an excuse for you to be filthy.**

Please. They love it.

Anyway . . .

To conclude this message, which has now far exceeded the length we intended it to—

**See what I mean?**

We'd just like to say that we are really looking forward to seeing all of you, and we can't wait to get back home to England – where we'll no doubt immediately come down with head colds, start complaining about the price of petrol and head into the nearest branch of Thomas Cook to look at holidays.

**That's right.**

**What we won't do is leave our camera phones lying around where other people can get hold of them.**

Or use cling film inappropriately.

**Or discuss other people's bowel movements in public.**

Or buy swimming costumes that give our bosses entirely the wrong impression.

**Or keep secrets from one another for no good reason.**

Agreed?

**Agreed.**

See you all soon.

**And no worries!**

Jamie, Laura and Poppy Newman.

xx

# Email to Jamie Newman
# Thur 29 Mar 12:32 p.m.

Dear Jamie,

Thank you for the submission of your book *Love . . . From Both Sides* for our consideration.

It's very unusual for my assistant to come rushing into my office first thing on a Monday morning, waving a manuscript and with a look of glee on her face. It's even more unusual for me to spend the next three hours of a Monday morning doubled over in my chair laughing, when I should be answering emails and taking calls from disgruntled agents.

*Love . . . From Both Sides* is crude, cringe-inducing and enough to put anyone off dating for life, but I haven't had such a good time with a book in years. I frankly can't believe your wife Laura let you get away with putting all that stuff in a manuscript and sending it to a publisher, but I'm very glad she did!

On the strength of what I've read I'd like to offer you a publishing deal with us, which will include a sizeable six-figure advance. You say in your covering letter that you have even more stories to tell about your relationship with Laura and the birth of your daughter Poppy, which I would also be interested in buying for publication.

I very much hope that you'll be interested in accepting our offer, Jamie. Please get in touch as soon as you can to discuss further.

Yours sincerely,

Penny Waters,

Commissioning Editor,

The Watermill Publishing Company.

P.S. Unfortunately we won't be able to make you a similar offer on your adventure novel *Max Danger and the Boobatrons*. While competently written, I feel that any story featuring seven explosions and twelve naked women in the first three chapters alone would only appeal to a very small cross section of the audience – the ones that dribble a lot and don't get out much. Why not try the guys who published *Fifty Shades Of Grey*? They like that kind of thing over there.

In the best books, the ending often comes as a shock.
Not just because of that one last twist in the tale,
but because you have been so absorbed in their world,
that coming back to the harsh light of reality is a jolt.

If that describes you now, then perhaps you should track down
some new leads, and find new suspense in other worlds.

Join us at www.hodder.co.uk, or follow us on
Twitter @hodderbooks, and you can tap in to a
community of fellow thrill-seekers.

Whether you want to find out more about this book,
or a particular author, watch trailers and interviews, have
the chance to win early limited editions, or simply browse
our expert readers' selection of the very best books,
we think you'll find what you're looking for.

And if you don't, that's the place to tell us what's missing.

**We love what we do, and we'd love you to be part of it.**

www.hodder.co.uk

 @hodderbooks

HodderBooks

HodderBooks